Helen Phifer is the bestselling writer of twenty-seven books, including the hugely popular Annie Graham, Lucy Harwin, Beth Adams, Maria Miller and Detective Constable Morgan Brooks series.

She lives in the busy town of Barrow-in-Furness surrounded by miles of coastline and a short drive from the glorious English Lake District.

Helen loves reading books that scare the heck out of her and is eternally grateful to Stephen King, Dean Koontz, James Herbert and Graham Masterton for scaring her senseless in her teenage years. Unable to find enough scary stories she decided to write her own and her debut novel *The Ghost House* released in October 2013 became a #1 Global Bestseller.

You can find her over on Instagram @helenphifer, or on her website at www.helenphifer.com

Also by Helen Phifer

The Annie Graham series
The Ghost House
Secrets of the Shadows
The Forgotten Cottage
The Lake House
The Girls in the Woods
The Face Behind the Mask

Detective Lucy Harwin
Dark House
Dying Breath
Last Light

Beth Adams
The Girl in the Grave
The Girls in the Lake

Detective Morgan Brookes
One Left Alive
The Killer's Girl
The Hiding Place
First Girl to Die
Find the Girl
Sleeping Dolls
Silent Angel
Their Burning Graves
Hold Your Breath
Stolen Darlings
Save Her Twice
Poison Memories

Detective Maria Miller
The Haunting on West 10th Street
Her Lost Soul
The Girls on Floor 13

Standalone novels
The Good Sisters
The House on West 10th Street
Lakeview House

The Forgotten Cottage

HELEN PHIFER

ONE PLACE. MANY STORIES

This novel is entirely a work of fiction. The names, characters and incidents portrayed in it are the work of the author's imagination. Any resemblance to actual persons, living or dead, events or localities is entirely coincidental.

HQ
An imprint of HarperCollins*Publishers* Ltd
1 London Bridge Street
London SE1 9GF

www.harpercollins.co.uk

HarperCollins*Publishers*
Macken House, 39/40 Mayor Street Upper,
Dublin 1, D01 C9W8, Ireland

1

First published in Great Britain by
Carina, an imprint of HarperCollins*Publishers* Ltd 2014
This edition published by HQ, an imprint of HarperCollins*Publishers* Ltd 2025

Copyright © Helen Phifer 2014

Helen Phifer asserts the moral right to be
identified as the author of this work.
A catalogue record for this book is
available from the British Library.

ISBN: 9780008737146

This book contains FSC™ certified paper and other controlled sources
to ensure responsible forest management.

For more information visit: www.harpercollins.co.uk/green

Printed and bound in the UK using 100% renewable electricity
at CPI Group (UK) Ltd

All rights reserved. No part of this publication may be reproduced, stored in a retrieval system, or transmitted, in any form or by any means, electronic, mechanical, photocopying, recording or otherwise, without the prior permission of the publishers.

This book is sold subject to the condition that it shall not, by way of trade or otherwise, be lent, re-sold, hired out or otherwise circulated without the publisher's prior consent in any form of binding or cover other than that in which it is published and without a similar condition including this condition being imposed on the subsequent purchaser.

*For my husband Steve, thank you
for your unwavering support*

Chapter 1

She looked out of the bedroom window onto the front garden – a garden full of flowers, some wild and some she had planted herself. The brightly coloured blooms were swaying in the breeze. She heard the men and the dogs before they came into sight; they were a good distance away but they were coming. She took one last look at the garden she had so nurtured and locked it into her mind, then she turned and ran. Annie Graham was running for her life. She held on to her left side to ease the stitch that was making it difficult for her to breathe. Running out of the back door of the house and over the dry stone wall, she wasn't familiar with the woods she was in, but she knew that if the dogs and men caught up with her it wouldn't end very well. The dogs were snarling. She could hear their teeth clashing together; they were getting too close.

Panting hard and clutching her side, she looked for a tree she could climb or a building she could take cover in. Her bare feet were cut, bleeding, and giving the dogs a trail to follow. It was no good; there was no way she could outrun them. She didn't even know why she was running; tired and overwhelmed, her body was telling her to give up and wait for them to find her. Whatever it was she had done could be explained. She was a police officer so she couldn't have done anything too bad. Slowing down to catch her breath, she heard the shouts of her pursuers closing in on her. They were hyped up and chanting the same words over and over:

'Thou shalt not suffer a witch to live; thou shalt not suffer a witch to live.'

Fear filled her heart. She wasn't a witch; this was stupid. Why would anyone think that? The voices were close now – too close. They were chanting in a frenzy. Annie looked down, expecting to see her police uniform, but was startled to see a long white cotton gown. She didn't even own anything that looked like this. An adrenalin kick started her urge for survival and she began to run once more. She heard the sound of the bubbling river, which wasn't too far away; if she could run into that it would clean her feet and throw the dogs off her trail. With the fast-flowing river in sight, she felt hope that this might not end as badly as she'd feared. She pushed herself on, so focused on reaching the icy-cold water that she didn't see the mossy boulder jutting out of the ground and ran straight into it. Excruciating pain shot through her foot and she lost her balance and began falling towards the water, jerking so hard that she woke from the nightmare and managed to wake Will at the same time.

'Oh, dear God, it was a dream. It was just a dream.'

A groggy Will reached across and switched the bedside lamp on. He looked at the clock: it was three a.m. 'Are you OK?'

'Sorry, I didn't mean to wake you. Bad dream.'

Will blinked and looked at her. She was covered in a film of sweat and her hair was stuck to her forehead. 'Want to tell me what it was about?'

She shook her head. 'No, thanks, I want to forget it.'

He nodded and then pulled her close to him. 'I'll protect you from your scary dreams. Do you want me to help you go back to sleep, take your mind off them?'

She laughed. 'Do you have sex on the brain permanently?'

'Only when I'm with you, but in this case I'll settle for a cuddle.'

He lay back and Annie lay next to him, his arms around her and her head on his chest. Almost immediately he began to breathe deeply and she lay listening to him, watching his chest rise and fall. She wished she could go back to sleep so easily. This was the second time in as many days that she'd had the same nightmare and had woken up at the exact same time. It left her feeling unsettled that there was something hovering in the distance, a dark shadow in the background that was keeping out of sight, and she had no idea what it was or what it could mean.

Pushing it to the back of her mind, she thought about the wedding, which was only fourteen weeks away. She lifted her hand to look at the beautiful engagement ring Will had given to her. Who said that dreams didn't come true? Hers certainly were and her life had never been so perfect. She felt as if she and Will were meant to be together; they were such a good match. Although it had taken some terrible detours to get this far, it had made both of them much stronger and surer about how much they loved each other.

She thought about the vintage wedding dress she had found in the small shop in Kendal last month and how straight away she had been drawn towards it. The high bodice, which had a whalebone corset and was covered in the most delicate lace, was so pretty she couldn't help but reach out to touch it. The dress had a full-length silk skirt, which was covered in the same delicate lace and the tiniest crystals and pearls were sewn onto it, making it sparkle. Lily had been busy pulling out dresses for her to try on when Annie had turned to the assistant and asked her if she could try this one on.

'I'm sorry but it's for display purposes and not actually for sale. It's very old but we do have some modern takes on it I can show you.'

Lily had turned around and seen the disappointment etched across Annie's face. 'Darling, everything has a price. Please let my friend try it on; it won't hurt and we won't tell if you don't.'

The assistant had dithered for a second then nodded and removed it from the mannequin. Annie had taken it into the dressing room and let the assistant help her into it. Deep down she knew that this was the one and it was the only one. It was so delicate and stylish, she had to have it; she would be gutted if they wouldn't sell it to her. It even fitted perfectly, thanks to her pre-wedding nerves and her loss of appetite.

An image of the first woman to wear the dress flashed across her eyes – she looked very similar to Annie but with much fairer skin and strawberry-blonde hair. Annie knew that the woman who had married in this dress had spent the rest of her life with her husband, happy until death separated them, and she took it as a perfect omen for her and Will.

When she opened the curtain and stepped out, Lily had gasped. 'Oh, Annie, you look amazing, simply beautiful.'

Even the shop assistant had agreed. 'Let me speak to my boss and see what we can do; it's as if that dress was made for you.'

Annie looked in the mirror and smiled. It was a lot different to the awful green suit she'd worn when she married her first husband, Mike, when she was just nineteen. She felt like a princess and knew Will would love it. Lily brought over a large diamanté slide, which she tucked to one side of Annie's hair.

'I don't care how much that dress costs, we have to buy it.'

'Well, if it's extortionate then I don't think so; there are lots of others.'

The assistant walked back into the room with a smile on her face. 'Phew, you caught her on a good day; she said if the dress was the one for you, and I've assured her that it is, then you can buy it. The only problem is it's eight hundred pounds.'

Lily whipped out her credit card. 'Done and thank you so much for all your help.'

Annie couldn't stop grinning; even she could afford to buy it. She'd been saving up and had more than enough to pay for the dress if Lily would ever let her. She lay in bed, snuggled next to

Will, thinking happy thoughts that pushed the nightmare away, losing herself in a world of weddings until she drifted back to sleep.

When she woke up she'd forgotten all about the nightmare until she tried to stand. Her foot was painful. She looked down at her left foot, which had a couple of scratches and the beginning of a large blue bruise on the side of it. She must have hit it on the bedside table when she'd been thrashing around in her dream last night. She hobbled to the bathroom, where she ran a bath and hoped a soak would take away some of the soreness.

Will had already left for work; he was on an early and she was on a late. Most weeks they were like ships that passed in the night but at the moment it suited both of them. Annie didn't want Will to get fed up of spending time with her and if she wasn't around all the time then he couldn't, although she missed him. She never got bored of being with him, unlike Mike; she used to do anything to escape spending time in his company, never complaining about having to work over her finishing time, and she hoped she would never feel that way about going home to Will. She got out of the bath and went downstairs.

The phone was ringing and she picked it up to hear a breathless Lily. 'Oh, Annie, it's Tom ... he's collapsed. We're on our way to the hospital. He's unconscious.' She let out a sob.

'Where are they taking him, Lily? Which hospital? We'll be there soon. He'll be OK. He's in the best hands.'

'Westmorland General.'

'We're on our way, Lily; I promise we won't be long.'

Annie hung up and rang Will, who answered on the first ring. 'Will, your dad's collapsed; he's on his way to Westmorland General in an ambulance with Lily.'

'How serious is it, Annie – did Lily say?'

'She doesn't know; I said we'd be there soon.'

'I'll be there in a minute.'

'I'll be ready; drive carefully, Will.'

She got dressed, grabbed her phone and some money then waited on the front doorstep for Will. His BMW turned into the street and she ran down the steps and climbed inside. Will's normally tanned face looked pale.

'Has she rung back?'

Annie shook her head. 'No, but it will take a while for them to get there. If you put your foot down we'll not be that far behind them. He'll be OK, Will; he's like you, made of tough stuff.'

'I hope so, Annie. I'd hate anything to happen to him now, especially before the wedding.'

Annie blinked back tears. She adored Tom and didn't know what she would do if the unthinkable happened.

They drove in silence, Will with his foot to the pedal. The roads weren't busy and they made it to the hospital in good time. They went to the accident and emergency department, where Lily was standing in the corner, her face pale and her arms wrapped around herself. Will ran over to her and hugged her; she hugged him back. Eventually they separated and Lily threw her arms around Annie.

'Thank you for coming so quickly … I don't know what to do. One minute he was fine, the next he collapsed on the kitchen floor. I heard a loud crash and thought he'd dropped a plate. I got such a shock to see him lying there.'

'Has anyone spoken to you yet? Did the paramedics have any idea what it was?'

'They said it could have been a stroke or a heart attack … The doctor said he'd come out as soon as possible.'

Lily burst into tears and Will stepped forward to hug her again. Annie looked at him and once more thanked her lucky stars that she had him, then she turned to go and see if she could find someone to speak to and find out what was happening.

1st July 1782

Betsy Baker listened to her mother groaning from her small bed behind the curtain in the front room and smiled. She did nothing but complain about the weather, the neighbours, what was for tea, what Betsy was doing, and on and on. Since she could remember, her mother had liked to use her fists on her; any excuse would result in a clip around the ear. If she didn't do her chores or was late to come in when she had been playing out, her punishment would be a sly punch in the ribs. Her mother had always been a drinker and how hard she would hit depended on how drunk she was.

Now that Betsy was much older and dared to hit her back, the punches were few and far between; instead, her mother preferred to use her vicious tongue to lash out at her, but Betsy was almost twenty-one and old enough to leave. If only she had somewhere to go, but her mother kept her there, always playing on her poor health. Betsy wanted a life of her own and a man. She wanted to live somewhere that wasn't damp and dingy or smelt of stale ale. She wanted to be free to do whatever she pleased with whoever she wanted. Her father had died when she was only five. She missed him. He would sing to her and tell her stories and she knew that he had loved her a lot more than her mother ever had.

Now, thanks to Betsy, her mother really did have poor health. Several nights ago Betsy had heard talk in the village of a powder called arsenic that could be bought from the chemist. Joss Brown, who lived at the farm not too far away, had been telling the rest of the men in the pub that he had bought some to kill off the rats that were overrunning his hay barns. Betsy worked behind the bar of The Queen's Head, where the men would gather each evening. Her mother hated her working in a pub but it gave Betsy a chance to get out of the cramped, cold cottage.

She had been flirting with Joss for weeks now. She was always quiet around the other men but she liked Joss, or she should say that she liked the big cottage that he lived in with his two sons. It was part of the farm that his mother and father owned. Joss was a widower; his wife had died last year and he had kept to himself ever since, but three times a week he would come into the pub for some ale and conversation. Betsy would do anything to escape from her mother and although she disliked children and did not want to have any herself, she would be able to put up with the horrible things until something or someone better came along.

This morning she had gone to the chemist and asked for some arsenic powder to kill the rats that had suddenly appeared in their house. The chemist had handed some over to her and told her to be very careful with it and she was. She had taken it straight home and put it into an old tin at the back of the larder, after first sprinkling some into her mother's broth. She thought that life would be much easier without her. Not half an hour later her mother had begun to complain of terrible stomach pain and feeling ill. She had taken to her bed and lay there all afternoon, moaning and groaning. Betsy had taken her a cup of tea with even more of the powder in and then left to go to the pub.

Her mother had begged her to call the doctor and she had said she would go and fetch him, but she had no intention of doing that. She wanted to leave her to it while she went to work, hoping that by the time she came home the woman would be dead and then she would call the doctor.

As Betsy was walking through the front door of the pub she walked into Joss, who was on his way out.

'Sorry, Joss, I'm running late. I never saw you there. Are you leaving so soon? It's only early.'

'Good evening, Betsy. It's been a grand day, hasn't it?'

Betsy nodded in agreement; if her mother was dead when she went home it would indeed be a grand day.

'Yes, Joss, it has been a wonderful day. Why don't you come back inside for one more drink? I like to see you and who will I speak to all night if you go home now?'

She could see the redness creeping up his cheeks and he was looking at her as if he was seeing her clearly for the first time. He noticed her long black hair, ice-blue eyes and her ample bosom.

'I want to come back in, I really do, but my father isn't well and I said I would milk the cows and take my boys back home. They're up at the farm with my mother.'

Betsy reached out and let her fingers brush along his bare arm. 'I am sorry to hear that, Joss. I hope he is better by the morning and then you can come back and talk to me tomorrow night. That is, if you want to?'

Joss shivered at her touch and she smiled.

'I'll be here waiting for you. Do not forget that, Joss Brown.'

She turned away from him and entered the pub, but she felt his eyes on her. He was standing watching her until she let the heavy wooden door shut and he could no longer see her. Betsy was having a grand old day. If everything went to plan, Joss would call round to offer his assistance. She could cry and tell him she couldn't bear to live in her cold, damp house, which still smelt of death. She hoped he would offer her a room at his cottage in exchange for some cooking and cleaning. Then she would work on him until he was besotted with her and ask for her hand in marriage.

The pub was busy and Betsy worked hard all evening. Old Jack Thomas would not leave her alone. For an old man he was like an octopus and whenever she passed him he would grab a handful of her behind. She'd laughed at him and slapped his arm away, telling him to behave himself or she would have him thrown from the pub. The other men had laughed. The talk in there had been good-humoured, the warmth from the sun today having a good effect on everyone's mood.

When it was time to go home she felt her stomach begin to churn. She hadn't seen a dead person before and hoped her mother didn't look like something from a nightmare. She put her cloak over her shoulders and declined an offer from one of the younger men in the pub to walk her home. She didn't want any gossip to get back to Joss and this was such a small village it would; there was no doubt of that. Her house was not a two-minute walk from the pub and she was home in no time, even though she had dragged her feet, uneasy about what she was about to find. She stood outside for a minute, trying to calm her shaking hands, then Betsy pushed the front door open and stepped inside, listening for any sound. It was so quiet; she couldn't remember the last time she had heard such peace in this house.

'Mother, I'm home now. How are you feeling? Do you still want me to fetch the doctor?' There were no candles burning as there would be every other night. The house was filled with darkness. Betsy's heart was beating fast with fear and excitement at what she might find behind the tatty, moth-eaten curtain that separated the living room from her mother's bedroom. She felt her way into the small kitchen, and then along the shelf above the stove for a candle and matches. She struck a match and the orange flame lit up the room briefly. She held the flame to the wick before it went out; it soon caught and the candle began to burn.

Not realising how much her hand was shaking until she lifted the candlestick up, she looked in the direction of the curtain. Her feet did not want to move but she forced them to take a step forward one at a time until her outstretched hand was touching the coarse material.

She drew it back and screamed. Not for one minute had she expected her mother to look as she did. Her face was frozen in an expression of contorted agony. Her head was turned towards the curtain. Her eyes were wide open, staring at Betsy, accusing her of murder, and there was blood around her mouth – so much blood. Betsy had no idea what she had expected to see but it had not been this and she carried on screaming until the neighbours came running to see what was the matter. She was led away by Mrs Whitman from next door, who had taken one look at her mother's body and gasped, crossing herself.

'Come, child – there is nothing you can do for her now.'

Betsy let her lead her by the hand to her house next door. This one was full of light and did not smell like her house had. A bleary-eyed teenage boy came down the stairs and Mrs Whitman ordered him to run and fetch Dr Johnson.

Chapter 2

The bell rang to tell them visiting time was over and Annie bent down to kiss Tom's cheek. He was so pale and had aged since he'd been admitted three days ago but at least he was alive. Will also bent down and kissed his dad, who grinned at the pair of them. His speech slurred, he spoke slowly. 'He really is a big softie underneath that cool exterior.'

Annie nodded. 'He is adorable, but you had us all worried, Tom. Don't go doing anything like that again.'

'I'll try not to.'

They turned and hugged Lily then left them to it. After closing the door to the private room behind them, Annie and Will left the hospital hand in hand. Neither of them spoke until they were outside.

'You know he was really lucky. It hasn't affected his speech too much and he can still walk and move his arms. I think he'll need someone to help at home, though. It's not fair to expect Lily to look after the house and my dad when he can afford to pay someone.'

'Oh, I don't know; plenty of people don't really have a choice, Will. They just have to get on with it and I don't mind popping in every day on my way home from work.'

'I know, but my dad isn't most people; he could afford a housekeeper or a nurse to help out. Even if it's only until he's back on his feet. I'll speak to Lily. I bet she refuses point-blank but it would make sense. I just wish we lived a bit nearer to them.'

'We could always go and stop with them for a little while.'

'Yes, we could, but it's not as if either of us are around much. We both work long hours and opposite shifts. What would you think about moving somewhere up there – a bit closer for you for work and nearer to my dad?'

'I'd love to, Will, but it depends on what we can afford. I love your house; it's perfect and buying something similar in the Lakes would cost a lot more than we can afford.'

Will pulled her close and kissed her. He loved the way she was so practical with money. She never expected anything like a lot of people would, given his dad's wealth.

'I love you,' he said.

'I love you too. Now, come on, take me home. I need a long soak in the bath and my pyjamas.'

'You also need me to scrub your back.'

'True, but I need a glass of wine and some chocolate more at this very minute.'

Will opened the car door for her and she got in. It had been a long day. She'd started work at eight so had been up since six, then she'd worked a ten-hour shift, which had been busy, and then she'd gone straight to the hospital to meet Will. She sank back into the soft leather seat of Will's BMW and closed her eyes.

He looked across at her and smiled. He was going to start looking for a house that Annie would fall in love with and was much nearer for her to get to work and nearer to his dad. He didn't mind being the one to have the longer commute; he enjoyed driving. It gave him time to think things through. A few of his cases had been solved on long car journeys when he'd had the time to really think about them. All he wanted was to make Annie happy, give her the life she deserved.

He'd heard from his dad's friend about a farm cottage that had been empty for twenty years. It was going up for auction and tomorrow he would make an appointment to view it. It was on the outskirts of Hawkshead and not as close as he'd like, but it was a beautiful village. There was the car ferry which ran most days so Annie could get across to Bowness. They'd gone to the quaint village for a wander round the last time they had a weekend off together and Annie had said how much she'd love to live somewhere like that, so it would be perfect for both of them. When he finally pulled up outside his cottage he gently shook Annie, who was asleep.

'Come on, sleepyhead. I'll run your bath while you see if you can find any chocolate in the cupboards.'

* * *

The silver CD player on Henry's bedside table played soothing classical music that filled the small room. The bed was comfortable, he had his music and the view from the window was impressive. His room looked out onto the landscaped front gardens and the water fountain. He couldn't really complain; it was like living in a hotel free of charge, every need tended to. The only thing that spoilt his view were the metal bars across the outside of the window and the locked metal door to stop him leaving his room whenever he felt like it, but that was OK. Since the day he'd come to the secure hospital he'd kept his head down. He'd always been polite and quiet – oh, so quiet. He'd spent six months in the medical ward where they had treated his severe facial burns until he was well enough to go up to a secure ward.

Henry turned from watching the nurses who were just finishing their shift and walking down the path to the main gates and the guard house. He caught his reflection in the mirror and for a second he didn't recognise himself. His dark hair had been burnt off in the fire and his scalp badly scarred. The skin was pink, shiny and puckered, the scars running down one side of his face. He had never been a vain person, not particularly thinking he was handsome, yet he still didn't like the face that stared back at him. Of course a hat and some dark sunglasses would cover the worst of it, should he ever be allowed back out into the real world, which he doubted would ever be possible; he was too much of a risk towards women, the judge had said at his trial, and Henry couldn't argue with him. There had been a lot of anger towards women, which was how he'd ended up in this predicament.

The nurses never looked at him, not directly, except for Megan, with the pink streak in her hair and the tattoos running up one arm. She was young enough to be his daughter and she would often sit on the end of his bed, talking to him about the weather or asking him how he was feeling. She would tell him her latest boyfriend troubles, which Henry wasn't the least bit interested in, but if he'd thought he lived a lonely life before he came here then it had got a whole lot worse now he was locked up and treated like a freak.

He knew that Megan was morbidly fascinated by him; she was probably dying to know why he'd done what he did, but she would never ask. She was forbidden from talking to him about his crimes. That was saved for Dr Grace Marshall, who had been there to see the drama unfold and watch him get caught so he did have a sneaking respect for her because she'd almost seen him in action. He didn't think he would ever kill her because she was far too valuable and he did enjoy their little chats, even if everything he told her was a distorted version of the truth. Henry wasn't stupid and he only told her what he thought she should know.

He had a bit of a soft spot for Nurse Megan, though; he wouldn't call it a crush because that was ridiculous, but he did like the attention she paid to him and he was working on her: feeding her snippets of his life before it had come to this in exchange for information about how the hospital worked, what she did on a typical day, how many guards were in the guard house and patrolling the grounds. Because Henry had no intention of staying locked up in this place for the rest of his life. Once he was well enough he had a couple of old acquaintances that he needed to visit and a plan he wanted to put in place.

When he had first been admitted and the pain had been excruciating and his days were nothing more than a morphine-induced haze, it had been the thought of meeting Annie Graham and Will Ashworth once again that had kept him going. It had given him the will to survive, against all odds.

The bolts on the door slid back and, bang on time, Megan entered with his lunch. He was supposed to eat with the other men on this wing but they were violent towards him, which was both a laugh and an insult. His crimes were no worse than any of the ones they had committed but for some reason they didn't like him, so he stayed in his room until he was collected by the nurses and guards each day and taken for his solitary walk around the grounds in what he called the giant birdcage. He enjoyed his hour of exercise and fresh air. The feeling of the sun, wind and rain on his face was one he would never take for granted ever again. Even in the torrential rain he would go out and walk, never missing a day.

His guards hated him even more in the bad weather and would shelter against the wall of the building or in one of the many doorways. Henry always promised them that he would behave and he did because he didn't want to jeopardise anything until the time was right for him to leave and not come back. It would be a bad day when Henry left. The weather would be terrible so as to hinder any searches that were made for him and his scent would be washed away by torrential rain. Unless, of course, he could get Megan to help him and he thought that he might be able to do just that. It would be a shame to kill her but needs must and she reminded him a lot of a girl he'd known briefly a couple of years ago. He would never forget Jenna White – she had been his first kill.

Chapter 3

Annie was glad to finish work. She'd been stuck all afternoon directing traffic in the glaring sun for the Windermere air show. It had gone fast but it was too hot to work, especially in the direct sun with frustrated motorists driving at you from every direction and not one of them understanding what a stop sign meant. A woman with a car full of grey-haired friends had almost taken her out and she had to stop herself from calling her a 'fucking idiot'. This would not have gone down very well with the public and probably would have resulted in a complaint to her sergeant, even though it was deserved.

The small station was empty when she got back; everyone was out enjoying the show, even Inspector Cathy Hayes, who always managed to worm her way out of as many public gatherings as she could. Annie was relieved because it meant she had time for a quick shower and could get changed in peace, then drive to the car ferry to meet Will on the opposite side of Lake Windermere at the Queen's Head in Hawkshead village. He had promised to buy her tea and a cold glass of wine and the thought of it had kept her going all afternoon.

She dried herself and got dressed in a pair of grey linen trousers, which were much cooler than her thick black combat pants, and a pale green blouse. She clipped her hair up and did a five-minute make-up job. Her nose was sunburnt so she covered it as best she could and left the station.

A door banged along the corridor. Annie paused. She knew the station was empty – it must be the resident ghost. She smiled to herself. Although she hadn't seen this one because it was very shy and kept itself to itself, it did like to bang doors and let her know it was around. She wasn't threatened by it or afraid because she knew it meant no harm; it was just going about its daily business and wasn't interested in her. Sometimes it was like that – not all ghosts were hanging around because they were stuck in this realm or didn't know how to move on. Some stayed because they wanted to.

She knew all of this because after sustaining a serious head injury two years ago that had been inflicted on her by her now dead husband, she had started to see ghosts. Which had totally freaked her out at first but after a while she had come to realise that it was a special gift and one that had helped her to overcome a serial killer by assisting a lovely ghost called Alice. She thought about poor little nine-year-old Sophie, who had desperately needed Annie's help to be set free from the Shadow Man who had taken her away from her family and kept her in the shadows for twenty years. She had come to Annie for help and fighting the Shadow Man had been the scariest thing Annie had done up to now.

Her friend Father John had tried to send him back to hell but had almost failed and it had been Annie who had stood her ground in sending him back, setting Sophie free in the process and reuniting her with her dead mum. Annie was lucky she wasn't plagued by dead people all the time, but if they needed her help they would come to her. Will had been scared by it at first but he and Jake, her best friend, had come to accept that Annie was now psychic and not mentally unstable, and it was just a part of her life.

She walked to the door and shouted down the corridor, 'Bye, you're on your own now but someone will be in later and I'll be back tomorrow afternoon.' Another door banged in answer and Annie smiled to herself. She would like to actually meet whoever it was when they plucked up the courage to show themselves.

She got into her convertible red Mini and put the roof down. It was stuffy inside and she wanted to freshen up and, besides, she only got to do this about six times a year with all the rain there usually was. The roads were still busy and it took her much longer to get to the car ferry than normal. There was a queue but she managed to squeeze into the last spot on the boat, which had just loaded. She paid her £4.50 and looked out across the water at the view. It was beautiful. There were lots of boats out sailing on the calm blue lake. The trees, houses and hills that surrounded the lake blended in seamlessly. The ferry was full of families and the sound of laughter as excited children were led from their cars by parents to take in the views.

Annie closed her eyes. She didn't think there was anything nicer than the sound of children's laughter and wondered to herself if she and Will would ever have any kids. Will was forty-five so he wasn't too old to be a dad and she was only thirty-four, but it wasn't something they'd ever discussed. She had always thought she didn't want kids, especially with Mike. It wouldn't have been fair to subject them to his violent outbursts. It was a relief that she had managed to escape from him when she had. Lately, every time she saw a woman pushing a pram or a man carrying a toddler through the busy streets of Bowness she would picture Will with a cute kid in his arms and her heart would ache just a tiny bit.

Maybe once they were married and settled down she would broach the subject with him and see how he felt. Of course if he didn't want kids that was fine as well, but she thought that he would make such an amazing dad it would be a shame not to give him the opportunity.

The ferry docked on the opposite side of the lake with a loud groan and a squeal of metal against stone and then it stopped suddenly. The barriers lifted and she turned the Mini's engine back on – last on, last off. There was a long line of cars waiting to board the ferry and go back to the other side. She drove off and waved at the ticket collector. Then she drove the short distance towards Hawkshead and the man of her dreams, who had texted her to say he was waiting for her at the pub and had managed to get a table out the front. She parked in the car park, emptying her purse of ten-pence pieces, feeding them into the machine. She got a ticket and then hurried to go and meet Will.

The early evening sun was still warm and the village was full of people wandering around. Annie walked towards the pub and felt her heart fill with joy at the sight of Will and the ice-cold glass of wine on the table in front of him. He looked up from the menu and grinned at her, his blue eyes crinkled and full of mischief. He looked so like his dad. Annie squeezed past a loud American couple who were blocking the way and bent down to kiss him on the cheek. He turned and kissed her on the lips and it was her turn to grin.

'Phew, am I glad to see you – what a day.'

She sat on the wooden bench next to him and picked up the glass, taking a large gulp. 'It's amazing.'

'What is – me or the wine?'

'You, of course, and the wine.'

He nudged her softly in the side. 'You liar – you meant the wine. I don't know about you but I'm starving and I'm having the biggest steak and chips they can drag out of the fridge.'

Annie looked at the menu and nodded in agreement. 'I'll have steak and a jacket potato, please.'

Will stood up and made his way to the bar to order. Annie sipped her wine as she people-watched. She could spend all evening people-watching. The American couple sat next to an older couple on the bench opposite and had struck up a conversation about how beautiful the village was and Annie agreed with them. It truly was. She could see the church, which was on a steep hill above the village square and she thought about Father John. She hadn't seen him for a while; she should really go and pay him a visit. Now that he'd taken over the church in Bowness permanently she wanted to ask him about the wedding. When she'd saved his life last year he'd told her he owed her one and would marry her and Will on the house. She wasn't after a cheap wedding but she would very much like him to marry them both.

Will reappeared and sat back down. 'I've got a surprise to show you after, but it will have to wait until we've finished eating.'

'You know I don't like surprises. Can't you just tell me what it is now?'

'No, sorry, I can't. For once you will have to be patient and anyway I will have to take you to it.'

Annie scrunched up her face. She had no idea what he was talking about but she didn't care; she could manage to wait an hour. They talked about Tom, Lily, the wedding, anything and everything, until the food arrived and Annie's stomach let out a groan at the size of the plate. Then they ate in complete silence, until the American woman leant over and asked her what she was eating because it looked divine. When they were both finished they left the pub and walked hand in hand back towards the car park.

'What do you want to do – follow me or leave your car here and I'll bring you up to get it tomorrow?'

'I'll come with you and you don't need to bring me back up. Cathy is working in Barrow until dinnertime; I'll ask her to pick me up on her way back up to Windermere and she can drop me off here.'

'Sounds like a plan. Come on, you're going to love this – I hope.'

They climbed into his car and he drove the opposite way than they would normally come down the small road that led through the village until they passed a big farmhouse and lots of barns. He carried on driving for a couple of minutes and then turned off at an old broken gate onto an overgrown gravel drive. It was bumpy and the hedges were so overgrown it was impossible to see where they were going. Will drove slowly until the drive opened onto a large house, which was unloved and in desperate need of repair, but it was love at first sight for Annie.

'Oh my, what an amazing house. Whose is it?'

Will stopped the car under a huge drooping lilac tree and picked up her hand. 'Well, that depends on how much you like it, because if you do like it then it could be ours.'

She looked at him. 'How?'

'Well, you said you'd like to live in this area and it belongs to my dad's friend who owns the farm we passed. He wants to sell it and was going to put it up for auction but he said if we like it then we can have first refusal. It will save him the hassle of trying to sell it.'

Tears glistened in her eyes and for the first time in months she felt speechless. 'But how could we afford it?'

Will laughed. 'This is cheeky, I know, but your house sale should complete soon, so that would be almost enough to pay for it. We can sell mine and then use that money to renovate it. But, to be truthful, you really don't need to worry if we can afford it. All I care about is if you love it enough to want to spend the time renovating it and then living in it. The rest will work itself out.'

Will didn't want to sound pretentious but he could more than afford it without using Annie's money, but she would want to contribute and he didn't want to take her independence away from her.

'Will, I love it. Have you been inside? How bad is it?'

'I had a look around before I went to the pub and, believe it or not, considering it's been empty for over twenty years it's not in too bad a shape. The roof is sound and so is the structure. It needs new windows and doors, damp-proofing, and there are a lot of small rooms downstairs that could be knocked through to make it more open-plan and spacious, but see what you think.'

They got out of the car and Annie squealed. The garden was

overgrown but amongst the weeds and brambles were cornflowers, lavender, roses and wild foxgloves. Will took hold of her hand and led her towards the front door, which had its own porch built around it. The trellis on either side was rotten and the creamy white rambling rose that covered it was holding it all together, but it could all be replaced.

As she followed Will under the porch, she shivered and the hairs on the back of her neck prickled. Her inbuilt supernatural radar was telling her it was already inhabited by someone that Will would never see, but there was no way she would let that stop her because she knew that she wanted to love this house from the inside as much as she loved the outside. As Will pushed the wooden door open, she looked at the faded wooden sign above it – Apple Tree Cottage – and sighed. The house was empty for now and Will led her by the hand from room to room. It was a good job neither of them were overly tall, as the ceilings were low. Each one had exposed wooden beams. Jake would struggle because he was very tall, but after hitting his head a few times he would remember to duck.

The kitchen was the only room that still had most of its cupboards and a huge old-fashioned range cooker. It wasn't very big and Will read her mind. 'If we knocked through this and the other two rooms we could have a really big kitchen-diner where you could practise your cooking skills.'

He winked at her and she laughed.

'Cheeky – it's a good job you can cook or we'd starve. Will, I love it. I can see a huge pine table and chairs and a sofa and a bookcase in the corner.'

She could also see children running and playing but she didn't say this because she didn't want to him to get scared before they'd even finished looking.

'It's everything I've ever dreamt about, but what about you? Your house is equally gorgeous, just a lot smaller.'

'I love it around here, Annie, and I would very much like to live here, in this house. I think it has so much potential and it will make an amazing family home. Of course, it will also be a major pain in the arse with the planning and builders and mess, but if you can put up with it then so can I.'

Annie held her breath. He'd said 'family home' and she wondered if perhaps he'd been thinking the same as she had but was too afraid to say anything. She threw her arms around his neck and kissed his lips hard, then just as quickly she pulled away, taking his hand and dragging him to the rickety, steep staircase. They climbed up the stairs and Annie was surprised at how large the landing was; there was enough room by the small window, which looked out over the fields and woods at the back of the house, to put a desk and chair.

They went into each room. There were five bedrooms in all and a bathroom. These rooms were much larger than the ones downstairs and the master bedroom was bigger than the one they had now. Annie paused in there to look at a painting on the wall; it was of the house when it was lived in. The exterior walls were white and the window frames painted pale green and Annie knew then that this was how she wanted it to look – exactly the same. There were wisps of smoke coming from the chimney and in the garden under a tree in the corner she could just make out the figure of a woman who was wearing a long white dress and had long straight dark hair. She had a basket on her arm but she was only visible to the naked eye if you squinted. Annie wondered if this part of the painting had been damaged somehow because the rest was in good condition.

She heard a scratching sound and whirled around. It sounded like fingernails being scraped across a blackboard. She shuddered but it stopped as suddenly as it had started. Will, who had wandered into the next bedroom, called her to come and have a look at the view. She pushed the noise to the back of her mind. The house had been empty so long it was bound to have mice, birds and God knows whatever else living inside. A voice whispered, *And ghosts*. She followed Will's voice to the room, which looked onto the front garden from the large window. As she crossed the creaking floor to look out of it she was hit by a sense of déjà vu so strong that it made her knees tremble. She had looked out of this window before – the last two nights in a row in her nightmare. Will looked at her, taking hold of her hand.

'What's wrong Annie – is everything OK?'

She smiled at him, afraid to tell him anything when she didn't understand it herself.

'Wow, it's truly beautiful, Will. I can't believe it's just been left to go to ruin for so long. I wonder why the owners moved out?'

'I do know, but I don't want to put you off.'

'Oh, God, please don't tell me someone was murdered in here.'

Will laughed. 'You're funny, Annie, and you have the nerve to call Jake a drama queen. No, nothing as horrible as that. The couple that lived here were called Bill and Margaret and they left because Bill became quite poorly, mentally. He had to be put into a mental hospital and back then it wasn't as easy to get out as it is now. His wife was elderly and she moved into a flat to be near her husband, but his health deteriorated and he died. Margaret was devastated and didn't want to live here on her own so she never came back.'

'Aw that's so sad, but kind of romantic too. And now we might be able to live here and bring it back to life.'

'Yes, say the word, Miss Graham, and it can be ours. I'll call and see the owner on the way back.'

Annie chewed her lip and looked around. She loved it and it would make the most amazing house once the wildlife and the ghost had been cleared out. The house was begging to be renovated.

'Yes, please. I would so much love to live here with you for the rest of our lives.'

This time it was Will's turn to kiss her and as he pulled her close she thought she heard that high-pitched scratching again, but she blocked it out. Sending a message to whomever it was that she would deal with them when the time was right and she was ready, she leant forward, kissing Will back.

'Eek, I'm so excited to live here – I'd live in a caravan in the grounds until it's ready if we have to.'

Will laughed. 'If we have to, we can stay with my dad and Lily. I'm not too keen on caravans. Wait until you see the back garden; there's an orchard full of fruit trees and over an acre of pasture land, so if you ever fancied owning a horse, now's your chance.'

'I've never really been the horsey type but I might agree to some chickens and a potbellied pig.'

They went out and, as Will locked the front door, Annie saw a shadow pass over the bedroom window they had just been looking out of. She looked up and strained her eyes but there was no one there, or so she hoped because she didn't want to have her chance of a happy-ever-after spoiled by some restless spirit.

Chapter 4

Annie had promised Lily she would call in on her way home from work to meet the new housekeeper that Tom had agreed to before they had let him leave the hospital. Tom had accused Will and Lily of blackmail, but eventually he had said yes. He had told Will when they were alone that he'd only put up a fight because he didn't want Lily to think he didn't think she could cope. Tom and Will both knew quite well that she could cope, but Tom wanted to be able to spend as much time with Lily as he could without her worrying about the cleaning or shopping.

Annie parked out the front of their house and sighed. It didn't matter how many times she visited, she just couldn't believe that someone could live in a place so beautiful, although the cottage that she and Will had just signed the contract for would one day look beautiful too, just not on such a grand scale. She walked up the stone steps and patted the head of one of the stone lions that flanked the front door. It was force of habit and one that tickled Will every time he saw her do it, but he'd never teased her about it – well, not much. She rang the doorbell and waited patiently instead of using the key Lily had insisted she have in case she ever needed somewhere to hide and they weren't in.

The door opened and Annie was surprised to see a woman

around the same age as she was; she had envisaged an older woman wearing a black and white maid's uniform opening the door. This tall blonde woman wore a pair of black three-quarter jeans and a black T-shirt and had a duster in one hand and tin of polish in the other.

'Hello, you must be Amelia. My name is Annie. I'm Tom's soon-to-be daughter-in-law.'

The woman's mouth formed a smile but it never quite reached her eyes. 'Yes, I am. I've heard a lot about you, Annie.'

She stepped to one side to let Annie pass. The way she looked at her made her feel uneasy.

'They're in the library.'

And then she walked away, back to whatever it was she was polishing, leaving Annie to it. Annie didn't like her but had no idea why. She'd never seen her before in her life and wondered why she felt so strongly about the woman. She was blonde and pretty with a look of Laura, one of Will's work colleagues who was now dead, so that might be why. Although she and Will had got over the one-night stand he never actually had with Laura, it still plagued her on the odd occasion. She walked along the hall until she reached the library door and knocked. Tom's voice told her to come in and she opened the door, surprised to see Tom sitting at the desk and Lily sitting on the chair. Annie walked over and bent down to kiss Tom's cheek. She grinned at Lily.

'How are you feeling today, Tom? I hope you're being a model patient.'

'I'd be a lot better if people would stop fussing over me.'

He looked at Lily when he spoke and she rolled her eyes at him. 'You're such a crank, Tom Ashworth; if I didn't love you I wouldn't want to be with you because you're driving me mad, as well you know with all your moaning.'

Lily winked at Annie and left the room.

'Sorry, Annie, we were just in the middle of a discussion and Lily was losing, badly. She's such a sore loser.'

'Ah, well, most women are. What's up? Is it anything I can help with?'

'Not really.' He lowered his voice. 'Lily doesn't like our new housekeeper. She wants me to tell her we don't require her services any more. I've told her she's staying until I don't need someone to run around after me and then she can do whatever she wants with her. I mean, we don't know the girl and you can't sack someone for giving off bad vibes, can you? Not that I can sense any, but super sleuth Lily can.'

Annie laughed. 'You do know that a woman is nearly always right, don't you, Tom, even when they're not?'

'I do – I've learnt that the hard way – but I also know when a woman needs a hand and Lily is too proud to ask for help, so I've had to take the lead. She'll get over it. I think she was expecting Mrs Doubtfire to walk in and take over the cleaning.'

He laughed and Annie joined him; it was the best sound she'd heard in ages. He was definitely on the mend.

Lily came back in with a tray filled with cups, saucers and a cafetière of fresh coffee. 'Has he told you what I think?'

Annie nodded. 'Yes.'

'Well, what do you think?'

'Ah, this has nothing to do with me so I'll keep out of it, if you don't mind. It's still early days. You can see how it's going in a couple of weeks and then decide.'

Tom looked at his wife. 'See? The voice of reason. Listen to the nice police officer; she talks very good sense.'

Lily poked Tom in the ribs then bent down and kissed his head. 'You drive me mad, Tom.'

'Yes, I suppose I do, but you love me all the same.'

They changed the conversation to Apple Tree Cottage and what Tom thought of the plans they'd had drawn up by Jake's partner Alex, who was an architect.

'It's a lovely old place. I think you and Will are going to be very happy in there. Now, how long do I have to practise lifting a glass to my lips without spilling a single drop of champagne at your wedding reception?'

'Eight weeks – I can't believe how fast it's coming around. I'm so glad I have you to help with the planning, Lily, because I really haven't got a clue.'

At the mention of the wedding Lily's face brightened and a smile spread across it. Tom winked at Annie and sat quietly, listening to the plans Lily had to turn their back garden into a romantic fairy-tale grotto. If it kept Lily happy it meant he was happy and he nodded along as the two women chatted about dresses, menus, guests and cake.

After an hour Annie stood up. 'Sorry, I need to get going; Will has promised that he'll be home in time for tea tonight so I want to be there to photograph the occasion.'

Tom laughed. 'I never knew that two men could be so lucky to find such amazing women.'

Annie kissed them both. 'I'll let myself out.'

She walked to the door and opened it, surprised to see Amelia standing on the other side, her cheeks burning. She nodded at her and then walked to the front door and let herself out. There was definitely something she didn't like about that woman and she hoped it wouldn't turn into something bad.

* * *

Will walked through the front door as promised at ten past six and Annie pretended to faint.

'Ha ha, very funny. Jake's on his way. Apparently he and Alex have something they want to tell you and it can't be done over the phone; it has to be done in person.'

'What is it; did he say?'

'Nope, it's top secret. You have to be the first to know, before anyone else.'

'I suppose we'll find out soon enough. I called to see your

dad on my way home. He looks so much better and he was very chatty. Lily is pissed off with him, though, about that Amelia.'

'Ah, yes, the ice queen. She's a funny woman. She didn't crack a smile once when I was joking with her the other day. In fact she wouldn't even look at me, apart from the odd sneaky glance. I'll have to tell Stu that I've finally found a woman who doesn't find me irresistible.'

'That's so vain, Will; I can't believe you just said that. But yes, I suppose there are some women who won't find you their type. Lesbians for one.'

'You're just jealous, Annie.'

He dodged the slap she aimed for his arm and grabbed hold of her, pulling her towards him. 'But I only have eyes for you.'

'Good, I'm glad about that because I can't live without you. So what's happening in the high-profile world of CID this week – anything exciting?'

'Not much, thank God. My department has had more excitement in two years than it has in the last twenty. Just the same old stuff really. The most exciting thing to happen this week was someone had their already broken petrol generator stolen from their shed by someone they already knew and identified.'

There was a loud knock on the door and Will opened it to see a beaming Jake and Alex standing on the other side. Jake was holding a bottle of champagne and offered it to Annie.

'To what do we owe this pleasure?'

Jake stepped in, followed by Alex.

'We wanted you to be the first to know. We're going to be parents,' Jake announced.

Annie threw her arms around Jake, squeezing him tight and then Alex. 'Aw, congratulations, but if you don't mind me asking, how?'

Will stepped forward to shake their hands. 'Congratulations, guys.'

Jake followed Annie into the kitchen. 'What do you think – we kept it quiet, eh?'

'You certainly did. Have you found someone to be a surrogate?'

'Oh, God, no, there are so many kids out there who need loving homes; we put our names down to adopt last year and have been going through the process for months now. This morning we got told that a three-month-old baby girl needed a home sooner rather than later. I can't wait! I never thought I'd say this but I guess looking after you has made me broody.'

Annie stared at him. 'What are you trying to say – that I'm like some big kid?'

Alex pulled a face at Will and the pair of them began talking about the latest football results, neither of them wanting to get involved.

'Of course not, Annie, but I do get to babysit you a lot and I'm just saying it made me realise how much I like taking care of people.'

Annie kept her temper in check, not wanting to spoil what was obviously an important day for both of them, but Jake had a knack of putting his size-twelve feet in his mouth without thinking almost every time he opened it.

'That's OK then. I'll let you off and I suppose that you are a very good babysitter.'

The tension in the room dissipated and Will felt his shoulders relax. He popped the cork on the champagne bottle and poured it into the four glasses he had just taken from the cupboard, handing Alex one first.

He downed it and smiled. 'You have such a way with words, Jake, I'm surprised anyone even bothers speaking to you most of the time.'

'I do, Alex; it's like a gift from the gods.'

This made all four of them laugh. You couldn't stay mad at Jake – well, not for very long. Annie wondered if she would ever have such news to tell her friends and, judging by the expression on Will's face, she thought that one day she might. He was looking very wistful into his champagne glass.

'Here's to Jake and Alex, who are going to be amazing parents.' Will toasted them and then downed his drink as well.

1782

Betsy didn't watch the cart that brought her mother's coffin to the front door; she didn't want to see it. Mrs Whitman had been the village's local layer of the dead for years and had gone in to wash and dress her mother in her Sunday best, ready to be laid into the coffin. The funeral was not for another three days but she felt as if she had already outstayed her welcome here, at the Whitmans' house. Tonight she must go back home and sleep in her own bed. She was tired and hoped this would make her sleep and forget the fact that her mother's body was lying downstairs, slowly rotting away. She wasn't sure whether it was guilt she'd felt or relief when the doctor had said she had bled to death from a burst blood vessel and there was nothing Betsy could have done to stop it. She had thanked him, knowing fine well it was nothing of the sort, but she didn't want him to suspect her of any wrongdoing.

Mrs Whitman and two of her mother's friends had been in and cleaned the house from top to bottom, ready for Betsy to go home. They had offered to go back in with her but she had told them, 'No, thank you.' They had done more than enough.

It was dusk by the time they had finished and Betsy said goodbye to them as they sat around Mrs Whitman's small kitchen table drinking tea. She went to her own house and paused at the front door. On the step was a bunch of freshly picked meadow flowers and a note. Bending to pick them up, she smiled to see Joss's name on the note. How sweet of him to have taken the time to bring them. Forgetting all about her deadly crime, she went into the house and over to the sink where, on the kitchen windowsill, there was a glass jar. Joss was so tall and handsome;

he had such a sweet smile. Her mother had rarely smiled at Betsy, even as a child, whereas Joss grinned the moment he saw her, making her feel special. No one had made her feel like that since her father had died, and she liked it.

Humming to herself, she filled the jar with water and put the flowers inside. Turning to put them on her small kitchen table, she gasped when she heard a groan coming from behind the curtain where her mother's bed was. Her fingers slipping on the wet glass, she almost dropped the jar, just managing to put it down before it fell to the floor and smashed into a million pieces. She stood still, her head cocked to the side, listening for the sound again. It was dark in the cramped room and she really needed to light some candles but she was afraid to move.

Behind the curtain, she could see the outline of the wooden coffin containing her mother's corpse. How could this be? Had she not been told herself that the woman was dead? The doctor had said that she was dead — maybe she had just been in a deep sleep and not dead at all. Betsy did not dare to move and stood there waiting, but there was no more noise so she convinced herself it had been her imagination then set about washing her hands and lighting candles. The curtain was drawn and there was no way on this earth she would open it and look at her mother's cold body. Mrs Whitman had placed fresh flowers around the kitchen and the sweet fragrance filled the air. Betsy took a candle and made her way up the stairs, as far away from the coffin as she could get.

Upstairs, she changed into her white cotton nightdress and climbed into the cold bed. She settled herself down and pulled the soft blanket up to her face. Her eyelids felt so heavy, she was glad for small mercies and leant across to the wooden bedside table and blew out the candle. She closed her eyes at the same time so she did not have to see the shadows that filled the corners of her room. Within no time at all she was asleep, too tired to dream.

The next thing she knew, the clock in the kitchen chimed three and Betsy opened her eyes. She had been restless for the last half an hour, too tired to wake up, but then she heard the scraping noise. This was different to the mice she could sometimes hear scurrying around up in the attic; it was much heavier, as if someone was moving a piece of furniture around downstairs. The hairs on the back of her neck prickled as she realised that someone was in her house. The sharp sound of breaking glass made her flinch.

Scared beyond anything she had ever felt in her life, she summoned the courage to get out of bed to go and see who it was. She felt around for the candle and managed to light it on the third attempt. Who would be so disrespectful to break into her home with her mother's dead body still inside? Opening her bedroom door, she took a step forward onto the small landing and froze. The dragging sound was approaching the stairs and every hair on her arms stood on end.

'Who's there?' Her voice wavered and she did not feel very brave, as whatever it was continued to move in her direction.

'I will scream if you come near me. Get out of this house at once before I open the window and scream until everyone in the village comes running to see what is happening.'

There was no reply but the dragging sound ceased. Betsy breathed a little slower. Whoever it was had gone, scared by her threats. She would give them time to leave the house and then she would go down to see what they had been doing. There were some rascals in the village but she did not think any of them would be so low as to come into her house when she was all alone in the middle of the night. She counted to one hundred and was about to step forward when the dragging started again, this time quicker and in the direction of the stairs. Terrified, she stepped back then turned to run into her bedroom, but as she turned she caught a glimpse of the figure that was now at the bottom of the stairs. It was almost bent double, wearing her mother's funeral clothes. She ran into her bedroom and slammed the door shut, throwing her back against it, and screamed.

It was Seth, Mrs Whitman's son, who came to see what was happening. He hammered on the front door and she ran to the bedroom window and leant out.

He looked up at her. 'Blimey, Betsy, you look as if you've seen a ghost. What's the matter with you? Screaming loud enough to wake the dead up yonder in the churchyard!'

She whispered, 'There's someone in the house, standing at the bottom of the stairs. Please help me.'

He rattled the door handle but it was locked. 'I can't get in; it's locked up tight. Did you leave a window open? How did they get in? I'll go fetch my dad; he might be able to get the door open.'

'No,' she shouted after him and he turned back to look up at her face.

'Well, what am I to do?'

'Please don't go, don't leave me. Kick the door in and if you cannot then break a window. I don't care as long as you come inside and chase away whoever is downstairs. I'm so scared.'

He bent down and ran at the door with his shoulder as hard as he could. The door, which was old and not in a very good state of repair, crashed open and he fell through it onto the cold stone floor of the kitchen. He couldn't see much because of the stars that were flashing in front of his eyes. Betsy shouted down to him and he dragged himself up onto all fours. He squinted as his vision adjusted to the dark and looked around. There was no sign of anyone standing at the bottom of the stairs or anywhere else and he shouted to her, 'Everything is all right; there is no one in here … well, except for you and me, oh, and your mother.'

Betsy ran down the stairs and threw herself into his arms. 'Oh, my Lord, I have never been so scared. Thank you.'

She lit two more candles and looked around the room. The flowers she had placed on the kitchen table were now lying on the floor in a damp puddle amongst the broken glass of the jar she had put them in.

'Look – see, someone was in here. It looked as if they were wearing my mother's clothes. Please take a look inside her coffin and make sure she is still wearing her best dress.'

Seth squirmed but then did as she asked; he didn't want her to tell everyone he was afraid of a dead body. Picking up a candle, he walked over and drew back the curtain. He paused and wrinkled his nose at the smell. Stepping closer, he looked down into the coffin then stepped away again and turned to Betsy.

'Your mother is still wearing her Sunday best that she wore to church every week. Are you sure you weren't having a bad dream? I mean, you've had a shock; it's bound to have been playing on your mind.'

Betsy, who had finished sweeping the broken glass, turned to look at him. Could it have been a dream or maybe it had been her guilty conscience? You couldn't just take another person's life and not expect to be affected by the matter. She nodded her thanks to him but she knew deep down that it had been no dream. How had the jar been smashed? There was no wind tonight and they had no animals in the house, not even a rat would be interested in a jar of flowers. She didn't want to stop in this house a minute longer.

'Please can I come back with you? I don't want to be in here on my own.'

He looked across at the coffin and then at Betsy. She was only two years older than him and he tried to imagine how it must feel to have to share a house with just your dead mother. A cold chill ran down his back.

'Course you can, but you'll have to stay on the chair downstairs. I don't want my mother accusing me of things that are not true.'

She frowned at him, too wrapped up in her own world to realise what he was trying to say, then she nodded. Too scared to look in the direction of the coffin, she left the house and shut the door behind her, locking it and leaving her mother inside.

Mrs Whitman was already awake when they went inside and

she took one look at Betsy's white face and went across and held her.

'Child, you can stay here until they take your mother away and bury her. I never thought it through. I'm so used to the dead, they don't bother me one little bit, but this is the first time you have had to deal with it and I should have been a bit more considerate.'

The relief that washed through Betsy was enormous and she would be eternally grateful to this woman who had shown her more kindness in the last few days than her mother had her entire life.

The day finally came for the funeral and, as they all lined up along the front street watching the coffin get loaded onto the handcart, Betsy had to stop herself from smiling. She was finally going to be free of that awful woman and she could go back into her own home and sleep in her own bed. The villagers who had lined up along the square all walked behind the cart as it was pushed through the narrow streets to the church.

Betsy noted that Joss was standing outside the pub with his cap in his hands and his head bowed. She turned her head to look back at him and as he stared at her she gave him what she hoped was a sad smile. Now in his eyes they both shared the same pain in their hearts: he had lost his wife and she her mother. Even though Betsy was glad to be free of her burden she would never let Joss know that because he genuinely grieved for his wife. She hoped he would still be there after the funeral because she very much wanted to talk to him.

The church service was short and the burial even shorter. As the priest said his parting words she stepped forward to throw down a bunch of daisies she had picked this morning from the fields at the back of the house and whispered, 'I'm sorry, Mother, but you have to rest in peace and leave me alone now. I have my own life to live.' Betsy stayed until the last and watched as her neighbours and the other villagers filed out of the church gate, down the steep steps until she was on her own. She felt a warm hand on her shoulder and turned to see Joss standing behind her.

'Come on, Miss Betsy, there is nothing more you can do now.'

She smiled at him and nodded. 'I do believe you are right, Joss. Will you take me to the pub so I can have a drink to toast her and drown my sorrows at the same time?'

She reached out and clasped his hand. At first he wasn't sure what to do but then he gripped it gently and together they left the grave and walked back towards the pub. It was busy inside, the locals loving nothing more than a funeral as a good excuse to not do any work and drink ale all day. She sat on a chair in the corner and waited while Joss went to the bar to get her a drink. He came back with one each and then he sat down next to her. The next couple of hours went past in a blur and Betsy got drunker and drunker until she could not stand straight.

When Mrs Whitman brought her back she nodded at Joss. 'I think you should take her home, Joss, make sure she's tucked up in bed and lock the door behind you.'

He nodded. He knew that Mrs Whitman trusted him but he did not know if he trusted himself. Betsy was all he could think about until an image of his wife would appear in front of his eyes and remind him he was a married man. He stood up and helped Betsy to her feet.

'Come on, Betsy. I think it's time you and me went home now.'

Betsy laughed. 'Why, Joss, are you finally propositioning me? I thought the day would never come.'

His cheeks burned but he grinned at the same time. 'Not as such. I just want to make sure you get home safely. Seth told me about the other night and how you thought there was an intruder in your house.'

He took hold of her arm and walked her towards the front of the busy pub and out of the door into the cobbled street. It was dusk now and he really should get back to his children; he'd been gone all afternoon. He walked Betsy across the village square and towards her house. They went inside and he lit some candles and closed the windows, which had been left open to air the house through and get rid of the smell of death. She stumbled as she walked across the room to where there was a curtain drawn across. Tugging it open, she nodded at the empty bed then turned back to him.

'Are you going to tuck me in, Joss; make sure I'm safe?'

He nodded, not sure if he should be taking a young woman upstairs to her bedroom, but he didn't want her falling. As she stumbled her way to the top and into her bedroom he followed her. She began to undress and once more he felt his cheeks begin to burn and he turned around to face the wall. He felt her warm hands wrap around his waist and, as he turned to face her, she hugged him.

'Thank you, Joss. Today you have been my protector and I like it. I like it very much. If I can ever repay the favour I will.'

'You are very welcome, Betsy. Grief is a terrible thing.'

Before he could finish what he was saying she stood on her tiptoes and put her soft lips against his much rougher ones. He paused, knowing this was wrong, but then he pushed the thought to one side and kissed her back. Wrapping her arms around his neck, she didn't stop and he didn't want her to. Scooping her up, he carried her over to the bed and laid her down, climbing up next to her. His hands ran up and down her legs and he marvelled at how soft her skin was and how good she smelt. She tugged at his trousers and he wanted nothing more than to bury himself inside her but he stopped, guilt at the thought of his dead wife and his two boys who were waiting for him back at the farm making everything that had seemed so wonderful only seconds ago feel so wrong.

He pulled himself off her and stood up. 'I'm sorry, Betsy, I really am. I shouldn't have acted like that with you, especially when you are so upset.'

'Joss, now is not the time to take the moral high ground. I want you and I know you want me ... well, you did a minute ago.'

She reached out and let her fingers trail over the front of his trousers.

'Yes, I do want you; I did want you, but I have to get home to my boys. They will be wondering where I've got to. They need me.'

Betsy felt a cold shard of jealousy stab straight through her heart. He thought the little bastards were more important than her and what she would have let him do to her would have made most men's dreams come true. Her eyes narrowed but she said nothing, just nodded.

He fastened his trousers and tucked his shirt back in. 'I will come and see you tomorrow. You get some sleep.'

And with that he turned and left her alone in her bed. She waited until she heard him close the front door and then she screamed and hit her fists against the pillow in frustration, hatred forming in the pit of her stomach against nine-year-old twin boys she had never even met. They would not get in the way of what she wanted – and what she wanted was their father and his big house. The alcohol made her brain foggy and her eyes closed. She drifted off to sleep, dreaming of a big cottage to live in, with just her and Joss and no horrid children running around in the garden, spoiling her life.

Chapter 5

Annie handed a plate of scrambled egg on toast and a mug of coffee to Will, then she sat opposite him with her coffee.

He looked up at her. 'Are you OK? It's just you were tossing and turning so much in your sleep last night I thought you were doing an aerobics class.'

She laughed. 'Maybe that's why I'm so knackered this morning then. I'm fine, thanks. Just a bit tired. I keep having the same nightmare – I'm running away from a group of men who are chasing me but, before I find out what happens, I always wake up at the same part.'

'Well, I hope it wasn't me you were running from!' He reached out for her hand. 'You're not having second thoughts about the wedding, are you? I understand if you are. I know you had a crap time with Mike. Plus it's all been blown up way out of proportion, hasn't it? I know Lil means well, but honestly, dancing lessons so we get the first dance right is going a little bit over the top if you ask me. What's wrong with a fumble in the dark and a bit of drunken swaying from side to side? I can ask my dad to tell her to take a step back if you want?'

'Don't be daft. I want to be Mrs Ashworth more than I want anything in this whole world. There is no comparison between you and Mike; you could never be like him if you tried, and yes, the dancing lessons are a bit too far but she's only trying to help. She wants it to be perfect and so do I. The first time round, it was more a marriage of convenience really. A quick "I do" in the register office and then back to the pub for pie and peas, all to get away from my mother. There's just so much going on at the moment that I don't know what to think about first. Alex and Jake are coming to the cottage with me this afternoon to go over Alex's plans with the builders again. It comes in handy having an architect as a friend; he's saved us a fortune.'

'I know and he's so good. I didn't recognise the downstairs when I called a couple of days ago – it's really taking shape. Are you happy with it?'

'I love it. It's everything I've ever dreamt of and more. Thank you.'

'Don't thank me; you own just as much of it as I do. I just want you to be happy, Annie, for us to be happy and spend the rest of our lives together.'

She stood up and walked around to where he was sitting and wrapped her arms around him, kissing him on the cheek. 'I am happy, Will, in fact I've never been so happy.'

She left to go and get ready, put a bit of make-up on so she didn't look like the Bride of Frankenstein, as Jake so lovingly called her. Will shouted goodbye as he went out of the front door and she ran to the bedroom window to knock on it and wave to him, blowing him a kiss. She tried not to think about the dreams that were threatening to take over but it was hard. They scared her because they were so real. Every morning she woke up at the same point, just as she fell over the rock and down the embankment into the icy-cold river. In a way she wanted to know what happened next: did she hit her head and die or did the men with the dogs catch up with her? Whatever it was and whoever the woman was, it must have been terrifying for her, all alone and being chased like a criminal. It never entered Annie's mind that the woman might have committed some heinous act and that was the reason she was being chased.

She got herself ready and then spent the next couple of hours browsing the internet for wallpaper and furnishings. She couldn't wait until the house was ready for the finishing touches. She'd already started painting the bedrooms as they had needed the least work doing to them. She decided to let Jake and Alex follow her up to the house in their car so she could stop behind to finish painting the master bedroom. She had picked out a soft grey paint for the walls and had ordered lemon accessories so it wasn't too girly for Will.

* * *

Tom was sitting up in bed. He hadn't slept well last night so Lily had insisted he had to stay in bed until he'd had a couple more hours' sleep. She walked into the bedroom carrying a breakfast tray even though it was mid-morning. She placed it on the bed and bent and kissed his forehead.

'Morning, sleepyhead – who said they'd never go back to sleep? You were snoring before I'd finished in the bathroom.'

'You're not always right, maybe just now and again.'

'Do you mind if I go and do some bits of stuff for the wedding? I said I'd go and see the florist and a couple of other people.'

Tom knew that Lily was having more fun planning this wedding than either Will or Annie, but they'd both assured him they were fine with it.

He nodded. 'Yes, I think I can manage without my nursemaid for a couple of hours.'

She kissed him again. 'There's a letter – well, it looks more like a card – for you on the tray. Probably a get-well one. I hope it's not from a secret admirer!' She turned and left him to it.

Tom looked down at the tray. She'd already poured his tea and buttered his toast so he wouldn't struggle too much. He picked up the envelope and ran his butter knife along it. It was a pale pink card decorated with balloons and a baby's pram, with 'Congratulations on the birth of your baby girl' written across the front. He frowned and picked up the envelope to check it had actually been sent to him. The name and address were written by hand in block capitals but it was definitely his name it was addressed to. He opened the card and a small black and white photo fluttered onto the floor.

Dear Daddy,

I don't think Mummy ever told you about me. I'm a big girl now and ever so lonely. Mum died last year and I'm all on my own. In fact, I've always been on my own.

It's time I had a family. It would be nice to meet you and my brother one day soon. You don't know me but I've been watching you all for some time now and I feel as if I know you all. I hope you're feeling better?

Love me

Xxx

Tom felt the tea he'd just drunk bubbling in his stomach as memories of an illicit affair that had only lasted one week thirty-five years ago filled his mind. He'd stopped it not long after it began because he couldn't do it to Elizabeth, his wife, and he'd come to realise pretty quickly that although Bethany had been a fun, wild, sexy girl she was also completely mentally unstable. Surely she hadn't got pregnant and had a child and kept it from him?

His hands shook and he felt as if he was going to be sick. He pushed the tray to one side and tried to get out of bed to go to the bathroom. In his hurry, he slipped and knocked the tray, which fell to the floor with a clatter, but he didn't try to pick it up; instead, he bent down and picked up the grainy black and white Polaroid photo that he hadn't seen before and he limped across to the bathroom, where he slammed the door shut and retched over the toilet bowl. The housekeeper came running up the stairs to check that he hadn't fallen out of bed or collapsed again. She took one look at the overturned tray and broken china that had spilt onto a small white envelope and grinned. Daddy hadn't taken it too well, by the look of things.

She knocked on the bathroom door. 'Mr Ashworth, are you OK?'

'Yes, sorry about the mess. I'll clean it up in a minute.'

She nodded to herself but set about cleaning it up anyway; it was her job to help with the mess and to look after him and she took it very seriously. Almost as seriously as her plans to kidnap her half-brother and hold him for ransom.

Chapter 6

Amelia drove slowly. She had missed the narrow road the first time and had to double back on herself after completing a rather scary six-point turn in the narrow lane, praying that nothing was speeding the other way. She found the road and turned off. It was so peaceful. There was hardly any traffic and she wondered what it would be like to be able to afford to live somewhere so quiet. Boring, probably. All the talk about this amazing cottage had piqued her interest and she was desperate to know what her big brother was spending all her money on. Lily had let her finish work early so she'd decided to come and check it out for herself.

She drove along until she saw the house and felt her heart begin to beat faster. Well, well, it was pretty spectacular, or at least it would be when it was completely finished. She slammed her car door shut in anger. All this time she'd missed out on everything that could have made her life so much better. Walking across the gravel driveway to the front door, which was wide open, she strolled inside as if she was supposed to be there. Two workmen were busy at the far end of the kitchen and when they looked up to see who she was, she smiled at them.

'Is Annie around?'

'No, she hasn't been here today. Can I help?'

'Oh, she said she was meeting me here. Never mind, I'll give her a ring. I'm the interior designer; we were going to talk curtains and cushions.'

The older of the men nodded. 'She might be held up. Why don't you take a look around while you're waiting?'

'Thanks, I'll do that.'

She turned and made her way to the stairs. She wanted a house like this. When she got her money off Daddy, that was what she was going to buy. She looked in all the bedrooms, saving the master bedroom until last.

* * *

Annie drove through the narrow country lanes with Jake and Alex following closely behind. Finally reaching the gates to the cottage, which were open, she drove straight through and stopped her car near to the builders' van and got out. What a difference since last week! The house had been painted white, making the windows, which had all been replaced with newer oak versions of the originals, stand out. It looked just like it had on the painting in the bedroom. They got out of their cars and stared.

'What do you think?'

'Oh, Annie, it's gorgeous! I can't believe what a difference from the last time I was here, when it was a peeling, dirty hovel.'

Alex frowned at Jake but she laughed.

'Say it as it is, Jake, but it was pretty grim. Wait until you see the inside; you would never believe it was the same house. Alex and the builders have done a pretty amazing job.'

She looked up and saw a woman in the upstairs bedroom window. Her heart almost exploded out of her chest but then she recognised the blonde hair and felt her fear replaced with anger. What on earth was Amelia doing in her bedroom?

Before she could go inside to find out, two men came flying

through the door as if they were being chased. Annie looked at their pale faces, concerned.

'Hiya, is everything OK?'

They both nodded at her. 'Brew time.'

They walked to their van, throwing open the doors and climbing inside, one of them pulling out his phone. The other waved at them and pointed to the flask on the dashboard. Jake muttered under his breath, 'Typical bloody builders and they wonder why they have such a reputation.'

Annie smiled. 'Don't be mean. They've worked really hard the last few weeks. They're entitled to a break.'

But something had made them run out of the house. You didn't look like they did because it was time for a cup of tea. They both looked petrified. She walked under the newly rebuilt porch, which had the original wooden structure, and shivered. She did it every single time without fail. She needed to man up; it was time to face facts – whoever or whatever it was that was still attached to this house needed to be told to leave. This was her home now. There was no way after spending all this money on it that she was moving into it feeling uneasy all the time.

A sheepish-looking Amelia came down the stairs and smiled at Annie. 'Sorry, you caught me. I was just passing and realised that this must be the house you and Will were renovating. Tom does nothing but talk about it and I thought I'd pop in to see if you were around and if you fancied a coffee. I realise how busy you are so I'll get going now; maybe we can have a coffee some other time.'

'Oh, OK … Yes, that would be nice. How did you get in?'

'The front door was open. The builders said it was OK to look around and wait for you.'

'Ah, I thought so. Sorry, Amelia, but maybe some other time.'

Jake watched the strained exchange with interest but kept his mouth shut. Annie walked Amelia to the door.

'Bye, Annie. It's a beautiful house, by the way.'

'Thank you, it is. Bye.'

Annie shut the door behind her, puzzled as to why the woman even thought that Annie would want to show her around her new house, but then she shrugged it off. Maybe she was just being friendly.

'Who was that?'

'Will's dad's new housekeeper. Did you find her a bit odd?'

Jake shook his head. He was still muttering about the builders, who were sitting in the van, but he stopped as soon as he walked into the completely rearranged open-plan kitchen-diner and lounge.

'Wow, what a difference! I can't believe it. It looks so modern, yet still fits in really well. I love the bare stonework.'

Annie squeezed her arms around Alex's waist, forgetting about her strange visitor.

'It's amazing, isn't it?'

It was Alex's turn to grin. 'It looks fabulous, Annie. I bet you can't wait to get the kitchen units and cooker in.'

'I can't and I've seen the most perfect Aga but it's so expensive. I don't know if we can justify spending that much money on a cooker for me just to burn food on and dry Will's socks.'

'I agree with you there, Annie; we all know what a crap cook you are, but surely you can't really put anything else in a kitchen this size except a range cooker. If you're going all country you need the right equipment, even if it is just to burn pizzas in.'

She shoved Jake, who was laughing.

'Anyway, I bet Will would buy you anything you want if you ask. I don't know what hold you have over him but he's like a changed man, and if Will won't buy one I bet if you told Lily what you want it would be here the next week, regardless of how much it was.'

'You know I'm not like that, Jake. I don't care about the money and I wouldn't dream of expecting Lily or Tom to provide me with an overly expensive cooker. But the one I've seen in a magazine is pale pink and it's to die for. With those off-white kitchen cupboards it would look amazing, but I'll wait and see if there's enough money left over before I order it.'

Jake walked over and lifted his hand to her forehead, pressing it against her skin to feel if she was warm or cold.

'Just checking you're not coming down with something. Since when did you like pink, my little wannabe Goth who lives in black clothes and has tattoos in places no one can see?'

'Cheeky! I like black because it's slimming. I got the tattoos when I lived with Mike and had to keep them hidden. I saw the cooker in a magazine and it looked so nice – I designed my whole kitchen around that cooker.'

'You designed your kitchen around a cooker that you're too scared to ask for? I'll tell Will about it and if you feel so bad about the cost it can be his wedding present to you instead of some soppy diamond bracelet he's been dithering about that you'll only lose anyway. At least you can't lose a whopping great cooker.'

Alex gently shoved Jake. 'Can you not keep your whopping great mouth shut for five minutes? I have no idea why anyone would tell you anything confidential because you can't keep that extra-large mouth shut long enough for your brain to store it.'

Alex took hold of Annie's hand and got her to lead him around the rest of the house while Jake stood by the kitchen window watching the builders, who were now in a deep discussion and kept pointing at the house. He took out his phone and typed a message to Will: *Don't bother with the diamonds. Annie wants a pale pink range cooker but is too scared to ask.* He might be unable to stop himself from saying what he was thinking but at least it got him what he wanted most of the time, and he knew that Will would order some brochures and then be the one to approach Annie about it so she wouldn't feel bad. After everything his friend had been through she deserved to be happy and so did Will.

Jake was mid-text when he stopped as a high-pitched scraping sound sent a shiver down his spine. It came from directly behind him. He felt the hairs on the back of his neck stand on end and he flinched when an icy-cold blast of air caressed the back of his neck, bringing him out in goose bumps and making him shudder. Afraid to look but even more scared not to, he slowly began to turn, his legs feeling as if they were too wobbly to hold his own weight. He hadn't heard Annie or Alex come back down the stairs and if he strained he could hear their muffled voices somewhere above him. It took a lot to make Jake scared but the fear that gripped his heart was suffocating. He could hear someone breathing and he knew it wasn't him.

He turned the last bit and was so relieved there was no one standing in front of him that he laughed, but then directly behind him he heard the sound of long nails being drawn across the glass window pane and another blast of cold air on the back of his neck. He forced himself to move forward and ran to the stairs to find Alex and Annie, who were just about to come down. Annie took one look at his face and knew something was wrong.

'What's the matter, Jake – why do you look as if you've seen a ghost?'

He shook his head, not quite knowing whether to tell her or not. She was supposed to be the psychic one, not him. Should he tell her there was something scary in the house, or let her go on unaware? He didn't want to be the one to break it to her that her dream house was haunted.

'Nothing – I just scared myself and thought I'd come and see what you two are doing.'

Alex walked forward and grabbed his arm. 'Is there something we should know, Jake? Because right now you look like you're about to pass out from fright. I think Annie has a right to know if you've seen something that most of us can't.'

'No, honestly, I heard a scratching sound and then I got a cold shiver and scared myself. I hate to be the one to break it to you, Annie, but this house might have mice.'

She laughed. 'Mice I can live with, ghosts I'd rather not. Are you sure you don't want to tell me anything?'

He shook his head once more, feeling like a total wimp for not being his usual self and blurting it right out, but if he spoke about it that might mean it was true.

He led Alex towards the front door. 'Come on, let's go to the pub for a drink and something to eat – my treat.'

Annie watched her friend, who was acting very strange – much stranger than usual.

'I'm OK, thanks; I'll wait here. I want to finish painting the master bedroom. Will said if he gets finished early enough he'll drive up and help.'

Jake nodded and stepped out of the front door and into the garden to feel the warmth of the sun on his face and he immediately felt better as it didn't feel so oppressive outside. The builders were now standing outside the van and they nodded at Annie. Jake didn't know if he should leave her alone but the builders were still here and surely they would be finishing their tea break any minute and going back to work. He leant down, kissing her on the cheek.

'Are you sure you don't want to come with us?'

'No, thank you; I've got too much to do here.'

Alex kissed her cheek and whispered in her ear, 'I think he's finally freaked. I'll ring you later if I need to get him sectioned.'

* * *

She watched them get into Alex's car and waved, then turned to face the builders, who were still hovering by their van.

'Is everything OK, guys?'

The older of the two of them looked at her. 'Erm … sort of. We've only a bit of plastering to do around the patio doors and the new electrics so we should be finished in the kitchen by tonight. Are you stopping here on your own, Annie?'

'I am for a bit; I wanted to finish painting the bedroom. Is there something wrong?'

For a minute it looked as if Callum, the younger of the two, was going to say something but then he thought better of it. She shrugged her shoulders, wondering why all the men were turning into total freaks, and walked back into the house, leaving the front door open so they might get the hint and follow her back in.

The air was much cooler inside, which was a welcome relief. She went upstairs to what was going to be her and Will's bedroom and took the lid off the paint. Before she could dip the paintbrush into the tin, the picture that she'd taken off the wall and placed on the chair toppled over with a loud bang, making her drop her paintbrush. She turned to look at it and wondered how on earth it had fallen. She walked across to pick it up and lifted it to see if it was damaged. She almost dropped it again, seeing the woman who had been barely visible a few weeks ago now in the centre of the painting, hanging from the front porch of the house, her head bent forward and hands dangling loosely at her sides.

Annie blinked and lifted it nearer. How had that happened? Could a painting move of its own accord? She knew that in reality it couldn't but still it chilled her to the bone because this one had and the woman was all too familiar: she looked like the one from her dream. She studied the figure of the woman. The paint didn't look as if it had just been altered; in fact it looked the same age as the rest of the painting. Annie put the picture down on the chair, puzzled as to how the woman had appeared and why she had been hanged from the front porch.

She walked back to pick up the paintbrush she'd dropped. Annie needed to find out the history of this house and pretty quick, before they moved in, so she could make sense of it all. She pulled her earbuds from her pocket and plugged them into her phone, scrolling through until she found her favourite playlist. Soon she was painting away, her head nodding in time to the music. She couldn't hear the breathing that filled the room or the sound of long fingernails on the small panes of glass in the window.

The builders on the other hand, who were downstairs, were working faster than ever to finish the plastering because they could hear the breathing. Neither of them spoke until the older one, Eric, let out a grunt as an invisible pair of hands curled themselves around his neck and pressed hard onto his windpipe. He stumbled backwards and ran towards the front door, his face pale and gasping for breath.

Callum quickly followed. 'What's the matter – why are you choking?'

Eric threw his head from side to side and ran out into the front garden. Suddenly able to breathe once more, he bent double, taking in huge gulps of air. 'I'm not going back in there – something just tried to bloody choke me to death!'

Callum, who was watching his friend, shook his head. 'You're having me on; it's not even funny now.'

They had left Annie alone in the house, oblivious to whatever was going on.

'What are we going to do, Callum? We can't just leave that woman alone upstairs in that house. What the fuck is going on? Someone was choking me! I couldn't breathe … I swear I could feel bony fingers wrapped around my throat.'

Callum shrugged. 'I'm not going back inside; that's it. First of all the tools kept moving on their own and a couple of times I heard voices telling me to leave, which I just put down to you lot messing around. But that scratching sound and the breathing is just too much … I've never had so many bad dreams in my life as I have while I've been on this job.'

Eric nodded. 'Phone Paul and tell him to get here pronto and then we better go back inside and tell Annie she needs to leave; it's too dangerous in there.'

Callum phoned their boss and relayed the events of the last

ten minutes to him. He ended the call and turned to look at Eric, whose face was still white.

'Well, is he coming?'

'He called us a pair of fucking fannies, said we were winding him up and if we thought it was a good excuse to knock off early we can think again.'

'Cheeky bastard – is he coming or not?'

'Yes, said he was already on his way here and only a few minutes away.'

They sat in the van in silence, both watching the upstairs bedroom window, where Annie was busy painting away. They were too scared to go back inside unless she started screaming for help. Five minutes later the sound of tyres crunching on gravel made them both turn their heads to see Paul park his van up behind them. They jumped out and walked towards him, ready for an argument, but he took one look at Eric, who had been working for him for the last ten years, and changed his mind.

'You look like you've seen a ghost; are you winding me up or is it for real?'

'I'm telling you now, Paul, there's something in that house and, whatever it is, it tried to choke me. I've never been so scared. I'm not going back inside but the woman who owns it is still in there. Someone needs to tell her it's not safe in that house, not on her own.'

Paul nodded. 'And do you think she's going to pay us for not finishing the job because you got spooked over something? I promised her the kitchen would be finished today, ready for the units to be fitted, and if it isn't I'll lose money because I gave her a set price. What if I come in with you and all three of us get the job done? Is there much to do?'

Callum looked across at Eric, who was shaking his head. 'Not really, boss, just a couple of bits. I'll go back in with you to finish off and Eric can wait out here. Whatever it was, it didn't touch me, just him. It was probably your aftershave; I told you it stunk.'

Eric gave him the finger then stuck his hands in his pockets and watched them walk back into the house. He realised that he didn't really want to be stuck out here on his own either. Safety in numbers and all that, so he followed them in and they began to finish off the tasks they'd been doing. The house was quiet now; there was no raspy breathing coming from out of nowhere and the house didn't feel quite as cold as it had before. Eric stayed close to Paul, who mucked in, and pretty soon the last bits of plaster were smeared on the wall. Paul told Callum to start cleaning up and gathering the tools together. He went to the staircase and shouted to Annie. There was no reply and Eric looked at him with panic across his face.

Paul climbed the stairs with Eric close behind. Callum took the tools out to the van and loaded it up, not wanting to be inside any longer. The two men reached the master bedroom, where Annie was so engrossed in her painting with her earbuds firmly in place that she hadn't heard any of the commotion. Paul stepped in and touched her arm to catch her attention. She jumped off the floor and both Eric and Paul jumped back, scaring themselves.

'Jesus Christ – you gave me a heart attack.' Annie pulled the earbuds out and laughed.

'Oh, my God … Sorry – I never heard you. Did you shout me?'

'Yes, and I think you've almost killed me off – bloody hell, my heart's racing. We just wanted to tell you the kitchen is finished, the plaster's going to need a while to dry out but this weather should speed it up.'

'Eek, I can't believe it! Thank you, guys. You've been great.' She grinned at them and Eric smiled back at her.

It was Paul who spoke. 'You're very welcome. There's something the lads have asked me to talk to you about. Have you got a minute?'

'Of course. It sounds serious. What's the matter?'

The two men looked at each other and Paul gave Eric the chance to speak, but he didn't.

'Well, they've told me that there's been some strange things happening in the house while they've been working – tools keep getting moved and all sorts. This afternoon Eric felt as if someone was choking him and he couldn't breathe.'

Both men held their breath and waited for the backlash from Annie. Instead, she put the paintbrush down and nodded.

'What else? Have you heard anything like the sound of nails scraping against a chalkboard or glass?'

Eric nodded frantically. 'Yes, all the time, and breathing, heavy breathing, and it filled the room; even Callum heard it. At first I thought I was going mad but when he heard it I guess it sort of made me think it had to be real.'

Paul looked at her. 'You don't seem too surprised or shocked.'

'I am, but not too much, and I don't want you to think I'm nuts because this isn't common knowledge and I'd appreciate it if you kept it to yourselves … but I have a bit of a psychic streak and I'm used to seeing and hearing things. A couple of times I've had a cold shiver and heard the nails scraping but not much else. Nothing has ever made itself known to me. Shit, I don't want a house that's haunted by something that wants to hurt people. I'm sorry and I hope you're OK.'

He nodded once more. 'What are you going to do? We need to get going now. Are you going to be OK here on your own?'

Annie looked around. She loved this house and wouldn't let some unhappy spirit chase her from it, especially one that was scared to show itself.

'Thank you, yes, I'll be fine. I'm not scared and I have a friend who is a priest; he'll come and bless it for me.'

The men looked at her as if she was completely insane and they shrugged. She thought about the painting and the woman who was hanging from the front porch. They turned to leave and she walked to the window to watch them get into their vans. Callum waved at her from the front seat and she waved back. A shiver ran down her spine but she crossed her arms over herself.

They left and Annie was truly alone in the house for the first time since they'd bought it.

She looked over at the picture on the chair and wondered if she should take it out of the house – maybe show it to Father John and see what he said – but could she drag him into something like this again? Although last time it had been him who had dragged her into a fight with a Shadow Man, who had terrified her. Still, she had managed to defeat the thing that collected souls for pleasure and save Father John, so technically he owed her.

She put the lid back on the paint and picked up the painting and the paintbrush, then she ran downstairs to the sink in the utility room to wash the brush. She placed the painting on the side and washed it and her hands; she dried them on an old towel then turned to pick the painting up. She walked around the house, checking the doors were locked and the windows were shut. The last thing she wanted now the house was almost done was someone getting inside through an insecure door or window. As she reached the front door she heard the scrape of nails against glass and turned around.

'I don't know who you are or what you want, but this is my house now. It hasn't been your home for a very long time and you shouldn't be here. It's time for you to leave. I want you to get out of this house and go to wherever you should be. Why are you haunting my dreams? You won't stop me from living here and if you don't leave of your own accord then I'm bringing in a priest to bless this house and have you removed.'

She heard nothing more so she walked out of the front door and shut it, locking it, and trying her best not to look above her head at the beams, where the woman was hanging in the painting, just in case she was hanging there now and she was about to walk straight though her. She walked across to her car and opened the door, putting the painting on the back seat. She needed to show it to Will, John, Jake or anyone really.

She drove off and as she began to make her way along the

winding road she wondered if Jake and Alex were still in the village, though it was Will she really wanted to talk to. She passed a dense wooded area and thought she saw a flash of white darting through the trees. Slowing down, she looked again. The woods looked awfully familiar and she saw the flash of white again. It was a woman and she was running, holding on to her side as if she had a stitch. Annie gasped and wondered if she was dreaming, pinching herself to make sure that she wasn't. She remembered that she was driving and brought her attention back to the road in front of her, grateful she hadn't wandered across the single white line into the path of an oncoming tractor.

She rounded a steep bend and saw the same woman, who was now standing in the middle of her side of the road. She was wearing the familiar white cotton gown; her head was bent forward and her long dark hair hung around her face, covering it. Annie slammed the brakes on, afraid it was too late and she was going to hit her. She turned her wheel sharply to the left and screamed as her car ploughed straight through a hedge and down a steep hill. She tried to put her brakes on but there was no traction and the car spun around on the damp grass. The oak tree that loomed in front of her car was enormous and her last thought before she hit it head-on was: *I'm going to die*.

There was a crunch and a loud squeal as the metal hit the trunk. Her head slammed forward against the steering wheel and she saw the woman out of the corner of her eye, with her head held high and her piercing blue eyes staring straight at her, and then the world went black.

1782

Betsy woke up late the next day. She had fallen asleep after her little angry outburst and not moved an inch all night. The sun was shining through the window and she stretched out. She had a headache from all the ale she had drunk but it wasn't as bad as she'd feared. How perfect would it have been to wake up next to Joss? She had never been in love but he was so kind to her that she thought she was falling in love with him. The only thing that spoilt her chances of being with him were his children, but she knew that they could be taken care of. She would continue to work on him; it was only a matter of time before he gave in. He was a man and they had needs, or so her mother always used to tell her.

She wanted to be out of this cramped house, the sooner the better, and the only way that was going to happen was if Joss asked her to stay with him. She would offer her services as a maid to his brats if she had to – anything to escape. She had been told she didn't need to go in to work today but if she didn't she might miss seeing Joss and that would serve no purpose at all. It was all about the timing. She wanted to be a lady of a house, his house, and not have to work in a smoke-filled, stinking pub forever.

She rolled onto her side, thinking about Joss, when a loud knock on the door made her jump from her bed and look out of the window. He was standing outside her door, as if her thinking about him had summoned him to her doorstep. She was naked and grabbed the sheet from her bed, wrapping it around herself, then she ran down the stairs. She opened the door a crack, to see him grinning at her like an excited schoolboy and she smiled back.

'Good morning, Betsy. I trust you slept well and are not feeling too ill today?'

'I did, thank you, Joss. I would have slept better with you beside me, though.' She noted the faint redness that worked its way up from his neck to his face. 'Oh, come now, Joss, do not tell me you are that shy. I find that hard to believe.'

She stepped away from the door so he could come inside the house. She had the sheet wrapped around her naked body so tightly he could not miss the soft curves it was hiding. He stepped in and shut the door behind him, taking off his flat cap.

'No, Betsy, I am not that shy and I have come today to tell you that I have hardly slept a wink all night for thinking about you. I lay in my cold bed yearning to have your soft, warm body next to mine and I kept on telling myself I was a fool for walking out last night. But I have my sons to consider and I still love my wife, even though she died more than a year ago now.'

Betsy tried not to growl at the mention of his boys. If Joss noticed the look of distaste that darkened her pretty face for a moment he didn't speak of it. She made herself smile at him then walked towards him, letting the sheet drop to the floor and exposing her naked body. Joss paused then stepped forward and wrapped his arms around her, pulling her close, his lips finding hers. She ran her fingers through his hair then held it tight so that he couldn't pull away and this time he didn't. He groaned and then scooped her into his strong arms, carrying her to the bed in the corner, in which her mother had died only five days ago. Betsy didn't stop him and lay there on the clean sheets, waiting for him to undress and come to her.

That the front door was unlocked did not bother her one bit; she would quite like it if someone had walked in on them. It would have made Joss squirm and he would have had to ask for her hand in marriage so he didn't ruin her reputation in the village.

After they had finished and Joss was breathing heavily from the exertion he rolled off her and lay next to her, stroking her hair. 'That was wonderful, thank you, Betsy.'

She laughed at him. 'Thank you? Do you thank all the women you sleep with?'

'No, I do not … You are the first one. Well, except for my …'

He didn't say anything else, pushing the guilt and betrayal to the back of his mind. He was too young to spend his life a widower and he had to think of his boys. Betsy was only young but she would make a good wife and mother, given time. He shut his eyes and began to snore ever so softly.

Betsy stood up and went to wash herself and get dressed,

humming the whole time. There was no way he wouldn't fall in love with her now; she had given him what most men wanted. She would tell him when he woke up that it had been her first time and watch him think about proposing to her there and then. Of course, it wasn't her first time but he wouldn't know that; her first time had been with the travelling preacher who came to the village four years ago. Her mother had welcomed him into their home, offering him food and shelter, and while she was asleep Betsy had offered him her bed.

He'd left after four days, telling Betsy he was becoming infatuated with her and he had a wife and children at home. She had laughed at him and watched him saddle up his horse, leaving the village with his head hung in shame when she had told him her age. There had been a few more since then – some of the village idiots and the occasional traveller who came into the pub for refreshments. Her mother would have been distraught to know her daughter was nothing more than a brazen whore but Betsy didn't care; she did whatever she wanted and sometimes having a man was exactly what she wanted.

She walked over to the bed and shook his shoulder. Joss opened his eyes and blinked, confusion filling his mind, and then he realised where he was and grinned at her. She bent down to kiss him and he tried to pull her back down but she playfully shoved him away and stood up.

'Haven't you got some cows to milk or something?'

He sat up. 'Bloody hell ... What time is it, Betsy? I only came to check on you. I wasn't supposed to ...'

He didn't finish his sentence as he clambered from the bed, pulling his trousers on and then his shoes.

'I do have cows to milk and pigs and sheep to feed. Would you like to come to the farm for supper, Betsy? I'd like you to come and meet my boys and spend some time with me.'

'Why, thank you, Joss, I would love to come for tea and meet the boys.'

She had to stop herself from grimacing at the thought of the children but she knew she would have to put up with them if she was to get what she wanted.

'What time shall I come to your house, Joss?'

'We don't eat until six – gives me the chance to have finished my jobs and then I spend the rest of the night with the boys, unless my mother takes them back to the farm for the night, and then I come to the pub to see your pretty face.'

Betsy blushed; no one had called her pretty before. She knew she wasn't ugly but it was nice to hear Joss say it to her. She crossed over to him and kissed him again, letting her fingers trail over the front of his trousers.

'Thank you, Joss; it is very kind of you to say. I think I am falling in love with you.'

He smiled then turned to leave. 'Please come for some tea, Betsy. I would really like it if you did. Although, I have to confess, once I get you in my house I may not let you go, for I'm falling in love with you as well.'

She pushed him out of the front door. 'Go and milk some cows. I will see you at six, Joss, and not a minute before.'

She watched him jog off down the small cobbled street towards the village square and could not help smiling. Perfect – her plan was going just as she'd imagined. It wouldn't be long before she had moved into that lovely cottage Joss owned. The only black cloud hanging over her was the children, but she had a plan for them if she did not like them as she feared: one that involved a small box of white powder she had hidden in a tin in the pantry.

Chapter 7

It was Will's turn to make the brews and he stood by the kettle waiting for it to boil. He could see the whiteboards which, thankfully, had no photos of dead women Blu-Tacked onto them. Since the last murder spree the town had quietened down, thank God, although he no longer took anything for granted. The national papers had begun to nickname Barrow as the murder capital of England. For such a small town the murder rate was incredibly high. Two serial killers in the space of twelve months was quite unbelievable: one locked in a secure mental hospital and the other a policeman who was now locked in solitary confinement for his own safety for the rest of his life.

Lost in thought, he was brought back to reality by the loud click as the kettle turned itself off. His phone rang on his desk but he ignored it. If it was important they would ring back. He poured the boiling water into his and Stu's mugs and stirred the drinks. He passed one to Stu, who was sitting with his feet on the desk playing *Candy Crush* on his phone. Will shook his head at him in mock horror.

'You know, for a grown man you sure do act like a big kid. I mean, for Christ's sake, sending me a request for a life on that stupid game on Facebook is going just a touch too far, don't you think? Real men play *Call of Duty*, not some bollocks about sweets.'

'I play *Call of Duty* as well, you cheeky git, and I'm a real man. Just ask Debs; it's me who has to get rid of the spiders in our house.'

Will laughed. 'Yes, right, I believe you. Have you got a decent suit for my wedding then? I bet you've got a pink shirt and tie. If I was you, I'd let Debs pick one out for you, judging by your work suits. I don't want you letting the side down.'

He winked at Stu, who gave him the finger.

'Ah bollocks, you just made me die.'

Will spat coffee all over himself as he choked on his laughter and went to get a paper towel to mop it up. As he came back into the room a very white-faced Stu was standing behind Will's desk, talking on the phone.

'Yes, boss, I'll tell him. Thanks; we'll be there as soon as we can. Which hospital are they going to?'

Stu stared at Will, who felt his heart sink to the bottom of his shoes; he'd known it had been too good to be true. That was his fault for thinking how quiet it had been, the Q word was banned in the station because whenever anyone said it out loud all hell broke loose.

Will arched his eyebrows at Stu. 'Crap – tell me then, or are you going to dither for the next ten minutes?'

'That was the control inspector. There's been an accident on the road to Hawkshead ... A farmer found a car that had crashed through the hedge and ploughed into a tree.'

Will felt his world come crashing down on him. He knew the next words out of Stu's mouth would be that it was a red convertible Mini.

'Is she alive? Tell me she's OK, Stu, please tell me she is.'

'He said the fire service were cutting her free. Yes, she's unconscious but breathing. The air ambulance has just landed in the field next to her and she'll be in Barrow shortly. I'll drive you to the hospital.'

Will nodded; he couldn't speak. His stomach was churning and he wanted to throw up. He grabbed his jacket off the back of his chair and his mobile off the desk and followed Stu out of the CID office. Kav was running up the corridor, looking whiter than Will.

'Have you heard about Annie?'

Will didn't trust himself to speak; he nodded. Kav reached out and squeezed Will's shoulder. 'I want a full update as soon as you get one, please. Jesus, what's she like?'

Will half-smiled. She was bloody terrible. An accident magnet, she'd been through so much the last few years and he didn't know how to keep her safe. She wouldn't let him take care of her or provide for her, insisting on carrying on being a police officer after almost being killed twice. He wanted to blue-light it up to where she was but it would probably be too late and by the time he'd got there the air ambulance would have left; he would just have to wait at the hospital for them to arrive. He followed Stu out of the station and across the road to the car park, getting into the front passenger seat of the unmarked car. He didn't speak. He couldn't lose her now; his life would be finished. His hands were shaking so much that he couldn't fasten his seat belt and Stu had to reach over and plug it in for him.

The hospital wasn't far away but it felt like the slowest journey Will had ever made, even though Stu was driving faster than the speed limit. As they drove through the hospital grounds, Will told Stu to stop so he could wait for the helicopter to land. He needed to see her, to make sure she was still breathing. Tears filled his eyes and he blinked them back. He'd never cried in front of Stu before and hoped he could keep it together. He hadn't even cried at Laura's funeral and she was one of his own, one of his team of detectives who had been murdered. Will knew that he would forever blame himself for her death. If she hadn't being trying to make him jealous by leaving the pub with a complete stranger she'd probably still be here today. He had kept it together in the church when everyone around him had been sniffling into tissues but he didn't know how long he could keep the tears that were threatening now at bay.

As he paced up and down on the road, an ambulance pulled up, ready to transfer Annie from the helicopter to accident and emergency. God, she would hate this fuss and he hoped she was conscious and telling them exactly how much she hated the fuss. She would be upset about her car, which would be a write-off if the fire service had to cut her free from it, but he'd buy her a brand-new one with a reinforced steel roof – hell, he'd buy her an armoured tank as long as she would be able to drive one.

The paramedics climbed out of the ambulance and opened the doors and lowered the ramp. They nodded at Will and he nodded back, recognising the woman who had been to a couple of jobs he'd dealt with. She came over to talk to him while her colleague spoke on the radio to the control room. He nodded at her and she touched Will's arm.

'The helicopter will be here any minute. Don't worry; she's in safe hands. The air ambulance doctors are miracle workers. We've had an update to say that the casualty is unconscious. She has a head injury, fractured rib and a suspected punctured lung so she'll be going straight to surgery.'

'Thank you. I can't believe it. I really hope she'll be all right.'

The loud thwack of the helicopter's rotor blades carried on the wind and Will looked up to the sky to see the distinctive green and yellow helicopter fly into sight. His heart was racing so much he was scared he was going to have a heart attack and drop dead before he got a chance to see her. A porter had come out and shut the big yellow metal barriers to stop motorists driving through. Quite a crowd had gathered on the grass and in the car park to watch and he wanted to shout at them all to 'bugger off' but he knew it was wrong; they were only doing what he himself would probably do if it wasn't the woman he loved more than life itself inside, fighting for her life.

* * *

Henry sat in his room, listening to his music and waiting for the nurse to bring his medication that he didn't actually need and that he would not be swallowing. He'd got quite good at pretending to take his tablets like a good boy. They were a mixture of antidepressants and God knows whatever else they thought was needed to keep him calm and his serial killer mode turned off. The thing was, although he hadn't really wanted it to turn on in the first place and at the beginning he had been sickened by his crimes, the more he killed, the more the despair had turned to pleasure and sheer enjoyment. He knew that he could control the urges when he needed to or until the time was right. He also knew that the time to try and escape was getting near; he could not spend the rest of his life cooped up in the hospital. He needed to be free, to kill again.

This time he had very specific victims in mind – and anyone who happened to get in his way. He would rather die trying to kill Police Officer Annie Graham and Detective Sergeant Will Ashworth than sit here, day in day out, living out the fantasy he had created.

Megan unlocked his door and brought his medication in. She grinned at him. 'Good morning, Henry, how are you today?'

'I'm fine, thank you. How about yourself?'

'Oh, you know how it is: same shit, different day. Whoops, sorry. I forget you're a patient and we're not supposed to swear in front of you. Still, you don't mind, do you? I'm a good girl the rest of the time.'

She winked at him and he nodded in agreement.

'Megan, you are like a breath of fresh air to me. So you can say what you like – you're the only nurse in here who actually talks to me like I'm a normal person.'

She laughed and tucked a strand of fuchsia-coloured hair behind her ear. 'Yes, well, I don't care what you did outside of these walls, as long as you're nice to me then I'm nice back and you, Henry, are always nice. You don't try and stare down my top when I bend over, you don't try and grope my bottom, and you definitely don't do some of the things the other patients do, or at least not in public anyway.'

'I'm afraid some men have no manners, especially around a pretty young thing like you. They have no self-respect so they don't give any to others. So have you any news to tell me today? How's that creep of a boyfriend of yours? Have you dumped him yet?'

She handed him a small plastic cup with his assorted tablets in and a plastic cup filled with water.

'Not yet; I think I will tonight, though.'

She sat on the end of his bed, waiting for him to take his tablets, but she didn't actually watch him because she started to pick at one of her fingernails, which had the remains of some silver glittery nail varnish on it. Henry went through the motions and slipped the tablets into his hand and down the side of his chair.

'Tut, tut, Megan. You'd better hope Nurse Wood doesn't catch you with nail varnish on. You know what a stickler for the rules she is; she'll have you suspended and then what would I do?'

'You'd die of boredom, Henry, that's what. It's OK, the old bat is off today, anyway. She rang in sick so let's hope she's off for at least a week and gives us both a break.' Megan winked at him. 'Anyway, she loves having me to moan at; it keeps her off everyone else's backs. So they owe me because I'm doing them a public service, so to speak. Henry, can I ask you something?'

Henry smiled at her. He had wondered how long it would be before she plucked up the courage.

'I mean you don't have to answer and I'm just being nosy so you can tell me to get lost ... but I can't stop thinking about it.'

He sat up straight in his chair, keeping his hands tucked down the sides. He rarely got the chance to talk about how good he was at killing.

'What is it, Megan? What can you not stop thinking about?'

She paused, as if unsure whether to continue or not, but then she lifted her head and looked him straight in the eyes.

'Did you really kill those people? I just find it so hard to believe. You're always so nice and polite. You don't act like a freak like most of the others on this ward and I just can't imagine that you would.'

He looked at her then slowly nodded. 'Yes, I did, Megan, and I'm not proud of myself. I don't know what came over me but I'm ever so sorry about it. I really wanted to apologise to the policewoman that I kidnapped and her friend who rescued her. I owe her so much because she was the one who stopped me and made me realise exactly what I was doing. They wouldn't let me speak to her after it was all over. I couldn't speak at first because of the burns. They hurt so much I thought I was dying. In fact I wish that I had because I can never make it up to the families of those girls or the policewoman. I would like the chance to say sorry to her; I hope one day I will get it.'

Megan nodded. 'You might one day, Henry. Have you tried writing to her?'

He laughed. 'They won't let me send any post out, especially not to her. I just wish there was something I could do. I'm not like that now; the thought of hurting anyone repulses me and I feel sick just thinking about what I did. I honestly believe at the time I had no idea of what I was doing or the harm I was causing. But now, thanks to everyone's help, the doctors and yourself, I feel like a different man. I think the tablets must help a lot.'

Megan stood up to leave but before she did she reached out and squeezed his hand. He shivered at her touch. It had been so long since a woman had touched him.

'I'll see what I can do, Henry, leave it with me.'

She walked out, slamming the metal door behind her and turning the key in the lock. He sat in his chair, staring out of his window with a huge grin on his face. The girl was too gullible for her own good. This was going to be much easier than he'd thought. He held a morbid fascination for her, which was a good thing. He would continue to manipulate her until he had her right where he wanted and an escape plan set in stone. He hoped that he wouldn't have to kill pretty little Megan, but if he did then so be it.

Chapter 8

The helicopter landed on the grass and Will watched as the crew unloaded the stretcher and ran with it across to the waiting ambulance. He ran over and caught a glimpse of Annie's blood-covered face. She was unconscious and had drips attached to her arms. Stu grabbed his arm to hold him back as they loaded her into the ambulance but he pulled free from him and jumped in with her before they had a chance to tell him to follow behind. It was only a short ride through the hospital grounds to the accident and emergency entrance but it felt like forever and he wasn't leaving her.

He sat at the side of her, holding her hand. 'I'm here, Annie. It's OK; you're going to be OK.' He kept on repeating it over and over. The ambulance stopped and they unloaded her and rushed her through to the resuscitation cubicles, where the curtain was drawn across and Will was told firmly to wait outside.

Stu came rushing in. 'How is she? There's never anywhere to bloody park here. I've just abandoned the car on the double yellows. They can give me a ticket; I don't care.'

'I don't know … She's unconscious; they're working on her.'

He turned and went to the reception to book her in so they had her details and could access her medical records. All he kept thinking about was her head. Jesus, she needed a crash helmet – surely all these injuries couldn't be a good thing. What if she was brain-damaged or worse? He shuddered. After he'd given her details, the receptionist led him to the relatives' room, where he looked at her, aghast.

'No, it's OK – she's OK. I just thought you might want somewhere private to sit and wait and not out there with everyone else.'

'OK, thank you … Will you come and get me straight away?'

'Yes, the doctor will be out as soon as she's stabilised to let you know what's happening.'

Will walked over to the window. How many times had he sat in here when the shoe was on the other foot and he was supporting families waiting for news of their loved ones? He'd never liked this part of the job, though when he'd first joined it was all he'd seemed to do for six months and he'd been so depressed by it all he'd been tempted to pack it all in, hand in his notice and get a job as a postman, anything that didn't involve dealing with incidents like these. He'd stuck it out and now he was a detective sergeant. In a couple of years he might even go for his inspector's exam if he could be bothered. What he wanted most was to marry Annie and settle down in their new home together.

He watched a man outside who looked a similar age to him, playing with a little boy, and he felt his heart ache. The man who'd never wanted to settle down or have kids now wanted nothing more than to be married with a couple of kids to play with. He wondered if Annie would feel the same. At least if she was pregnant she would have to take it easy at work. His dream was for Annie to leave the police and get a safe job, one that didn't involve driving through windy country lanes at ridiculous speeds to go to a domestic or an accident.

He snapped out of his daydream as his phone rang. He pulled it out of his trouser pocket to see Jake's name flashing across the screen.

'Will, the house is gorgeous, mate. I'm so jealous. We left

Annie painting your bedroom and went to the pub but we're on our way back. We've been stuck in traffic for ages because there was an accident and they had to close the road to let the air ambulance land. Is she home yet? Because Alex has something he wanted to show her. I've tried ringing her phone but it's just going to voicemail.'

Will turned away from the window and spoke quietly. 'I'm at the hospital, Jake. It was Annie who was in the accident. Her car went off the road and hit a tree.'

'No way. Is she OK? Jesus Christ – I knew we shouldn't have left her alone; I've had a funny feeling in the pit of my stomach since we did.'

'She's unconscious, has a punctured lung and I can't even remember what else. I'm in the relatives' room, waiting for a doctor to come and tell me that she's going to be OK.'

'We're on our way. I swear to God she needs locking in a house and never let out in public on her own again. What's she like?'

Will didn't know whether to be relieved that Jake was coming or not. He was a drama queen but Will would rather have him for company than Stu, who was sitting on the chair not speaking. At least Jake's nonstop talking would keep his mind occupied.

'You can go if you want, Stu. Jake's on his way with Alex.'

'No, it's OK, Will. I don't want to leave you here on your own.'

He didn't finish what he was going to say but Will silently finished it off for him: *Just in case it's bad news and you need someone.*

'Honestly, it's fine. Annie will be fine; she's come through worse than this. She's tough. You get back and then you can tell Kav the latest update. If I need you I'll ring and, anyway, when they come to get me you'll only be sitting here on your own.'

Stu stood up. 'You're sure?'

'Positive.'

'OK, I'll go then. Ring me if you need anything or want a lift home to get some stuff.'

Stu squeezed Will's shoulder and then opened the door and left, pulling out his mobile to no doubt ring Debs and fill her in.

The man and little boy were still playing outside on the small piece of grass and Will smiled at them. His eyes filling with tears, he turned and sat down on a chair that was slightly softer than the hard plastic ones in the waiting room, waiting for either the doctor or Jake to come and find him.

* * *

Amelia left Tom's house. He hadn't come out of his room all morning since he'd read her card. He had rung the bell and asked her to bring his laptop up to him from the study, which she had done, knowing fine well he was about to start searching for her mother. Well, he could look all he wanted; she'd never been on Facebook or had an email or Twitter account before she'd died. In fact she hadn't owned a computer full stop, refusing to even look at one.

Amelia drove her battered Corsa through the lanes until she reached the cottage she was renting. It was only small but it had a cellar, which had been the main requirement when she had been looking for it, and it also had a long private drive so the cottage couldn't be seen from the roadside, which was perfect for her needs. When she brought Will home she didn't want any spectators.

She walked in to see her boyfriend Luke playing on his Xbox. 'Do you know what really makes me sick to the teeth? They live in that huge house and drive Mercedes four-by-fours and BMWs and I have to drive that clapped-out piece of shit that's held together by the rust. Every time that Annie comes, all they talk about is the wedding that Lily is spending my money on like there's no tomorrow. Spending my money while I have to clean the toilets they sit on so I can afford to eat, when it should be the other way around. I hate the lot of them. It will serve them right to worry what has happened to precious Will when the time comes.'

Luke nodded. It was easier for him to agree with whatever she said, otherwise she was prone to get violent. He'd already had a split head and a black eye off her this year. She looked at him in disgust. If he thought she was keeping him around when she got her payout he had another think coming. He would be told to pack his bags once her plan had been carried out and given some cash to keep quiet, but for now he would have to do, because she couldn't do this on her own and she had no one else to trust. She made her way upstairs for a shower.

She came back down naked, her damp hair hanging loose around her shoulders. She walked in front of the television and he groaned. 'What did you do that for? I just died!'

Then he looked up at her and realised she was naked and grinned. 'Oh, I'll let you off.'

She strode up to him and took the control from his hands, throwing it to one side, then she straddled him.

'Tell me the words I want to hear, Luke – tell me you've finished my cellar or I won't let you fuck me. I don't want to wait much longer. I want to put the plan into action and get Will as soon as it's done. I want him tied up in the cellar while Daddy is panicking and getting me a suitcase full of cash together.'

He kissed her then pushed her off. 'Come on and see for yourself.'

He took hold of her hand and led her into the kitchen and the cellar door. He slid the two bolts across that he'd fixed to it just this morning and opened it, pulling the cord and illuminating the uneven stone steps. The smell of damp lingered in the air but the cellar was pretty watertight. He led her down the steps to the small room at the bottom, which must have been used as a food storage place years ago. She looked around. He'd nailed planks of wood over the one window, which led onto the back garden; he'd also attached two black cast-iron ring pulls to the wall so she could tie Will's ropes to them and secure him to the single bed that he'd put up. There was also a bucket for him to pee in.

Amelia nodded her approval. 'I'm pleasantly surprised, Luke. You've done well.'

She grabbed him and dragged him down onto the bed, kissing him hungrily, and he let out a sigh of relief that for once she was pleased with him.

1782

Betsy arrived at Joss's cottage just before six and was greeted by two identical twin boys who were playing on a rope swing hanging from a huge oak tree in the garden. She forced herself to smile at them and they waved at her. She opened the gate and walked in.

'Hello, is your father around?'

'He might be – who's asking?'

Betsy felt the hairs on the back of her neck stand on end – the cheek of the little brat. She had told herself that she had to give it time to get to know them if she wanted to make it work with Joss and that she would do her very best, but she knew it was pointless. She'd only spoken to them once and she already hated them even more than she had last night when Joss had left her to come and be with them.

'Tell him Betsy is here, please.'

The slightly smaller one of the two nodded and jumped off the swing, running to the house and through the front door, shouting for his father. The other one jumped on the rope and began swaying himself. The whole time he never took his eyes from her and she stared right back at him. Two could play that game.

Joss came through the door and grinned at her. 'That was good timing, Betsy; I've just this minute taken the pie from the oven. Boys, this is Betsy, my friend. Betsy, these two terrors are my sons, Arthur and Cuthbert.'

She gave them her best smile, even though it hurt her cheeks. 'Well, I'm very pleased to meet you both; what a handsome pair of young men. I bet you look even better with all that mud scrubbed from your hands and faces.'

The boys looked at each other and giggled. Joss marched across the garden until he was standing directly in front of them. 'The pair of you get in that house and clean yourselves up. Did I not tell you not to get all muddied up?'

They stopped smiling. 'Yes, Father, sorry.'

With that they both ran off into the house and Joss turned to look at Betsy.

'You'll have to forgive them. They don't see many people, other than my parents and their schoolteacher. They are good boys most of the time, but they do like to make a mess, climb trees and do everything I liked to do myself when I was a lad.'

Betsy laughed. 'They are adorable, Joss; they remind me of you so much. I don't mind them at all.'

As she spoke she kept her fingers crossed behind her back and hoped the contempt she felt towards them did not show on her face. He led her inside his home and she marvelled at how big and light it was. There were lots of windows, unlike her damp, cramped cottage in the village, which still smelt of death.

'Oh, Joss, this is a fine home; you are so lucky to live here.'

'I reckon I am very lucky to live here but I work hard for it. My father is a hard man to please and if he did not think I deserved this house then he would make me leave it and he would move someone in here that he deemed worthy of it.'

She was standing looking out of the big windows, which overlooked the orchard at the back. She turned around to face him.

'You are a good man, Joss, and you would make someone a good husband.'

His cheeks flared red and he turned away, going back into the kitchen. Betsy could have kicked herself. Why had she just reminded him of his dead wife? Stupid girl – she would have to watch everything she said from now on. She wanted him to think she was pure of thought and not see through her disguise.

The boys came thundering down the stairs, looking much cleaner than they had ten minutes ago, and they smiled at her. She smiled back. This was much better. As much as it pained her, she had to pretend to like them until she could move in and then she could do what she had planned. She followed them into the kitchen, where the huge table was set with a steaming pie and a big pot of vegetables. It smelt good and she felt her stomach rumble for the first time in days.

'That looks a fine pie, Joss. Did you make it yourself?'

The boys giggled and Joss smiled.

'I cannot lie to you, Betsy; no, I didn't. I just put it into the oven. My mother makes a batch of them and sends them down so we don't starve ourselves.'

'Well, your mother is a very good cook then and also very kind. Did you tell her I was coming for tea?'

'I did and she thought it was a very good idea, didn't she, boys?'

They both nodded in unison as they waited eagerly for Joss to dish the pie out. He stood up and filled four plates with pie and vegetables, passing Betsy hers first, then his sons and finally he sat down himself. The boys put their hands together, ready to say grace, and Betsy followed suit as Joss said a prayer of thanks to the good Lord. Then they ate. They talked about the weather, the crop of apples that were ripening on the trees out the back and lots of other things. When they had finished, Joss sent the boys upstairs to play before they had to go to bed and they ran off, glad to be on their own. Betsy helped him to clear the table and then she filled the sink with water from the kettle, which had boiled on the stove. Joss told her to leave it; he would see to the dishes when she had left, but she pushed him away.

'It's the least I can do, Joss, please let me.'

He nodded and stepped back from her, sitting at the table to watch her. When she had finished drying the pots she wiped her hands and walked across to him.

'You have a beautiful home, Joss, and a lovely family. I used to dream about living in a house like this when I was a child – a home filled with love and laughter. My mother was always in bad health from the day I was born and I spent most of my childhood looking after her and cooking and cleaning. This is a terrible thing to say, but I felt relieved when she died, as if I was free to finally have a life of my own.'

She bowed her head and lifted a finger to wipe away a tear that wasn't there. Joss stood up and pulled her close to him. She lifted her face to stare up at him and he bent down and kissed her. It was Betsy who pulled away, not wanting him to think her too forward, but inside she was gloating.

'I know this is probably far too soon, but how would you like to live here with us, Betsy? I don't mean as my wife … well, not yet, unless you wanted to, but more like a live-in helper. You could help to look after the boys, which would make it a lot easier for my mother, who isn't getting any younger, and if you wanted to help with the cooking and cleaning that would be up to you, but I would very much like it if you said yes. We could see how it goes and then, when you are ready, if you wanted to be more than a helper then I would be more than happy to marry you, Betsy Baker.'

'Oh, Joss, I don't know what to say.'

'Say yes, please. I haven't been able to stop thinking about you for weeks. I want you so much that it hurts.'

She smiled and lifted her lips to kiss him, then pulled away. 'Yes, I would love to live here with you and look after you all. But I want to be more than some housemaid, Joss. I want you just as much.'

Loud shouting from upstairs and thudding broke the moment and Joss pulled away from her, running towards the stairs.

'Boys, stop it now. If you can't play nice then you can go to bed. I'll be up in five minutes and I want you tucked up under your covers.'

Betsy wanted to go up and smack the little bastards for spoiling the moment. She would soon change them once she moved in. There was no way they would get in the way of what she wanted and that was Joss. She didn't care one bit about the brats – she only wanted their father and his house.

Joss came back to her. 'I'm sorry, Betsy. I'm so pleased that you want to move in. When should I bring the horse and cart to collect you?'

'Tomorrow would be fine. I have very little to move. There is nothing in that house except for my clothes and books that I would want to keep. You have everything in here that I could ever need.'

'It's grand that you want to move in so soon. I will come and fetch you tomorrow afternoon. Would you like to come upstairs and pick a room to sleep in now and then I can get it cleaned out and ready for you?'

'Joss, I would sleep anywhere as long as you are close by. Is there a room next to you so the boys will not notice me slipping in and out of your room when they go to bed?'

He nodded. 'Yes, come on. I'll show you the one that the boys are in now. I can move them further down the corridor to give us some privacy, if you like.'

Yes, she liked that idea very much indeed, and it would show them she was to be in charge if they had to leave their room and give it to her. Things were happening very fast but that was fine by her. The sooner she left that dingy hovel she called her home the better.

Chapter 9

The door opened and Will didn't know if he wanted to hear what the doctor was going to tell him. The woman smiled at them – Jake and Alex were standing next to each other behind him.

'Mr Ashworth?'

Will stepped forward and nodded.

'I'm pleased to tell you that we've managed to stabilise Annie. She has a punctured lung and is being prepped for surgery. The bad news is she is in a coma due to the head trauma. I see from her previous X-rays that she's already sustained quite serious injuries to that part of her brain. Her signs are all good, though, and once we've sorted out the lung she'll be transferred to the intensive care unit, where they'll take good care of her until she decides to come back to us.'

'Oh, thank God for that – thank you. Do you have any idea how long she could be in a coma?'

'I'm afraid I have no idea. That will be down to how fast her injuries take to mend and how strong she is. Would you like to come and see her before we take her down to theatre?'

His eyes moist with tears, he nodded and followed her as she turned and led him through the curtains into the resuscitation room, where Annie was wired up to so many monitors and tubes he hardly recognised her.

'It's just until she's breathing properly on her own. My colleagues inform me that Annie is a bit of a legend here in the department and they all think she'll make a full recovery.'

He looked at the doctor and nodded. 'Yes, I suppose she must be.'

Then he stepped forward until he was close enough to bend down and kiss her cheek. 'Oh, Annie, I love you so much. Please get better soon.'

Tears fell onto her cheek and he reached out to wipe them away. He straightened up.

'Can I stay with her until they take her down, please?'

The doctor nodded and walked away. Will picked up Annie's hand and held it, stroking his finger along her thumb. He'd heard countless times about how someone in a coma could hear what was going on around them and that you should talk to them, so he told her all about his not so exciting day at work and anything else that entered his mind until the nurses and the porters arrived to wheel her down to surgery. He kissed her once more then watched as they wheeled her away.

A young student nurse came over to him. 'Are you OK? Would you like to go back to the relatives' room? Or you can come and sit on a chair near theatre if you like. It's a bit busy in there though, so you might want to stay up here.'

'If you don't mind, I'd like to be as near as possible. Can I just tell my friends they should go and I'll ring them if there's any news?'

'Of course you can. I'll wait in reception for you and then I'll take you down.'

Will walked back to where an anxious Jake was pacing up and down.

'She's gone to surgery then she'll be going into intensive care so you might as well go home and I'll ring you once she's out.'

Jake looked at Alex, who shook his head, and for once Jake didn't argue.

'Are you OK on your own? I can stop if you want me to.'

'No, there's not much point, but thanks, anyway. They'll only let me in to see her tonight. You'll be able to come see her tomorrow and I don't mind being on my own. In fact I'd rather be on my own.'

Alex reached out and squeezed Will's arm. 'We understand and you'll let us know if there's any news?'

'I'll ring you as soon as there is. Thanks, guys, I appreciate it.'

Jake stepped forward and hugged Will. 'She'll be OK; she's used to being battered and abused so this is just a glitch. She'll be back to normal in a few days, looking for the next disaster to walk into.'

Alex looked at Jake in shock. He never failed to say the wrong thing. He grabbed Jake's arm and led him to the door, pushing him out.

'If you need anything at all, Will, give us a ring. One of us can be here in less than five minutes.'

He shoved Jake out into the corridor before he could say anything else. Will smiled to himself. Jake was right; Annie had been battered and abused by her husband, Mike, but she'd come through it and escaped him. She'd beaten a serial killer in a fight for her life and saved them both, so this should be like a walk in the park for her. He just hoped she had the strength to fight back this time because he didn't want to imagine a life without her.

He watched Jake and Alex for a minute. They were standing outside Alex's car having a domestic. No doubt Alex had been mortified at what Jake had just said, but that was Jake. They both got into the car and he heard the doors slam through the double glazing.

He turned and walked out into the reception area and the waiting nurse, who smiled at him. She led him down to the theatres, where there were some chairs partially hidden behind a screen. He thanked her and sat down. He thought about ringing his dad and Lily but they had enough to contend with and he didn't want to make his dad come down here when he wasn't in the best of health. Lily would insist on coming. So he didn't bother. He would wait until tomorrow before phoning them and then they could decide whether Tom would stay at home with Amelia while Lily came.

Will had thought a lot about why he had taken a dislike to Amelia when he didn't even know her and he'd never seen her before in his life. But it was the fact that she seemed so at home in his dad's house and she gave the impression that she knew him and didn't really like him. Which he thought was odd, but at least she wasn't a permanent fixture. Lily had made sure that it was agreed Amelia's position was only a temporary one.

* * *

Tom had stayed in bed all day, his stomach churning and his appetite non-existent. Lily had come back and fussed around him, wanting to call the doctor out. What was he going to say? He wasn't well because he'd just found out he'd fathered a daughter he knew nothing about and hadn't provided even a pair of shoes for her since she'd been born? Tom wasn't like that; it wasn't in his nature. If he'd known, he would have made sure she was taken care of from the day she was born. It wasn't fair that he'd never been given the chance and, if it was true, he could understand why she would be angry with him. He didn't know what to do. He was embarrassed that he had never stepped up to the mark. He didn't want Will or Lily to think he was a disgrace and he didn't know how to even contact whoever had sent the card; of course it could be a total hoax from some jealous person – but why now?

He shut the laptop. The only link he'd found when he'd searched the internet had been the death notice for Bethany

Jackson, who had died last year in a hospice near Blackpool. It had said 'dearest mum to Amy' so she did indeed have a daughter. He'd then tried searching for Amy Jackson but there were hundreds of them so he gave up. His head was hurting and he felt sick to the very bottom of his feet.

Lily came back in to check on him, feeling his forehead with the back of her cool hand.

'Lily, for the love of God, I'm fine. I just feel a bit run down and I need to sleep. Will you please stop fussing?'

'If you're not any better by tomorrow I'm ringing the doctor, Tom. I'm not taking any chances with you. I'll leave you be and sleep across the hall tonight; if you want me just shout. I hope you feel better soon.'

She went out of the room, softly closing the door behind her, and he felt even worse. He'd never lied to her since the day they had met. He didn't lie to anyone. He turned on his side and shut his eyes, hoping that he'd wake up and this would all be a bad dream.

1782

Betsy had settled into Joss's home as if she was meant to be there. The boys were a bit of a handful but she had locked them in the bedroom one day whilst Joss was out at work and neither fed nor watered them. After six hours they had begged her for a drink and promised her they would no longer be bad for her. That was a week ago and it seemed to be working, although they were keeping away from her full stop. She had expected them to go running to Joss but they had not said anything to him because she knew that if they had he would have taken the belt to them for not doing as Betsy had told them in the first place. Joss was such a gentle father, unless the boys needed disciplining, but she respected that and enjoyed it. A couple of times she had told him little white lies about his boys so Joss had sent them to bed, banishing them to their room, so it gave her some time alone with him.

She liked cooking and cleaning. It was such a pleasure in the large bright room that was his kitchen, which was nothing like the squalid corner of her mother's house. Most of all she liked to potter around in the garden. Joss had built her some raised beds to plant some herbs and vegetables in, and she liked nothing more than digging in the soil and planting seeds, weeding and watering them. There was something so satisfying about the feel of the earth underneath her fingers. She also enjoyed picking the fruit from the trees out the back of the house in the orchard. Joss's mother had spent a morning with her, showing her how to make jams and chutneys to store in the larder. Betsy would not say that she liked the woman much but she had been kind to her and still took the boys to the farmhouse to sleep every weekend, giving her and Joss some time on their own.

The only problem was that Betsy wanted Joss to herself all the time and she didn't want to share him with his horrible boys or his parents. She wanted it to be just the two of them in this big house, but she knew he loved his boys a lot more than he loved her. She had made a point of studying him carefully at first whenever they walked into the room and had seen that his face lit up. He would play fight with them and tell them such stories even she enjoyed to listen to them, because she loved the sound of his voice.

A fistful of brown earth splattered against the kitchen window she had cleaned only an hour earlier, making her jump away from the stove and the broth she was stirring. It was followed by some loud shrieking. She ran outside to see what was going on and felt time stand still as every single part of her body filled with a bright red rage. The boys were knee-deep in her vegetable garden. The rows of seedlings that had begun to sprout were trampled and spread all over. Clumps of soil had been thrown onto the lawn and at the house. Betsy looked at the mess and then the boys, who stopped mid-throw, the expression on her face making them realise the gravity of what they had done as it began to sink in. They looked at each other and then at Betsy.

'Sorry, we were just playing. We forgot this was your part of the garden.'

She couldn't speak. She wanted to drag both of them out of the soil by their hair and beat them with the sweeping brush until they could not move and then beat them some more. Instead, she turned and walked back into the house, not trusting herself to speak or to look at them. She knew exactly what she was going to do. She went into the kitchen, slamming the door closed behind her so the boys couldn't come inside, although she didn't think that they would dare. Then she went into the larder and moved the assortment of jars to one side until she could reach the small tin she had hidden at the back, containing the arsenic she'd used to poison her mother. The little swines could have a taste of her medicine; see how much trouble they got into and how much mess they could make when they were lying in their beds vomiting blood.

Joss had said his parents were coming for tea so she might as well use some on their broth as well and be done with them all. She separated enough mixture into another pan for her and Joss and left the biggest pan on the stove, adding the contents of the box of arsenic then as many spices as she could to disguise the taste. She was furious but she wouldn't tell Joss about it because then he would have a reason to suspect her when they began to take ill. Her life would be perfect with just her and Joss – no horrible children or interfering parents.

Betsy set the table and put the bread she had made into the oven so it would be warm when she served it with the broth. She wanted it to be just right. After the broth, she had a chicken that she had roasted and some potatoes. She hoped the boys would begin to feel ill and go up to bed, leaving her and Joss alone for the night. Joss arrived home just minutes before his mother and father and Betsy shooed him to the bathroom to clean himself up a little. He laughed at her as she slapped his arm when he tried to grab her and pull her close to him. He came back down with the boys, who had cleaned themselves up and were being very quiet. Joss sat down, nodding at them to follow suit.

'Now then, what's the matter with you two – cat got your tongue? It's not like you to not be talking my head off.'

'Nothing, we are just being quiet for a change so Betsy doesn't get mad at us.'

She put the warm bread on the table and smiled at them. 'As if I could stay mad at you two for long. I have never known two boys who cause so much mischief, but I think the world of you both so think yourselves lucky for that.'

They looked at each other and smiled, relieved that she wasn't about to tell their father what they had done earlier. The kitchen door opened and in came Joss's parents, who walked straight across to the boys and fussed over them. Joss's mother bent down and kissed both of them on the cheek and then she turned and kissed Joss, and nodded her head at Betsy, who gritted her teeth. The woman could be so fickle, only speaking when the mood took her.

Betsy smiled at her and turned to stir the broth. She took the heavy pan and ladled it into four bowls then carried them over to the table, first giving it to the boys and then Joss's parents. She turned her back and then poured hers and Joss's broth into two more bowls. She carried those over and then sat down, waiting for Joss to say a prayer. Her stomach was churning. What if they could taste the poison she had laced their soup with? They would know what she had tried to do and then she would be in trouble, but before she knew it they were all dunking thick wedges of the soft white bread she had made and smothered in butter into their broth and talking about the news from the neighbouring village that the blacksmith there had been struck down with some illness that might even be a case of the Black Death.

If they thought the soup tasted funny, none of them complained and for a minute Betsy had second thoughts; did she really want to kill two boys and their grandparents? Then she thought about the mess they had made of her little garden and the fact that she and Joss deserved to be on their own and decided that yes, she did. Of course Joss would be devastated but she would be here to comfort him in his hour of need. It never occurred to her just exactly what would happen to her if they all died and someone realised she had been the one to administer the poison. Too wrapped up in creating her perfect life, Betsy laughed and talked away with them until they had finished. She cleared away the dishes and then served the next course. Up to now, none of them looked as if they had noticed anything amiss.

Halfway through the chicken and vegetables, both boys groaned and held on to their stomachs. Joss's mother stopped and asked them what was wrong.

'I do not feel well … my stomach is hurting.'

The other boy nodded in agreement.

Betsy looked at them both. 'Maybe it was all the dirt and mud you were throwing around this afternoon. They made such a mess and they were filthy.'

She looked at Joss when she said this and he looked at the boys.

'Did you wash your hands, both of you, before you ate?'

They nodded in unison.

Joss stood up and walked across to feel their heads, which were hot and clammy.

'I think you should both go and lie down for a while until you feel better.'

They stood up from their seats and made to leave the room.

'Goodnight, boys. I'll come up and tuck you in shortly. See if there is anything you need.'

Joss's mother stood up. 'There's no need; I will take them to bed and make sure they are not wanting for anything.' The two groaning boys and Joss's mother left the room. Joss and his father discussed whether or not they should sell some of the cows and buy some new ones. Betsy felt sick. She looked down at her plate and hoped that she had not got the pans mixed up and poisoned herself, then she told herself to stop being stupid. She had been very careful. After half an hour Joss's mother came down the stairs, her face white.

'They are asleep now, Joss, but if they don't get any better by the morning then make sure you send for the doctor. Come now, I do not feel that well myself. I want to go home and lie down. I fear whatever the boys have, I may have caught it as well.'

She walked to the kitchen door and Joss's father followed her.

'Thank you both. I hope the boys are better by the morning.'

Betsy picked up the plates from the table and turned to put them in the sink. She did not want Joss to see the smile that had spread across her face.

Chapter 10

Annie found herself in her house. It was very different to how it looked now and she realised that this was what it must have looked like when the painting had been commissioned. She walked under the porch but this time she didn't shiver or feel uneasy. Inside, she could hear a woman humming to herself and the clatter of pots and pans from the kitchen. Annie froze: it was the girl from her dreams. She didn't notice Annie because she was too busy mixing something into the soup. Not wanting to stay and watch her, she heard the sound of laughter coming from upstairs and wandered up to see two young boys playing in their bedroom, which was next to the one that she and Will were going to share.

One of the boys looked at the other and lowered his voice. 'You do know we're for it when she tells Father what we did, don't you?'

'I'm not daft, of course I do, and she'll tell him all right. I don't like her, Arthur; she only makes a fuss of us when Father is around.'

'I wish that Mother was here. Why did he need to get her to come and keep an eye on us? We were doing just fine on our own.'

'Shh, if she hears you she won't give us any supper and I'm hungry.'

'Well, I'm not going down there until Father calls us; I'd rather starve than sit with her on our own.'

Annie felt sorry for them. They didn't like the woman – whoever she was – so that made three of them. A man's voice broke her trance and she found herself back downstairs in the kitchen. The man who the voice belonged to had come in and was washing his hands in the sink. He was tall with crinkly blue eyes like Will's. He looked so familiar. He kissed the woman, who still had her back to Annie, and then he went to shout to his boys. As he called their names Annie could sense the contempt that radiated off the woman. She had a terrible sense of foreboding and knew that something bad was about to happen and she was helpless to do anything. Opening her mouth to warn the man, she almost choked, gagging on something in her throat that made her unable to speak.

An older couple came in and she wanted to yell at them all to get out while they could – but she couldn't. The woman was ladling soup into four bowls and she passed them out to the boys and the couple she assumed were the man's parents. Annie watched her fill two more bowls from a separate pan, using a different ladle. Why was she doing that? The first pan had been more than big enough and then it hit her. The woman had poisoned the soup. Annie, who was comatose in her hospital bed, began to twitch.

Will sat down on the chair next to Annie's bed, repaying the favour of two years ago when it had been him lying there and her keeping guard. She'd been unconscious for three days now but she had been restless today, which he took as a good sign. Her hands kept twitching and her eyes were rolling underneath the closed lids. She was either dreaming or trying to wake herself up. He hoped it wouldn't be long before she did wake up. He lifted his hand and scratched at the stubble on his chin. He looked rough. He hadn't slept at all and the nurses had kicked him out at one this morning, telling him to go and get some rest. He'd wanted to sleep next to her on a fold-up bed but she wasn't a child and they'd told him no.

Her car that she adored was a total write-off and he knew the first thing that she would ask him when she woke up would be how her car was. He was even thinking of letting Jake be the one to break that news to her. He'd buy her a brand-new one as long as she was well enough to drive it. He hadn't thought about if there could be any lasting brain damage. They would deal with that if it came to it but Will didn't care if there was. The doctors seemed hopeful that once she woke up she would be OK, but he knew they were unable to say for definite.

Lily had been every day, leaving his dad with the ice queen taking care of him. She'd taken him to the canteen for a coffee and a bacon roll this morning, where he'd sat picking at the bun as he had no appetite. 'She'll be OK, Will. It's just her body's way of saying: leave me alone while I get better.'

'I know she will but I just want her to open her eyes; even if she doesn't speak, I just need her to look at me and remember me. You hear horror stories of people waking up from a coma and having amnesia. I couldn't bear it if she didn't even know who I was.'

'You're thinking the worst, which is only natural, but we both know what a little fighter she is. Do you think she won't be lying there demanding her body to do what her mind is telling it? Because I don't think for one minute she's lying there taking it easy.'

'How's my dad, Lily? Is he any better?'

She paused, taking a sip of her coffee. 'He's not too bad.'

'What does that mean?'

'I didn't want to worry you; you have enough with Annie.'

'But?'

'But I'm worried about him. He hasn't been himself since the morning before Annie had her accident. He was sick and feverish. I asked him if he wanted me to call the doctor out but he shouted at me and told me to leave him alone. Will, he's never spoken to me like that in all the years we've been married. Something's bothering him but he won't tell me what.'

'I'll give him a ring later. Did you get the doctor to check him out? Is it the side effects of the stroke, do you think?'

'I don't know, to be honest, although I told him if he continues and doesn't make an effort to get out of bed then I'm getting the doctor whether he wants him or not.'

Will felt even worse than he had ten minutes ago. He knew that Lily must be worried to have mentioned it when Annie was so poorly. It wasn't even as if he could leave here to go and see his dad; he wanted to be here when she woke up. He would ring him and try and get it out of him when Lily left.

They finished their coffee and made their way back up to the intensive care unit. Lily walked in with him and across to the bed where Annie lay and bent down to kiss her on the cheek. She then turned and kissed Will on the cheek and said goodbye. Will hugged her and watched her walking out, wishing that none of this had ever happened. If he hadn't shown Annie the house she wouldn't be lying here now. Why had he even bothered? He told himself to stop being stupid, that Annie loved the house; it was one of those things that a hundred 'if onlys' could not have changed.

In her dream Annie watched the two boys eat all their soup and smile at their dad. She found herself begging God not to let them die. *Please God, let me be wrong.* As she asked for some divine intervention she felt the woman on the opposite side of the kitchen turn and look directly at her. Every hair on the back of Annie's neck stood on end as the woman opened her mouth, smiling at her. She nodded once and then a voice as clear as anything echoed in her ear. 'Welcome to my life, my nightmare. I'm glad that you can watch how it all ends. Now you will see why this is my house. It was always meant to be my house and it always will be. So get out.'

Annie's body stiffened up and her hands clasped at the sides of the bed. Her head moved from side to side and her eyes were all over the place. Will jumped up and shouted for the nurses, who were in the corridor discussing something. Two of them came running in and looked at each other.

Annie was frantic. The woman in white had lived in their house a long, long time ago. She knew that now and she also knew the reason why the men had been chasing her. Horrified and powerless to do anything to stop it, she had watched as the two cute boys and their grandmother had been taken ill. Annie felt her heart break in two at the sight of them crying in pain. Then it began once more as she found herself in the usual position – staring from her bedroom window, listening to the chanting men and snarling dogs that were coming for her. This time they had caught up with her because Annie had felt the rough rope that had been looped around her neck, the other end thrown across the beam of the porch of her house.

The woman had been struggling to get the rope off her neck as three men had taken the end of it and hoisted her up from the ground, chanting over and over again: 'Thou shalt not suffer a witch to live.' Her hands had been clawing at the rope, which was biting into the soft flesh of her neck and she'd frantically tried to loosen its grip around her with her nails, which hadn't made one bit of difference. Knowing there was nothing she could do, she had stopped struggling and looked across at the men who were gathered in her own front garden. The man whose family the woman had killed was standing at the back of the crowd, his face a mask of horror. The woman had smiled at them all. She hadn't been a witch, just a woman who had wanted her man and no one to get in her way.

Will, whose heart was racing, kept talking to her. 'Annie, it's OK. You're in hospital … open your eyes.'

Her head tilted back and she opened both of her eyes wide with fright. She stared at Will for a minute and he felt his blood run cold. Did she even know who he was? And then she blinked a couple of times and looked at him again. He had hold of her arm, stroking it to calm her down. Her breathing slowed and she relaxed. She smiled and he felt his heart jump for joy. Thank God she recognised him. The nurses pushed him to the side and checked her heart rate and blood pressure, talking to her and asking her questions the whole time.

Will stood back and for the first time since he'd walked through the hospital doors three days ago felt his whole body relax. His hands, which had been in tight fists, uncurled. He wanted to hold her more than anything but he could wait another five minutes. One of the nurses went to bleep the on-call doctor and Annie turned her head to look at Will. Her voice hoarse, she whispered, 'Hi.'

And it was the best sound he'd ever heard. He leant down and kissed her tenderly on the cheek. She pointed to the jug of water on the bedside table and he poured a small amount into one of the glasses and sat on the bed next to her. She lifted her hand to take it off him but it was trembling so he held it for her and lifted it to her lips, where she took a small sip then laid her head back against the pillow and nodded.

'I had the most terrible nightmare.'

'Good, because I think it woke you up.'

'How long have I been in here?'

'Three days – three very long days.'

She squeezed her eyes shut and the memories of the woman in white running through the woods being chased filled her mind.

'Did I run someone over? I must have hit her. She was standing in the middle of the road.'

Will shook his head. 'No, you didn't.'

'A woman – well, she was only a young woman, about twenty. She had long dark hair and the clearest pale blue eyes I've ever seen. She was running through the trees and I kept seeing her, then I rounded the bend and she was in the middle of the road.

I slammed my brakes on and turned the wheel; I was sure I'd hit her.'

'No, you didn't hit anyone … well, except a bloody huge tree and that didn't do too badly. Your car didn't fare too well, though.'

She shook her head. 'Are you sure I never hit her, Will? She would be dead if I did. Did they check the fields near to where I was to see if her body had been thrown over the hedge by the impact? It happens – I went to an accident years ago and we missed one of the wounded passengers because they'd been thrown so far from the car.'

'Annie, I promise you never hit anyone, just the tree.'

Annie felt Will's warm hand take hold of hers and felt the mattress go down as he sat on the bed next to her. She didn't open her eyes, feeling sad for the family the woman had murdered horrifically, but she did squeeze his hand so he knew she was OK and he gently squeezed back. She had to find out who the woman was. The men had been chanting that she was a witch but that hadn't been true, although she was a cold-blooded killer. When she was out of here she would do some research. By the look of the cottage and what they had all been wearing it would have been a couple of hundred years ago.

Her head was pounding and she felt as if she wanted to drink the full jug of water down in one go and she was tired – so tired, even though she'd been asleep for three days. The doctor came across to her bed and began to examine her and she let him get on with it, answering his questions as best she could. After thirty minutes he left with the nurse and Annie looked at Will.

'Take me home. I've had enough of this place.'

He laughed. 'Now there is nothing in this world that I want more than to take you home with me because our bed is so cold without you tossing and turning all night long, but I want you to be well enough to go home.'

She tutted. 'Well, regardless of how I am tomorrow, if you

don't take me home I'm not speaking to you ever again. But I'm too tired now to argue.'

'I'm so glad you're back. I'll let you get some rest and I'll be back first thing in the morning to rescue you.'

She opened one eye. 'You better had, Will; you know how much I hate hospitals.'

He bent down and kissed her dry, cracked lips. 'I love you, Annie Graham. Try not to get into any trouble while I'm gone.'

'For once I'm too tired. I love you too, Will.'

He turned and walked out of the unit and waved at her but she was already asleep. Taking out his phone, he sent texts to Jake then Lily and finally Kav, her old sergeant and friend, who had been up every day to check on her. Then he was going home for a large glass of Jack Daniel's, a long soak in the bath and a shave. He walked along the corridor, his feet automatically guiding him without needing to look up from his phone, along the passage that led to the accident and emergency department and through the sliding glass doors that led outside. He walked straight into a woman and lifted his head to apologise, surprised to see Amelia.

'Oh, it's you, sorry about that. Is everything OK?'

'Yes, thanks. I've been to visit my neighbour, who had a fall, and then I went down to my car and it won't start and my phone has died. I was just going to use the payphone.'

'Do you want me to take a look at it? I'm not a mechanic but I know a little bit. You might have a loose cable or need a jump-start.'

'Would you mind? That would be great.'

Will, who was so happy he would have driven her back to wherever it was she lived, nodded. He followed her out of the entrance to the hospital and along past the maternity unit to the steep steps that led down to the car park at the bottom of the hospital. It was dark along here, with only a couple of lights working that kept flickering. As they reached the bottom step she led him across the car park to the darkest corner.

'I hope you have a torch in your car because it will be a struggle to see what's what. I know everyone's skint but surely the hospital can afford to buy some light bulbs. This is ridiculous – it's an accident waiting to happen.'

Amelia agreed with him and led him to her car. She opened the door and pulled the catch to release the bonnet. Will lifted it, turning the flashlight on his phone on and shining it in the direction of the engine. He fiddled with some wires. As he turned to tell Amelia to try the engine, he felt a massive crack against the side of his skull and his knees gave way as he lost consciousness.

1782

The walk home to their farmhouse was not a pleasant one for Joe and Mary, even though it wasn't far away from Joss's cottage. Mary stopped every couple of minutes, doubled over with cramps in her stomach, and Joe, who was also feeling ill, was trying his best to support his wife and keep standing upright. He was feeling dizzy, his sweat felt cold and clammy yet he felt as if he was on fire. He didn't tell Mary he felt so ill because she was so poorly herself. They managed to shuffle towards the gate of the farmhouse and then Mary coughed, racking her lungs, and when she lifted her head Joe was frightened to see blood running down her chin. Her lips were bright red and there was blood frothing from them.

'Come on, Mary, we best get you into bed and then I will call out the doctor.'

Mary, who would normally shoo him away, nodded and then carried on shuffling towards the front door of their house. After what seemed like forever they reached the door and Joe had to drag his wife through it and to the stairs. Breathing heavily and on the verge of collapse himself, he helped her upstairs to their bedroom, where she fell onto the bed, not bothering to undress or get under the blankets.

He kissed her feverish forehead. 'I'm off to get the doctor, Mary. Hold on, lass.'

He stumbled out of the door but, losing his balance, he fell to his knees and coughed, which hurt his stomach even more. His throat was dry and his head felt as if it was going to explode. He dragged himself up and managed to get downstairs, where he fell onto the floor in front of the fire and could move no more.

* * *

The boys were moaning and crying and Joss was getting more worried by the minute. They were so hot to the touch he had never seen anything like it. Betsy was downstairs making cold compresses and trying not to faint. What had she done? She had wanted them to die this afternoon but now she didn't and she wished with all her heart she could take it back. Joss would be sure to find out it was her who had poisoned his entire family and then he would not want anything to do with her and she would probably hang for her crimes. She washed out the pan in which she'd poured the arsenic, scrubbing away every last trace. Then she set about washing the bowls and spoons.

A loud thud from upstairs made her drop the bowl she was washing and it cracked into a hundred pieces as it hit the tiled floor. She ran to take up the compresses and was shocked to see Joss on the floor, cradling his son in his arms. The boy wasn't moving and was clearly dead. The grief on Joss's face brought her to her knees and she cried out to him, but he shook his head at her.

'Get Dr Johnson now, Betsy … he's not breathing. Please.'

She ran as fast as she could downstairs. If she went for the doctor they would know what she'd done; it would be all over. She didn't want to get caught. Instead of running for help, she went outside to get the heavy spade she used to dig her herb garden and went back inside the house. She knew what she had to do as she crept back up the stairs towards Joss and his boys.

She could hear loud sobs coming from the room and knew that the only thing she could do that might save her neck was to kill Joss and then bury all three of them in the garden.

She inched her way along the corridor towards the bedroom and paused at the sight of Joss, who was now holding both his sons in his lap on the floor. He was rocking them back and forwards and sobbing. For a moment she regretted the pain she had caused him but then her sense of self-preservation took over and she crept behind him and raised the spade above his head, bringing it down with such force he didn't speak a word, just fell to the side with a stream of blood running down his face. Then she turned and ran to the stairs and back outside to the patch of soil she had prepared for the carrots and potatoes. The sun was setting but she began to dig as fast as she could a hole big enough to put all three of them in.

Joss murmured and blinked his eyes. The room was spinning and he felt sick. Something was heavy on him and he looked down to see the lifeless bodies of his sons. He knew then that this was all Betsy's doing. Why had she not called for the doctor? Instead of that she had hit him with something. Tears streaming down his cheeks, he forced himself to stand up and lifted both boys onto one of the beds. He bent down and kissed them, pulling a blanket over them to keep them warm. He stumbled towards the window and saw Betsy's hunched-up figure digging a hole in the ground and he knew without a doubt it was meant for them.

He turned and ran out of the bedroom to the back door of the house. He needed to get some help before she finished digging their grave. He had been so foolish and now he had lost everything. He went out and ran through the orchard until he reached the dry-stone wall that bordered the edge of his cottage and the woods. After climbing over it, he then ran through the woods away from the cottage towards his parents' house. When he was out of sight of his cottage he ran back onto the road and covered the short distance to the farm. As he reached the gate he saw Dr Johnson coming out with two of the farmhands.

The doctor looked at Joss with concern. 'Why, Joss, whatever has happened to you?'

'I need help … My boys …' He let out a sob so loud it racked his entire body and threatened to undo his composure all over again. 'My boys are dead and she tried to kill me.'

He walked towards the front door and the doctor, who was a man much older than Joss, stood in front of him.

'You can't go in there just yet, Joss.'

'Why? I need to see my parents.'

'I'm afraid both your parents are dead.'

Joss felt his knees buckle and he fell to the ground. Both of the men he worked with every day ran to help him up.

'She's killed my family; she must have done. We were all eating our tea when both boys fell ill and then my mother. Oh, God, and then she hit me over the head with something and I've run out of my house and she's in the front garden digging a grave. What are we going to do?'

Marcus King, who was a loud, brash man but a hard worker and one of Joss's friends, looked at him. 'Betsy Baker, whose mother died a month ago, has killed your entire family. She must be a witch; no mortal woman would kill children. Let's go and get her, see what she has to say for herself.'

Joss was at a loss for words. His head was a throbbing mess and his heart felt as if someone had reached into his chest and ripped it in two. He shook his head. 'Someone should go and get the constable.'

Dr Johnson was whispering into Seth Whitman's ear and he nodded then turned and ran towards the village. The doctor helped Joss over to the low wall that bordered the front of the farmhouse.

'Let me take a look at your head. Seth has gone to get some help and then we will go back and see what young Betsy has to say for herself. I'm very sorry about this, Joss. I cannot for the life of me imagine how you are feeling but we will go and see her as soon as we have a group big enough to deal with her.'

Joss didn't quite understand what the doctor meant but he knew, whatever it was, it was not good for Betsy. His eyes filled with tears at the thought of his boys, lying there without him, and he wondered why she had not killed him as well because she might as well have. He had no reason to live now. His life had ended along with his boys'.

* * *

Betsy wiped the sweat from her eyes. She was exhausted but she thought the hole looked big enough to put Joss and both boys inside. She had no idea what she was going to do once they were buried. She would have to move; there was no doubt about it. She wiped her dirty hands down the front of her dress and decided she was going to get changed. She ran into the house and up to the room where she slept. The only thing she could find was a long white nightdress from her drawers. Once she'd pulled the sticky clothes from her body and pulled it over her head, she felt better. She might even take to her bed and pretend to be as ill as her mother had been and she could say she did not know where Joss and his children had gone.

She walked into the boys' room, expecting to see Joss dead with his boys and felt her heart begin to beat wildly. He wasn't there. She ran to look in the corner behind the bed in case he had crawled towards it but it was an empty space. She felt sick. Where was he? He hadn't passed her so he must be in the house somewhere. She ran to the window and heard dogs barking out on the lane that led to the cottage, followed by the loud voices of a group of men. They were coming for her. They knew. Joss must have gone for help.

She left the room, running down the stairs and out of the

back door, taking the same path that Joss had taken less than an hour ago. No time to put her shoes on but not caring, she ran through the orchard, clambered over the dry-stone wall and slipped over into the woods, landing heavily on one side. The sound of the barking dogs was much nearer than she'd thought and she had to pull herself up and run for the trees to give herself some cover from them. The shouts of the men carried through the trees and the panic she felt almost made her want to throw herself onto the ground and wait for them to catch her but her mind wouldn't let her. She carried on running. The dogs were snarling and barking and she decided to run towards the stream to get rid of her scent.

Her feet were cut and bleeding and she had an awful stitch in her side, which she had clamped her hand over to try and ease. She ran towards the stream, not seeing the rock sticking out of the ground, and she hit it with her bare foot, losing her balance. The pain made her black out as she fell down the bank towards the stream and landed in a heap at the bottom.

Chapter 11

Jake parked the police car outside the entrance to the accident and emergency department and walked through the empty waiting room, along the corridor towards the wards and the intensive care unit. As he walked through the double doors he looked towards the bed that Annie had been lying in yesterday and his heart skipped a beat to see it was empty. His face drained of colour and the nurse rushed over to him.

'She's fine. I'm pleased to say we moved her up to a private room on ward five an hour ago. She's been awake on and off throughout the night and able to hold a conversation.'

Jake felt his shoulders relax. 'Oh, thank God for that. Thank you; I'll nip up there to go and see her.'

He left with a grin on his face and walked down to the lifts. He couldn't remember which floor ward five was on and he was too lazy to walk up the stairs. He got in the lift and blushed when an old woman got in next to him, asking him which floor he wanted.

The next stop was his and she chuckled to herself. 'You're as lazy as I am, young man.' With that, she shuffled out of the lift and in the opposite direction to where he was going.

The duty nurse looked up from the desk and pointed down the corridor. 'If you're looking for Annie Graham, she's in cubicle three.'

He walked towards the wooden door, excited to see his friend. It had only been four days since he'd spoken to her and it felt like a month. He knocked on the door and opened it. She was lying in the bed, her eyes closed. He walked in and bent down to kiss her on the cheek.

She opened her eyes and grinned. 'I thought you were Will.'

'Cheers, is that all the greeting I get? I mean, don't hide your disappointment on my behalf, will you.'

'You know what I mean. What time is it?'

He looked at his watch. 'Eleven-thirty, almost time for lunch. I'm starving. What are you having? Do you fancy sharing it with me?'

'You can have it; I'm not hungry for a dried-up tuna sandwich and some melted, tasteless vanilla ice cream. I'm so glad I'm awake; you would not believe the dreams I've been having whilst I was out of it. I dreamt I poisoned loads of people with arsenic and then I was chased through the woods by a group of men, all chanting about me being a witch.'

'I can sort of see why they would be calling you a witch. Did you have a broomstick?'

She threw a grape at him, which he dodged like a true professional.

'Have you seen Will, though? Seriously, he hasn't been yet and he promised me he'd come first thing and rescue me.'

'I haven't. I've been working, unlike some of us. You never cease to amaze me, what lengths you go to get out of an honest day's work.'

He winked at her, and then pulled his phone out of his pocket to see if he had any missed calls from Will. It wasn't like him to not turn up to see Annie when he'd said he would. The screen was blank. He dialled Will's number but it went straight to voicemail so then he typed Will's collar number into his airwave handset to ring him on that and it said 'party not available'.

'Have you checked your phone?'

'I don't know where it is. I should imagine it's probably in the car that I managed to write off. With being in a coma, I haven't really needed it for a couple of days.'

Jake called Kav to ask him if there were any jobs ongoing that Will might be tied up with. 'No, my friend. As far as I'm aware, CID are having an even slacker day than we are. Why do you ask?'

'Annie wondered where he is. He promised to help her escape from the hospital but he hasn't turned up yet.'

'Jake, have you got your earpiece in?'

'Yes, boss.'

'Has it occurred to you he might be in bed catching up on some sleep? He won't have slept much since Annie was brought in. Plus he might be leaving her as long as possible until she's seen the doctor. We all know how stubborn our friend can be.'

'Ah, yes. I didn't think of that. Good point.'

He finished the conversation then sat on the chair nearest to the bed.

'I think he's still in bed. He's probably knackered after keeping an eye on you for almost twenty-four hours a day since you got brought in. I'll give him a knock on my way from here and see how he is. So then, have they said when you can come home to wreak some more havoc and stress everyone out?'

'Piss off.'

He laughed. 'Oh, how I've missed thee, Annie Graham. I can't tell you how boring my life has been. Do you know that Annie Ashworth doesn't quite have the same ring to it? In fact, it makes you sound like some charwoman from the Nineteen-Fifties. Have you thought about keeping your own name when you marry Prince Charming?'

The door opened before Annie could reply and in walked the doctor.

'I'll leave you to it and go and check on Will. I'll come back up to see you after.'

He winked at her and she shook her head but grinned at the same time.

Jake drove straight to Will's house. He got out and ran up the three steps to his front door and pressed his finger on the bell several times. He waited for a minute then peered through the living room window. There was no one in there. He lifted the flap of the letterbox to see if he could see any sign of life and shouted, 'Will!' Concerned now that his friend wasn't answering, he hammered on the door with his huge fist.

The next-door neighbour, who was an older woman, opened her door and looked Jake up and down. 'Do you think that maybe he's not in?'

Jake bit his tongue. 'Maybe he isn't, but I need to know where he is. Have you seen him today?'

'No.'

'Well, can you remember when was the last time you saw him?'

'I think it was yesterday morning. He didn't come home until one a.m. and then he left just after eight yesterday. How's Annie?'

'She's OK, much better. Are you sure you never saw him come home last night?'

'I can't miss hearing his engine whenever he pulls up and my dog always starts barking every time Will opens his front door, and the dog barked yesterday morning when he went out but not since. I'm positive.'

Jake nodded. He felt uneasy. There was nowhere for Will to go. He walked around to try the wooden gate that led to the back garden but it was locked. So he dragged the wheelie bin close to it and jumped on it to climb over. Jumping down on the other side, he peered through all the windows but there was no sign of life. There were two patio doors and he tried them both but they were locked up tight. He looked at the wooden shed down the bottom of the garden and felt his stomach lurch. Surely not. Will had no reason to do anything stupid, but Jake couldn't get the image out of his mind of the man he'd found not that long ago, hanging in his garden shed after an argument with his wife.

He ran down to the shed, which was locked, and looked through the grimy window. All he could see was a lawnmower and a tool bench. Phew, no dead Will. He felt his heart slow down and pulled out his phone. This time he dialled Alex's number; he picked up straight away.

'I need you to do me a massive favour, please. Can you get the spare key for Will's house from the cabinet and bring it to me? I can't get hold of Will and I'm at his house now. It doesn't look as if he's here and his car isn't but I just need to check.'

'I'll be there in five minutes. Have you tried phoning his dad or Lily?'

Jake felt his cheeks burn. He was such an idiot – why had he not thought of that? Will had probably gone to see his dad and tell him Annie was OK. Panic over but there was still a smidgen of uneasiness that made him want to check the house anyway. Will's car was nowhere to be seen so it was highly unlikely that he was at home. He walked back to the wooden gate, this time unlocking it and letting himself out, and waited on the front wall until Alex's car turned into the street.

Alex got out and passed him the key. 'Did you phone Lily?'

'No, I don't have their number. I wanted to make sure he wasn't passed out in the house somewhere before I worried them.'

He turned and walked to the front door, inserting the key into the lock, praying he wasn't going to find Will's body somewhere. Alex followed him in.

Jake shouted, 'Will, are you home?'

He was met with dead silence. He looked at Alex, who shrugged. They checked the kitchen, living room and lounge. Then Jake took the stairs two at a time. He checked the bedrooms and bathroom but they were empty. The bed didn't look slept in and the sink and shower were dry.

He turned to Alex. 'He must be at his dad's. Where else can he be?'

Jake went downstairs to the small table in the hall, where he rooted through the drawers to find an address book. He had no idea what the telephone number was for Will's dad. He found a small black leather book and flicked through the pages until he found it. *Dad* was written in small black print. Jake pressed the numbers on his keypad and waited for it to connect. After a couple of rings it was answered by Lily.

'Sorry to bother you; it's Annie's friend, Jake.'

'Oh, my God, please tell me she's OK. Is everything OK?'

'Yes, Annie's fine – she woke up last night and they've moved her out of intensive care this morning. Didn't Will tell you? Is he there? I really need to speak to him.'

There was a slight pause.

'Will isn't here. I haven't seen him since I left the hospital yesterday morning. Have you been to his house? He looked exhausted yesterday. He might have slept in.'

'I'm here now and he's not. It's OK; he must have been called into work. I'll check there and get back to you. Did he phone you last night?'

'He sent a text to say Annie had woken up and he was tired and going home to bed. Tell him to give me a ring as soon as you find him, please.'

Jake hung up and looked at Alex. 'Where is he? He wouldn't have just taken off; something's not right. We need to go back to the hospital and double-check we haven't just missed him.'

Alex nodded. 'Should I wait here in case he turns up?'

'If you don't mind. If he's not at the hospital I'll let you know and you can lock up and come meet me there.'

Jake kissed Alex's cheek then left to go and get back into the police car. He phoned Kav, relaying everything to him. He ended by telling him he was worried. Kav agreed and told him he'd meet him at the hospital in five minutes.

* * *

Amelia and Luke managed to manhandle Will out of the back of the car. Luke, who had been hiding on the floor in the back, had helped to gag and tie him up, throwing him on the back seat with a blanket over him. Then Luke had driven back to their cottage, with Amelia keeping a watchful eye on the roads for any police cars. The roads had been deserted and they had made it back in record time. There had been a couple of moans from the back seat but Amelia had leant over and cracked him on the side of the head with her fist and he'd quietened down again.

'Watch it; you don't want to kill him, do you?'

Luke, who wasn't as violent as his partner, took his eyes off the road and she screamed at him, 'Just drive and let me deal with him.'

He knew better than to argue with her, so he focused on his driving and said nothing more. They managed to carry him into the house and down into the cellar after a bit of a struggle. The steps were narrow but they made it and dropped him onto the mattress. Will was still groggy and it was Amelia who tied him up so that he could still move a little but not far.

Luke searched Will's pockets, pulling out his phone.

'Make sure you take that somewhere and get rid of it; he might have some kind of tracker on it. In fact, go now and throw it in the lake or something, anywhere as long as it's not near here. Drive up to Ambleside or somewhere and then come straight back.'

'But it's a new phone. Do you know how much these cost? Can I not keep it?'

'Are you a fucking idiot, Luke? No, you can't keep his phone; it will lead the police straight to our front door. Get rid of it now.'

Luke was getting pretty sick of his psychotic girlfriend bossing him around but he was in it just as much as she was now so he might as well just do what she said until the money came in and then he was leaving her. All he wanted was a flat somewhere, a car and his Xbox. She could go and get fucked.

He went back out to the car and got in, no idea where he

was driving to. He did know one thing, though: there was no way he was throwing that phone in the lake. He would go somewhere for half an hour and turn the phone off but he was keeping it. He knew from watching television that the police needed all kinds of technology to trace a phone and they were in the middle of nowhere in the Lake District. It wasn't as if they were surrounded by some big-city police force who were used to dealing with shit like this. He imagined the worst crimes they had to solve around here were a bit of sheep rustling and poaching. He drove to Ambleside, glad to be away from Amelia for a bit of peace and quiet, where he parked up for a while and shut his eyes.

* * *

Lily picked up the post. There were three letters, all for Tom. One of them looked like another get-well card. She would take them up to him with his lunch; he had still been asleep when she'd gone in earlier with his breakfast. Amelia had phoned to say she was unwell and wouldn't be there today and Lily had felt nothing but relief. There weren't many people that she didn't like but Amelia was one of them. She couldn't put her finger on what exactly it was that she disliked but something bothered her.

She wondered if Tom had a virus and had passed it on to Amelia, which would explain his odd behaviour the last week.

She went into the kitchen to prepare him a light lunch and made two coffees and then she put it on a large wooden tray along with the post and carried it upstairs to Tom. She couldn't wait to tell him that Annie was OK. She knocked on the bedroom door then walked in. Tom smiled at her and looked pleased to see her, which made her feel a lot better.

'That's more like it. How are you feeling today, darling?'

'I'm a lot better, thanks. Where's Amelia? Aren't we paying her to be running around after me?'

Lily laughed. 'Yes, we are, but I have no idea why. I love running around after you and I'm much cheaper.'

'I'm sorry, Lily. I've been such a miserable bastard and none of it's your fault. But there's been a very good reason for it. There's something I need to tell you.'

She walked over to the bed and placed the tray next to him. He glanced down at the post and his face turned white when he saw the handwritten envelope.

Lily looked at him and felt her stomach flip. 'What's the matter, Tom? We don't have any secrets and you know you can tell me anything.'

His hands shaking, he reached down to pick up the envelope and slid his finger along the seal. It hadn't been licked and was easy to open. He tugged out the card that was inside. It had a grainy black and white photograph of Will stuck to the front – he was tied up in the back seat of someone's car and he looked unconscious. Tom felt sick. He opened the card and gasped.

Dearest Daddy,

I told you I was lonely so I've brought my half-brother to stay with me.

He didn't want to come but after he was hit over the head with a heavy hammer there wasn't a lot he could do about it.

Now he's all snug as a bug in my cellar, he can't talk much because of the gag but he's safe for the time being.

I don't want anything to do with you but I do want a share of what is mine and if you arrange to pay me what I want you can have your precious son back, relatively unharmed. There isn't a lot I can do about the gash on his head and the black eye but they will mend.

If you don't pay me what I want then you can have your precious son back in a box. I don't really care either way, he means nothing to me.

I want you to put a million pounds in unmarked notes

in a holdall and meet me to do a swap; I will give you two days to get the money together. If it takes longer then he dies.
  I hope you're feeling better today,
  Love me

Tom, his hand shaking, passed the card to Lily, who took it from him. She read the words inside and sat on the end of the bed next to Tom.

'What's this all about, Tom? Who is this and why are they calling you daddy? Is this some kind of sick joke?'

'I don't know who it is and I wish to God it was a sick joke … This is all my fault. Can you phone Will and see if he knows anything about this? It might be some stupid mocked-up image for my benefit.'

Lily looked at the photograph again. It didn't look as if it was a joke; it looked like fresh blood on the side of his head and Will wouldn't agree to anything so twisted when his dad had been so ill.

'Tom, this looks real … Oh, my God, poor Will. His friend Jake phoned an hour ago to ask if Will was here because he couldn't find him … What are we going to do?'

Chapter 12

Henry was restless. He knew it was getting near to the time to make his move. Megan had let slip yesterday that there was some kind of open day next Wednesday and there were some very special visitors coming to look around. Therefore, it could be the perfect opportunity for him; whichever ward they were visiting would be spruced up until it looked as if the patients were actually happy. He had no doubt it wouldn't be his ward – who the hell would want to come and shake hands with the likes of Henry and the other sick bastards who were kept prisoners here at Her Majesty's pleasure? It would cause a public outrage to see some honourable member of the royal family chatting away to England's most depraved and evil killers; they wouldn't be photographs for the family album to show the grandkids when they were having afternoon tea. He knew that the prisoners on his secure unit would all be locked up and left with minimum staff. They would probably sedate them all, slip an extra Valium or something stronger in with their breakfast meds so no one would cause any trouble.

It would be easier to get Megan to sneak him out when they were so focused on everyone else. She had been getting much more friendly with him, staying longer in his room than any of the others and chatting away. She had told him about some American television show that had a serial killer and an FBI agent played by Kevin Bacon and how this serial killer called Joe something-or-other was the sickest person she'd ever seen on television. Megan had said it was the best television programme she'd ever watched and was addicted to it. This Joe had followers who would do anything for him and she thought it was an amazing idea. It had taken him some time to convince her that it wasn't real, that it was all played by actors, as convincing as it might be, and she had laughed at him.

'Henry, do you think I'm stupid? I know it's not real but it seems like it is and if I could, I think I would jump at the chance to be in that cult.'

That was the last conversation he'd had with her and it had set Henry's mind wondering about just what exactly made his nurse Megan's mind tick.

* * *

Megan sat at the tiny breakfast bar in her flat, glued to her Kindle as she nibbled on her toast and jam. She was engrossed in a book called *Deadly Obsession*, which was all about her favourite patient – Henry Smith. From the very beginning there had been something about Henry that she had found very attractive. He was much older than her but he was always so kind. She was well aware of how violent he was, a deadly killer, from what the author of the book had written. It was so exciting reading about him and what he'd done and then to go and actually speak to him in person. Of course she knew he was lying to her about feeling guilty for what he'd done because she didn't believe for one minute that he did. He was very good at it, though, and totally convincing. He was so charming to her and such a good listener.

He liked his radio and to read books all day. Through her

training as a mental health nurse, she knew he displayed many of the traits of a psychopath but this only made him even more attractive to her because Megan shared many of the same traits. She smiled at the thought of Henry thinking she was all sweet and innocent. He had bought her story about being an abused girlfriend when, in reality, Megan hadn't had a boyfriend for six months.

She looked at the clock above the cooker and closed the cover on her Kindle, slipping it into her handbag so she could read it on her lunch break. She ran to the bedroom to get her phone off her bedside table and took one last look at her wall, filled with newspaper articles all about Henry Smith. She knew him as well as she knew herself. He would never admit it to her, but she knew that the thing keeping him going was the thought of finally exacting his revenge on Annie Graham. Megan wanted so badly to be there when he did, watching from the sidelines. She left the flat and got into her car for the short drive to work, excited to be seeing Henry again.

The key turned in the lock and he smiled to himself. She was always so punctual and he admired that in anyone. He smelt her perfume before she stepped through the door, something so floral but fruity and he liked it. She came in with his tablets.

'Morning, Henry, did you miss me?'

'I did, Megan. The days go by so slowly, but without seeing you they drag even more. I hope you have some good news to tell me.'

'Aw, you're such a sweetie; at least someone misses me. Yes, I do.'

She handed over the plastic cup filled with his assortment of tablets and he took it from her, his fingers brushing against hers, and he felt a thrill run through his whole body. It was hard to contain the shiver that ran down his spine. Megan pulled away from his touch as if she'd been burnt and he smiled.

'Well, then, are you going to put me out of my misery? Please.'

'I told him to pack his stuff and leave last night. I kept thinking about what you said to me the other day and I decided that you were right. There's no point keeping on with a relationship just because you don't like being on your own.'

Henry feigned taking his tablets whilst she was picking at her chipped nails.

'And how do you feel about that now? Do you regret telling him it's over?'

'At first I was terrified, my voice was shaking, but then, as I watched him pack his things and leave without so much as a "please don't say it's over, baby", I realised I was doing the right thing. He didn't even look bothered, just shrugged his shoulders and left. I mean, I would have hated it if he'd broken down and cried but it would have been nice to know he was the slightest bit bothered. You were right; he was just freeloading and he was a total waste of space.'

Henry suppressed the huge grin that threatened to break out. He loved it when he was right. 'I'm glad that you're not too heartbroken. You are a wonderful girl and the right person is out there for you; I'm positive. You will know him when you meet him and then you'll realise what love is.'

He reached out and patted her hand. He expected her to pull away from him but she didn't and he smiled.

'Do you think so, Henry? I really don't like being on my own. I suppose I should be thankful I have a job to come to and you to talk to, otherwise I might go crazy and end up in the women's ward.'

'So have you heard anything else about our special visitors next week? Will they be coming on this ward to meet a group of murderous freaks or will they get taken to the women's ward, where they can make polite conversation with the patients on there, who are much nicer and a lot less scary than us killers?'

Megan threw back her head and laughed. 'You know they won't want to shake hands with you lot unless it's some bunch of European do-gooders who don't care about anything but fighting for some cause. Don't tell anyone this but I heard them saying at handover they are going to sedate everyone on this ward and leave me and Julie in charge while they go and talk to all the nice important people. Should we have a party up here, Henry? If they do, you could actually come out of your room for a bit if the freaks are all off their heads. It would be nice for you to spend some time out of here.'

'Now, that sounds wonderful, but surely I'll be just as doped up as the others? I won't be in a fit state to have a grand old tour of the television or craft room.'

'Not if you don't take the tablets, you won't. Just make sure whoever gives you the medication that morning doesn't see you slipping them down the side of your chair. I know you do it sometimes but I don't give a shit. I wouldn't want to fill my body with crap I had no idea what the side effects were either so I don't blame you.'

Henry nodded. So sweet innocent Megan wasn't fooled by him. Maybe she wasn't so sweet and innocent after all.

'Ah, you know about that. Why haven't you told nurse bossy boots? After all, it's against ward policy for a patient not to take their prescribed medication, yet you know that I don't and haven't said anything to anyone.'

'Because, Henry, I like you. I can talk to you. You don't want to rape me and I hope you don't want to kill me like the others would if they were given the chance. I feel sorry for you and I don't think you belong here, cooped up in this room, day in, day out. I just want to make you happy.'

This time it was Megan who reached out and took hold of his hand.

'You know I would help you if you wanted to get out of here. I wouldn't tell anyone. It would be our secret; we could go somewhere and I could look after you. Do your shopping, run your errands, and you could be free to a certain extent. Obviously, we would be on the run from the police so it wouldn't be an awful lot of freedom but it would be a damn sight more than you have right now. Then I wouldn't be on my own. Have you ever thought about trying to escape, Henry? You must have. I know I would have done if I was you. I think I'd rather die trying than spend the rest of my life in here. Well, I'm offering you the chance to get away from this place but we'd need somewhere nice and quiet to escape to.'

Henry felt his mouth open; he didn't know what to say. This was a turn-up for the books, but one that he liked very much. Megan apparently had a very naughty streak in her, one that wanted to put her life at risk and help a murderer to escape. He nodded; she had given him an awful lot to think about.

He didn't want to say too much just yet but he already had it all planned out. His mum's friend had died a couple of months before he'd got caught and she'd left them her caravan on the very tip of Walney Island. The site fees had been paid up five years in advance and the key was taped under the top step of the caravan. They would be able to go there and hide out, in relative peace. The police had never picked up on the caravan and it wasn't in his name; it was in his mother's. Maybe he wouldn't have to kill Megan after all and it made sense that he wouldn't be able to survive on his own, not the way he looked. Because of Annie, he stood out from the crowd and would draw people's attention. It was something he would consider very carefully before agreeing to her offer.

* * *

Jake drove back to the hospital and parked on the grass verge outside the accident and emergency department for the second time in an hour. It was a good job he wasn't busy but Kav, his sergeant, would understand. He paced up and down and saw Kav coming in from the opposite side of the hospital and slowly driving towards him.

Kav got out of his car. 'Any sign of him yet? Because his car is parked in the bottom car park, but it's empty.'

'Really? That's all right then; he must be here. I must have missed him. Sorry, false alarm.'

'Don't worry. I wanted to come and see Annie anyway. Come on, let's go inside and see how she is.'

Kav followed Jake. Both of them kept their heads down, avoiding eye contact with anyone so as not to give them an excuse to come and start talking to them. When you wore bright yellow body armour you became a magnet for everyone and their friend to stop and tell you their life stories.

The nurse waved them on through when they approached the desk and Jake led Kav to the room Annie was in. The door was shut so he knocked and then walked in. His heart dropped to see Annie on her own – no Will. Jake looked at Kav as if to ask *What next?* and Kav shrugged.

'To what do I owe the pleasure?' Annie asked with a happy smile.

'I just wanted to come and see how my favourite ex-officer was; you know, make sure that you're behaving and not causing too many problems for the nice doctors and nurses.'

'One day you will see me when I look my absolute best and not like death warmed up.'

Kav laughed. 'If I saw you without a stitched head or black eye it would probably give me a heart attack. How are you doing, kid?'

'I'm OK, thanks, waiting for Will to come get me so I can go home. By the way, have either of you two heard from him? I've been ringing and ringing on this stupid hospital phone, which is rubbish, but all I get is voicemail. Has something bad happened at work that's keeping him tied up?'

Jake stepped forward. 'Not really. Annie, has he not been to see you at all today?'

She pulled herself up in the bed. 'No, I haven't seen him since he left last night.'

Jake felt as if there were a thousand alarm bells screeching inside his brain and he tried his best to come up with something that wouldn't scare her, but he found it hard to speak.

It was Kav who stepped in. 'We can't find him, Annie. No one has seen him since he left here last night. Is there anywhere, apart from your house and his parents', that he could be?'

Annie peeled the sticky pads off her chest and arms then swung her legs out of the bed.

'Only our new house, but we haven't even got a bed in there yet or a sofa; it's empty apart from one rickety chair in the bedroom. He said he was going home to bed. I don't think he'd have driven all the way there when he was so tired.'

Before Kav could say the words, Jake had stepped out into the hall and was passing the address of Apple Tree Cottage to the control room to get a Lakes officer to go and check if Will was there.

'If he had gone there he would have been here by now. Have you seen his car?'

'Oh, shit, his car's in the car park. Is there any other way he could get to your new house?'

Annie stood up on legs that wobbled as she tried to walk on them and Jake caught her as he came back in.

'Get back in bed. What do you think you're doing?'

'I'm going to find Will, that's what, and don't you dare try and tell me any different, Jake. He might be in trouble or ill.'

Kav nodded at Jake, then he stepped outside and asked if there was a dog handler on duty and for CSI to meet him at the hospital. Then he popped his head back into the room. 'I don't think he was in the car but I'll go and double-check.'

Kav jogged down the corridor towards the stairs and the exit that would bring him out near to where Will's car was parked. He made it out in record time, even though he had a stitch. Why was it he only ever had to run whenever Annie was involved in something? He reached the car and peered through the windows, thanking God that Will wasn't slumped over the steering wheel inside. He tried the doors but they were locked. Walking around to the front, he pressed the palm of his hand onto the bonnet. It was stone-cold. The car hadn't been used for hours, so where the fuck was Will? He stood waiting for the dog and CSI to arrive.

* * *

Jake paced up and down the small room whilst Annie tried to make herself look presentable but she was wearing a hospital gown and no clothes because they'd all been cut off her when she was brought in.

'Annie, I know you're worried but, seriously, you can't go out of here wearing just that gown; it's proper indecent.'

'Well, be a gentleman and give me your jacket, then when we reach the car you can drive me home so I can get some clothes and then bring me straight back.'

A nurse walked in with a tray of food and almost dropped it on the floor. 'What are you doing, darling? Get back in bed and get your feet up.'

'I'm sorry but I can't; there's an emergency and I need to go right now. I'm fine – thank you for all your help; I really appreciate it.'

The nurse looked at Jake as if to tell him to get a grip and he shook his head in apology and rolled his eyes at Annie.

'I'm sure this nice officer can deal with whatever the emergency is while you rest up.'

Annie looked at the older woman and took a deep breath to calm her down before she spoke. 'I'm sure the nice officer could, but I'm also a nice officer and I need to go right now.'

Jake unzipped his body armour and took off his black fleece jacket that he was wearing underneath it. He handed it to Annie, who slipped it on and wrapped it around herself, the sleeves dangling almost to her knees.

She walked to the door. 'Don't worry; I know it's my own fault if I go out of here and die but I'm sorry, I have to go. Thank you for everything.'

With that, she began walking barefoot down the corridor towards the lifts. Jake ran after her and took hold of her arm.

'Thanks, Jake, I owe you. What about the cameras? Should we go and check them before we leave the hospital, see if it has Will leaving on it last night? We only need to check the A & E and maternity exits; all the others will have been locked up by the time he left – it was past ten o'clock.'

'Cracking idea, Annie. You know I really miss working with you, even though right now you look like you've escaped from the mental health unit. People are going to think I've sectioned you.'

'I don't care what I look like, Jake, and don't tell me you wouldn't be the same if it was Alex we couldn't find because I know you'd be having a nervous breakdown.'

He nodded. She was right; he couldn't begin to imagine life without Alex in it and it didn't bear thinking about because he loved him so much. They went to the small office near the main entrance where the security guards hung around drinking coffee and watching the CCTV. Jake knocked on the door and walked straight in, Annie following. The two guards looked over to him then at Annie and one of them stood up.

'Cheers, mate, where did you find her? They didn't even let us know one of them had escaped. They normally do. I'm telling you, they need better locks on the doors down there; it's not safe.'

Jake couldn't stop the grin that spread across his cheeks. The guard walked over to Annie and took hold of her elbow.

'Come on, love, let's get you back down to your ward. It's dinnertime. Fancy a little walkabout, did you, a bit of fresh air?'

Annie pulled her arm away from his. 'How dare you? I'm not a mental health patient. I'm a police officer and I work with this idiot. We need you to check your CCTV from last night around ten o'clock to see if you have one of our detectives leaving the hospital.'

The guard looked at his mate then winked at Jake. 'By heck, she's good. Very convincing; you would have had me fooled.'

Jake felt Annie's fist bury itself into his left kidney, which wiped the grin from his face. 'Argh. She's telling the truth. She's a police officer who was a patient here on the medical ward and has discharged herself – without the doctor's consent, I might add.'

He rubbed his back. 'We need you to check the cameras, please; it's a matter of urgency. We need to see if the detective left the hospital or if he's still inside somewhere, because he hasn't been seen since he left Annie's private room last night.'

The guard's cheeks flushed red. 'Sorry, officer, no offence. You're not exactly dressed right – my mistake.'

He turned and walked over to the monitors, where the other guard was stifling a giggle behind his hand. After what felt like forever he got the video footage up of both exits, checking the A & E one first. After watching it for a few minutes, Annie told him to stop it and let it play. Will could be seen walking past the reception desk, his head bent as he was looking at his phone. Annie clenched Jake's arm, her heart racing. He walked out of the automatic doors and straight into a woman. Lifting his head, they had a brief conversation and Annie felt her world about to come crashing down.

Please, God, don't let him have left with her and gone back to her house, not now. Not after all we've been through. Annie could sense Jake squirming to the left of her and felt her cheeks begin to burn. The woman looked familiar but the footage wasn't very clear and they didn't look intimate; there was no kiss or touching, apart from Will walking into her, but it looked as if it had been a total accident.

Jake turned towards her. 'It's not what you're thinking; you can tell he wasn't expecting to see her. But it does look as if she knows him – sorry, Annie.'

They continued watching the screen. The woman turned and Will followed her out of the hospital.

Annie felt sick with worry. It wasn't right. 'Please rewind it to the point where he knocks into her.'

The guard obliged, rewinding it back then playing it in slow motion. Annie bent closer to the screen. She did know that woman – but she didn't know her very well.

'Oh, my God … I know her – I think it's the ice queen.'

Jake raised his eyebrow at her and the two security guards turned to look at her.

'Well, me and Will call her the ice queen. It looks very much like Amelia, Will's dad's new housekeeper. Why would Will go with her, unless she came to tell him Tom was poorly? Oh, God, have you spoken to Tom and Lily? Is everything OK with them?'

Jake relayed the conversation with Lily he'd had earlier.

'Give me your phone, Jake. I need to speak to Lily.'

He handed it over to her then turned to the guards. 'Please can you burn a copy of that off for me in case it's evidence? What about the outside cameras? Can you check to see if they are on that and which direction they headed off to?'

The guard who was sitting down nodded and brought up the view from the outside camera. It showed Will walking along with the woman, past the maternity unit and down towards the steps that led to the lower car park, where they turned the corner and were gone.

'Can you get them up once they've got to the bottom of those steps so we can see which car they get into?'

'No, sorry, mate, someone broke the screen on the camera down on that part of the car park a couple of days ago and it won't get fixed for a couple of weeks.'

Jake felt the hair on the back of his neck stand on end. It was all too much of a coincidence. Annie let out a sob on the phone and he turned to her.

'Don't touch it again. Tell Tom it's OK, we'll get someone up to you very soon.'

The guard handed a disc to Jake. 'Good luck, hope you find him soon.'

Jake ushered Annie out of the small office and into the corridor. 'Don't touch what?'

Annie, her face whiter than he'd ever seen it before, burst into tears, which was another first for Jake. With everything she'd been through the last couple of years, he'd never actually seen her cry and he felt his heart pounding.

'Tom got a card in the post this morning with a ransom note in it.'

'You're having a laugh … Why would anyone want to kidnap Will? I mean, that's plain stupid. What did it say?'

'Lily didn't really say; she was too busy crying. What are we going to do? Poor Will.'

Jake shook his head. 'Let's go find Kav and tell him, then get you home so you can put some clothes on and then we'll figure it out.'

They walked towards the exit and down towards the steps where Kav was standing next to Will's car with Debs the crime scene investigator already suited and booted and getting ready to start processing it for any evidence. Kav took one look at Annie's face and knew something was wrong. Jake began relaying it all to him then turned to catch Annie just in time before she passed out and hit the tarmac.

She woke up in the front seat of the CSI van being fanned with a crime scene logbook by Jake. He whispered, 'Kav's having a shit fit, wants you back in hospital and me and him to go to Will's parents along with someone from Kendal CID.'

'I'm OK; I haven't eaten for God knows how many days. Please don't let him send me back in there. I'll only do one when his back's turned – you know I will. Then I'll probably fall out of the toilet window while I'm trying to escape and break my neck and it will all be your fault when you're crying over me at my funeral. Just think of the guilt you'll have to live with for the rest of your life.'

'Fuck me, that's emotional blackmail and a half. I'll tell him but he's not happy. He wanted me to carry you up there.'

She laughed. 'Then you'd have been in the bed next door,

having a heart attack. Seriously, tell him I'm fine. I just need chocolate and Will.' She felt her eyes brim with tears but blinked them back. Now was not the time to turn into a blubbering wreck. Kav would definitely send her back into the hospital.

Kav walked across to them both. 'Right, plan of action is to take Annie home and get her dressed. We can't have her upsetting the upstanding citizens of Barrow looking like that, and then Annie can direct us both to Will's parents' house so we can speak to them, see what the hell is going on. Is that OK with you both? Annie, are you well enough for this because, quite frankly, I don't want you collapsing or, worse, dying on us; I need you to be able to keep it together.'

'I'm fine. I just need something to eat and some clothes. It will take me five minutes.'

Kav nodded, satisfied for now. He knew that she would only be a complete pain in the arse if he left her behind.

Jake handed his keys to Debs. 'Give them to whoever comes to get the car and tell them I abandoned it outside A & E. Thanks.'

She nodded, pocketed them and continued dusting for prints.

1782

Betsy opened one eye then tried to open the other and winced. Her head was throbbing, she couldn't see clearly and for a moment she had no idea where she was or what was happening. A shadow fell across her as a man leant over her and then she remembered that she had been running away from them. He poked her in the chest with a stick and she flinched.

'She's alive, bit dazed but still breathing, unfortunately.'

She blinked to make her eyes focus. There were at least seven or eight men standing around her in a circle, looking down at her, and for the first time in her life she felt pure panic fill her lungs and steal all the air from inside, making it hard to breathe.

Rough arms came down, gripping hers, and then she was lifted to her feet. She felt sick as the pain made her head feel as if it was on fire.

'Well, then, what have you got to say for yourself, you murdering whore?'

Another voice spoke to the left of her. 'Now, then, you all know what it says in the Holy Bible. Thou shalt not suffer a witch to live. I say we take her back to the house and hang her high from the beams. That will chase the Devil from her. Satan won't want anything to do with her once her body is left to rot. Let the birds peck her eyes out and the animals scavenge her flesh. It will be a lesson for everyone to see.'

Betsy felt bile rise in her throat and her stomach soured. It was all over. She knew that her life was going to end very soon and there was nothing she could do about it. She wanted to cry and beg Joss's forgiveness but she would not show these men such a sign of weakness, so instead she let out a loud chuckle. 'You foolish men, I am no witch. I tell you now; it is not the Devil inside of me, as you may have yourselves believe. But if it makes you feel better then go on and believe your rubbish.'

A hand slapped her across the face, leaving red fingerprints across her cheek. She lifted her head to see Joss standing in front of her and knew it was him who had hit her.

'Why, Betsy? Why would you want to kill my sons, my mother and father? Was I next? I loved you and this is how you repay me, by killing the people who mean the most to me.'

Before she could answer, he turned his back on her and walked away and she felt her stomach roll and a tear fell from her eye. She had wanted him all to herself; was that such a bad thing?

Another voice chanted: 'Thou shalt not suffer a witch to live; thou shalt not suffer a witch to live.'

Over and over again, it was getting louder as more voices joined in and she shut her eyes. She felt herself being dragged forward and knew they were taking her to the house that she had longed to be her home, but there was nothing she could do. She wasn't strong enough to overcome seven grown men and she had nothing left now that Joss had turned his back on her.

It didn't take very long before they reached her beloved house that had started all of this. Her vegetable garden was still a mess from when the boys had thrown the soil and seedlings everywhere and there was the big hole that she had frantically dug in the middle of the other patch. She wondered if dying would hurt. There was a lot of chanting, pushing and shoving. A rough rope was hooked around her neck, the strands so coarse they were cutting into her flesh even before it tightened. She opened her eyes to look at them, the men who were going to kill her and take her away from her beloved Joss.

'I'm no witch, you fools; I just wanted to be on my own with Joss. I'll tell you one thing, though – I do like to kill people … I very much enjoyed killing my mother, listening to her groans of agony. Don't think that I won't come back for you all once I'm dead, because I will haunt each and every one of you until the day you all die and then you can meet me face to face once more. This time it will be one on one and we will see how brave you are then.'

Betsy felt them pause. Her words had struck fear into some of them. She knew every single one of them because they all drank in the pub she had worked at. She knew where they lived and hoped they would spend the rest of their lives looking over their shoulders. She looked at Marcus, then nodded for them to get on with it.

The rope went taut and she gasped, her fingers automatically reaching up to try to loosen it. She felt her feet lift from the ground. She looked around to see where Joss was and saw him standing at the back of the crowd, a shovel in his hand ready to bury her, but what made her eyes pop open and her heart stop beating was the sight of her mother standing next to him, with rotting flesh hanging from her bones, her arms stretched open wide and a huge grin spread across her mottled green face that had black sockets for eyes. Betsy frantically kicked her legs and pulled at the rope around her neck, wanting to be free, not wanting to have to meet her mother again, but there was nothing she could do and she lost consciousness …

* * *

As Betsy took her last breath the men around her began to panic, and the two holding the rope bent their heads.

'What have we done?'

The words broke the silence. Joss looked around. He didn't know who had spoken them but he felt as if his whole world had crashed down onto his shoulders. He didn't look at the woman who had once held his heart in her hands and at the same time had taken it and ripped it in two. He turned and walked across to the vegetable beds he had spent a full day digging and preparing for her to grow her own vegetables in. She had been so sweet and funny when he'd met her.

He went to the hole that she had started – one almost big enough to put her body in. Two of the others joined him and they began to dig, and before long the hole was deep enough. Joss didn't want to touch her; he didn't want her corpse in his garden either but if the law got hold of this they would all surely hang as well, for were they not just as bad as she was? He wiped his brow with his sleeve; it was warm work digging.

He turned to Marcus, who had been the ringleader in all of this. 'Cut her down and put her in that hole.'

'I thought you might want to leave the witch there for a few days, let the locals see what happens when you dare to mess with us.'

'Are you serious? We have just killed her in cold blood, hanged her like a pig about to be slaughtered and you want to leave her there, dead and rotting, from my front doorstep for the whole village to see? Just bloody cut her down, Marcus, and be done with it and may God forgive us for our sins.'

Joss stood with his back to them; he couldn't watch. There was some grunting and a loud thud as Betsy's body hit the ground. He didn't watch them carry her over to the hole and put her in it. Instead, he passed his spade to the man nearest to him so he could begin to cover her. They worked fast and before long the only sign of what had happened was a mound of fresh soil.

Joss nodded at the men who had buried her. 'I have no desire to talk about this to anyone and neither should any of you. Let us all hope that no one cares enough to wonder what happened today or to ask the whereabouts of Betsy Baker. If anyone should ask, you should tell them that you don't know and the last you heard was she was leaving and going to the next village.'

Seth, who was the youngest of them all, looked across at Joss. 'Do you think she meant what she said? Was she a witch, Joss? I don't want to spend the rest of my life terrified she's coming to get me.'

'No, Seth, I do not believe that she was a witch and I do not believe that she can come and haunt us or scare us to death. I believe she was trying to scare us into letting her go and maybe we should have.'

The men all turned and looked at Joss and shook their heads.

'How can you say that? Are your family not lying dead because of her and, judging by the gash on your head, you would have been too. We did the right thing, Joss.'

Joss nodded then walked out of his gate and up the road towards the village and Dr Johnson's house. He was numb inside. His heart felt as if it was made of stone but he forced himself to move one leg after the other and keep on walking away from his home and the bodies of his children. He prayed to God the whole time for his forgiveness and for the souls of his family. He hoped that his wife, Flora, who had died so suddenly, had been waiting for their boys when they passed over and had been able to comfort them in their hour of need. Joss didn't really care what happened to him now; in fact he did not know if he wanted to live or die. He would bury his family and then decide whether or not to join them.

He finally reached the large house, which was Dr Johnson's home and surgery. The doctor's housekeeper, who was a cousin of his, stepped out of the front door to greet Joss, running down the steps to hug him.

'I'm so sorry Joss, I really am. Come inside and get your head looked at … it needs cleaning up.'

He followed her inside, weary and far too afraid to go home.

Chapter 13

It took Annie five minutes to get dressed, clean her teeth and put her hair in a ponytail. It took her ten minutes to stop herself from crying as she lay on Will's side of the bed, holding his pillow close to her face. She knew she was being overly dramatic but there was no way she could live without him; he was her life. She also knew that Will was just as competent at fighting as she was. They all learnt the hard way as new recruits fighting with the drunks on a Saturday night. They all did intense self-defence refreshers every single year so technically Will should be able to hold his own against a woman. It bothered Annie that Amelia must have an accomplice; she wouldn't be strong enough to do this on her own. What if she had a gun? What if …?

'Annie, are you OK? Still breathing up there?' Jake's voice snapped her out of the vision she had been about to see.

'I'm fine, thanks; coming now.'

She got off the bed and kissed Will's pillow, pulled a tissue from the box and blew her nose and then went downstairs and out of the front door, slamming it shut behind her. Jake and Kav were sitting in the front of the panda and she opened the door and climbed in the back. She opened a multi pack of chocolate bars and offered one to each of them. Kav shook his head but Jake took one. Neither of them spoke to her. She looked like shit and for once Jake didn't blurt it out and embarrass her. In fact she felt like shit; her head was pounding and she felt sick and her chest was so sore it hurt every time she took a deep breath.

With hands that were trembling, she ripped open a chocolate bar and bit it in half. There was something so soothing about it and as she slowly chewed on it she felt a little bit better. Finishing the first and starting on the second, she knew she needed the energy and the comfort that it brought. Kav was busy on the radio, speaking to someone from Kendal CID, and Jake was driving. Annie tried to blank everything out and just concentrate on staring at the road through the gap in the seats, otherwise she would end up being sick all over the car and then Kav would go mental. Jake had the blues on but no sirens and they got through the standing traffic at Ulverston and Greenodd in no time. Pretty soon, they were turning off on the road to Bowness.

'Just keep going; it's one of the houses just past the big hotel on the left-hand side. I think it's Storrs Hall. I'll tell you when to slow down.'

Jake drove fast but cautiously, which made her feel a little better as she hated his driving with a passion. The road was quiet, no traffic jams or coaches, and for once luck seemed to be on her side.

'Slow down now and it's the next one along; once you pull in there's a narrow drive that opens up.'

Jake followed her orders and indicated he was turning left. As the drive opened up so did Jake and Kav's mouths.

'Bloody hell! I never knew his parents were this rich. All these years we've known him and he's never said a word – no wonder you can't wait to marry him.'

'You can be such an idiot, Jake. I had no idea either until we split up. I got an invite to a barbecue from his parents and I didn't even know they were his parents until he turned up. So, for once in your life, shut up.'

Jake shrugged. 'Well, if you don't marry him I'm going to. I can just see myself living in a house like this.'

It was Kav who elbowed him in the side this time. 'Shut the fuck up, Jake; you're not helping.'

'Sorry, just saying.'

He parked the car at the bottom of the steps and, before he could get out, Lily came running down the steps and flung open Annie's door. Annie stepped out of the car and felt Lily launch herself at her.

'Oh, thank God you're OK and you're here. I don't know what to do. Tom looks as if he's about to have a heart attack … I've phoned for the doctor – I'm just waiting for him to come and check him out. Poor Will … I can't believe it.'

'I know, and poor Tom – it must have been such a shock for him. Don't worry, we'll get it sorted out. I'll find him and God help me when I get hold of her.'

'I kept telling Tom there was something about her that I didn't like but he thought I was being paranoid. Come inside, all of you, and we can talk about it and see what to do.'

Annie introduced her to Kav and Jake, who both looked a little bit out of their depth. Even in a state, Lily looked gorgeous. Annie couldn't help but smile when she saw the redness creep up Kav's cheeks when Lily shook his hand and thanked him for coming.

They followed Lily into the kitchen, where Tom was sitting at the table with a glass of whisky.

Annie ran over to him and hugged him; he put the glass down on the table and hugged her back, squeezing her tight with his good arm.

'I'm so glad to see you, Annie; we've been so worried about you. Should you even be out of hospital yet?'

'That's what I keep telling her but she doesn't listen to anyone, do you, Annie?' said Jake.

Annie pulled away from Tom, and Kav introduced himself, shaking Tom's hand, as did Jake.

'I'm fine, Tom, really. Look at us, both a couple of invalids and now this. I can't bear it. We need to find him, Tom, and the sooner the better.'

Tom nodded and pointed at the chairs. 'Please sit down. Would you like a drink?'

They all declined and Lily stood behind Tom, her hands on his shoulders, and they listened as Tom told them about the cards.

'I should have told Lily when I got the first one, and Will, but I was too embarrassed. I didn't want to upset him. He doted on his mum and so did I; it was a stupid, reckless affair that was doomed before it even started. She meant nothing to me and I regretted it every day of my married life. I always meant to tell my wife but she died so suddenly that I never got the chance … and now look at the situation we're in. I've thought about it and if she wants money then so be it. I can get it together in twenty-four hours. I don't want Will harmed in any way. My son means more to me than any amount of money.'

It was Kav who spoke. 'Let's wait until the detective from CID gets here. We all want to see Will safe but we need to think very carefully about this. We need as much information as you can give us. Jake, why don't you take Tom into another room and take a statement from him about anything and everything that could be relevant? I'll speak to Lily in here.'

Jake nodded and waited for Tom to push himself up from the chair. He shuffled along, leading the way to the library with Jake following. Tom nodded at Kav, grateful not to have to share every little detail in front of his wife and future daughter-in-law.

Annie filled the kettle and took cups and saucers from the cupboard. She didn't know what else to do except make some tea. She felt like a spare part but she couldn't go home and wait; she wanted to be here with Tom and Lily in case they needed her. Her stomach was churning and she hoped to God that Will was safe somewhere and they hadn't hurt him. As far as she was aware, kidnapping was rare in this part of the country. She just hoped that whoever got sent to deal with it actually knew what they were doing.

There was a loud knock at the door and Lily jumped up to go and answer it. Annie waited to see who it was. Two men in suits walked in behind Lily. They nodded at Annie and she nodded back.

'Detective Sergeant Nick Tyler, Kendal CID.' He held out his hand and shook Annie's. 'And this is Detective Constable Richard Ward. We've heard a lot about you, Officer Graham. I'm sorry that we're having to meet under these circumstances but I know Will; I did my CID course with him and I'm sure he's holding up as well as can be expected under the circumstances. We'll get him back, I promise.'

Annie nodded; if he knew Will then he would take it personally, which was good. It would mean more to him than someone off the street.

'Have you had any contact with them? Has anyone tried Will's mobile?'

Lily pointed to the cards on the kitchen worktop, which were lying side by side.

'These cards and that's it. I think we've all tried to phone Will but with no answer; it goes straight to voicemail.'

Nick wandered over, pulling a pair of latex gloves out of his pocket. He slipped them on and picked the first card up, opening it up to read inside. He then pulled an evidence bag from his pocket and sealed the card inside, passing it to John to write the time, date and other details on. Whilst he did this he took the gloves off and Lily lifted the lid of the bin for him to throw them in. He did exactly the same with the next card, putting on a fresh pair of gloves to pick it up and read it, then sealing it up so as not to break the chain of evidence. He didn't want to risk any cross-contamination, although there was a good chance it was already too late. Then he sat down and gently questioned Lily, who couldn't tell him much that she hadn't already told Kav.

'I need Amelia's full name and address. I think Sergeant Kavannagh will cover everything in your statement but I want to start the address checks immediately. Where did you find her? Was it through an agency?'

'We have a friend who runs a holiday cottage rental business; she asked some of her employees if any of them wanted some extra work a couple of days a week and there was only Amelia who said yes.'

'Then I need to speak to your friend as well; they should have Amelia's address on file. I'm pretty sure we'll get this sorted and have your son back pretty soon.'

Annie nodded. It didn't sound as if Amelia was a master criminal so, fingers crossed, they would have Will back within a few hours.

Nick stood up. 'I think that's all we need for now. I want to get to the station and begin our enquiries as soon as we can. Would you like a family liaison officer appointed, to come and be here with you all?'

Lily looked at Annie, who shook her head. 'No, thank you. If you need to know anything, you can speak to me. I'll stay here with Tom and Lily and be your point of contact. Thank you, Nick, and please hurry up and bring him home.'

Nick nodded. 'I'll do my best, Annie, I promise.'

Kav walked both officers to the front door and let them out. 'If you need anything – resources, information, extra officers to search, let me know. I'll have them up here in the blink of an eye.'

Nick nodded. He didn't smile because he wasn't sure if this was going to be as simple as they were all hoping. There was a good chance the kidnappers would be complete amateurs and panic, kill Will and do a runner if they thought things were going wrong. If he'd thought that he had a headache this morning after that bottle of red wine last night it was nothing compared to the sledgehammer that was pounding his brain at this exact moment in time. He'd never dealt with anything like this; he'd never dreamt he'd ever have to deal with anything like this and he couldn't admit it to Annie and Will's parents that he was completely winging it and didn't have a clue.

'Thanks. I'll be in touch as soon as we know anything.'

Chapter 14

Henry shivered, tugging his coat around him to shield his body from the driving rain. It had rained for two days solid; the courtyard that he exercised in had big puddles of water that he had to keep walking around. Tomorrow was the day of the important visitor. He still had no idea who it was and Megan didn't seem to know or care, to be honest, when he'd quizzed her several times about it. She'd come to see him fifteen minutes before she'd finished last night and taken her usual position, sitting on the corner of the bed.

'So, Henry, what do you think about my idea? I need to know before I go home so I can pack up what I need because I won't be going back to that flat again if we make a break for it. The police will be all over it in no time, not that there's any evidence there.'

He stretched his arms out in front of him, clasping his fingers. 'I think that it's very kind of you to offer to help me out, but do you honestly have any idea of the consequences?'

'I've been thinking about this for weeks now. I know that I'll never get a job nursing again. I'll go to prison if we get caught, and it's OK. My life is so boring at the moment, I'd give anything for some excitement and I think that running away with you might just be what I need to do.'

Henry stared at her; she seemed sincere. He noted that her fingernails were fluorescent pink today to match the streak of colour in her hair. She had a rebellious personality. She probably thought it would be very romantic, helping a serial killer to escape and going on the run with him. The one thing she hadn't taken into account, though, was the fact that he was a cold-blooded killer and, should the need arise, then he would think no more about killing pretty little Megan than he would about crushing an ant underneath his shoe. Maybe that was the attraction – the excitement of it all.

'Well, in that case, I don't mind if you don't. How are you going to get me out of here, though, Megan? Have you thought about it? I don't even want to attempt to leave if we're going to get stopped at the gatehouse on the way out.'

'I'm going to disable the disturbance alarms in the communal area; I'll pull a wire out of the main console. Then, when everyone is on lockdown, you will put on the clothes I give you in the morning and we're going to walk out of here as if you're supposed to. No one is going to give you a second glance as long as you don't freak out. If anyone asks you, tell them you're on day release and we're off to the post office, but they won't; they'll be far too busy monitoring the ward the visitor is going to. Trust me, Henry, it will work.'

Henry nodded. What option did he have? This was much simpler than trying to escape on his own. Megan had all the security passes to open the locked gates. He thought it was so brazen, simple and obvious that it would probably work.

'What time are you planning on doing it?'

'I'll play it by ear and come and see you first thing.'

She walked over to him, bent down to kiss him on the side of the cheek then turned and left, locking the door behind her. He shivered. What a turn-up for the books this was. It might end up that Nurse Megan was nothing at all as he'd expected and she could be even sicker than he was, but it was a chance he was willing to take. Anything to get out of here and see his dream woman again. He wasn't sure how Megan would react when she found out that she had some serious competition; it could go either way. Henry realised that the less he talked to Megan about Annie Graham, the safer it would be for all of them.

He would find somewhere that he could be all alone with Annie. If he had to knock her out or drug her that was fine, but when she woke up gagged and bound she would get the shock of her life. He had waited long enough to spend some quality time with her and he wouldn't be taking any chances. She would be easy enough to track down. All he had to do was to phone the police and ask to speak to her. They would be able to tell him there and then if she was available or if she had moved departments and then the fun would really begin. It was the stalking and watching that made it all the more exciting.

Henry turned his radio on and paced up and down his room, far too agitated to sit and relax. He needed to keep busy. The excitement of escaping and seeing her once more was too much for him. He continued to pace for twenty minutes, the whole time getting more and more worked up about what he would say and do when he finally had Annie to himself, and he had to go and take a cold shower to cool himself down. He couldn't act like this; the staff would notice and know something was wrong and then they would either increase his tablets or send in reinforcements to make him talk.

He took himself off into the small but compact bathroom attached to his bedroom, stripped naked and then stepped under the cold shower spray. The water bit against his skin, making it prickle with goose bumps, so cold that it actually hurt, but he forced himself to stand there until he shivered so violently that all he could think about was getting under the duvet on his bed and sleeping.

* * *

Henry woke at the crack of dawn. He'd told the evening shift nurse he felt unwell and wanted to stay in bed and sleep. So they'd left him to it, occasionally looking through the small square of toughened safety glass in the door to see if he was still breathing. No doubt they wouldn't leave him totally alone. He stared across to the window. He always slept with the curtains open, liking to see the outside world at all times. There was an oak tree not far from his window, which he'd often thought would be a good place to hang himself from, given the opportunity, but he was always exercised out the back in the secure courtyard and the fact that he always had a babysitter made it impossible.

He wondered if today would go to plan. Would he be a free man by lunchtime, or would he be in solitary confinement with no one to talk to? Megan would be arrested and led away in handcuffs, should they get caught, and that would be a terrible thing. He was almost tempted to tell her he'd changed his mind. Did he really want to risk losing what very little he had? Then his eyes drifted towards the metal door and he realised that yes, he did want to try to leave. He needed to see Annie again; it was a burning desire in his chest – very much like the fire that had started two years ago and resulted in him killing those girls.

Getting up from the bed, he washed and dressed himself and took up his position in the chair. He leant across to switch the radio on, closing his eyes. Images of Jenna White and Emma Harvey, before and after he'd killed them, flicked through his mind. They'd been suppressed for a while now but it seemed as if they were back and he knew that it wasn't going to end well for anyone who tried to stop him. A smile spread across his lips and he remembered the smell of fear and the feel of their delicate skin. Henry felt as if he'd been under a hazy cloud for months but now the cloud had gone and he could finally see clearly again.

He jumped at the sound of the key turning in the lock and waited with his eyes shut to hear who his early morning nurse was. That was the beauty of having nothing better to do in this place; he knew every one of them by the sound of their voice.

'Morning, Henry, I hope you're ready for the day ahead.'

He grinned and looked around to see Megan smiling back at him.

'Well, good morning, Megan. I wasn't expecting you so early.'

'I swapped my shift and told them I was willing to work longer hours.' She placed his breakfast tray on the table. 'I'll be back very shortly with your clothes. Nurse Happy is dishing out the extra drugs to our friends. When she gives you yours don't question her; just do what you normally do like a good boy.'

'I think I can manage that.'

'Good. I'll be back soon. Oh, and you best eat that breakfast. I've filled a cool box with lots of food and have plenty of bottled water and snacks in the back of my car but we won't have time to park up and throw down a blanket to sit on and have a picnic. Once they realise you've gone the sirens will sound and they pipe them as far as the neighbouring village to warn the nice, normal people to keep inside and lock the doors because there's a madman running around.'

Henry laughed. 'My dear, you're making it sound like something from a bad Nineteen-Fifties film. Surely they don't let sirens off?'

'Yes, they do because, back in the Sixties, I think it was, someone did escape and murder some poor kid in the village so they've kept the early warning sirens in place ever since.'

'Well, let's hope that we can be well clear of this place before they begin to terrorise the villagers and start a riot.'

Megan giggled. 'Henry, you are wicked. Have a little faith. Just because I look like a sweet, normal girl it doesn't actually mean that I am.'

She turned to leave then looked back at him. 'I'm just checking – you're not planning on killing any kids, are you? Because the deal's off if you are.'

'Megan, now you need to have a little faith. Just because I look like your typical serial killer, it doesn't mean that I don't have some standards.'

She nodded. 'Touché, Henry.'

Henry ate his mediocre breakfast of cereal with cold milk, followed by two slices of wholemeal toast, as he watched the rain fall against the glass. It was perfect weather. The door was opened by another nurse, who came in with his medication. She nodded at him and handed him the small plastic cup; he thanked her and lifted it to his lips, throwing his head back and tipping them into his mouth. He passed her the container. Some loud shouting from out in the corridor drew her attention away from him just long enough for him to spit the tablets into the palm of his hand. He picked up the plastic water cup and took a large sip. Satisfied, she turned and left him alone – so far, so good. Now he just hoped Megan had her side under control.

Twenty minutes later, she came in with the laundry sack. Leaning inside, she brought out a neatly folded pair of black jogging pants, a hooded sweatshirt and a baseball cap. She passed them over to him.

'Really, Megan?'

'Really, Henry; we need to cover the scars on your head and the cap will do that, then you can pull the hood up to cover the side of your face. What were you expecting, a three-piece suit?'

'Well, maybe not a waistcoat but a jacket and trousers would have sufficed. No, you're right; I do need to hide my face so they are an excellent choice. Thank you.'

'I'll be back in fifteen minutes. Nurse Happy will be going on her break in ten minutes and it gives all our other friends time to be feeling the effects from the extra pills. We'll leave through the fire exit at the back of the ward and take the stairs down to the basement and go out through the staff entrance. There is only ever one guard on down there and they will be monitoring the cameras to make sure the special visit is going without incident and that no one is trying to get in who shouldn't.'

She left and he went into the bathroom and dressed himself, then looked in the mirror and smiled. With the cap on and the hood up, you couldn't even really see the scars. He felt excited and it had been a long time since he'd felt like this. Today would be a great day; he had a gut feeling that it would. Unable to settle, he paced up and down, keeping away from the door so no one could see him, especially as he was supposed to be comatose and drooling in his chair. He was sure it was illegal to drug patients to keep them quiet, just for an easy life. He stood still and listened; the ward was unusually quiet.

Finally his door opened.

'Are you ready to do this, Henry? If you've changed your mind then it's fine.'

He turned to face her. 'I'm ready.'

She nodded and he walked out of the door into the corridor. She shut it and locked it behind him. Then she walked towards the fire exit at the opposite end of the ward and he followed her, his hood up and head bent down, not sure if she'd managed to do anything to the internal cameras. Megan swiped a card and the door clicked. She pushed it open and he followed her through into the much colder fire exit. She jogged down the stairs and he followed her down several flights to the basement. She swiped her card, which opened another door, and held it open for him to step through.

'When we reach the guard station I'll keep him talking. You just wave and carry on walking towards the doors.'

Henry could see the small booth in the distance and felt his hands grow clammy; it had all been too easy up to now. He wondered if this man would be the one thing between him and his freedom and then he realised that if he did try to stop him he would kill him, no doubt about it. There was no way he was going back inside that glorified cell.

As they approached the booth a phone began to ring, so loud that it echoed around the basement area, and Henry jumped. The guard picked it up and spoke loudly to whoever was on the other end. The talking soon turned into raised voices and Megan started to walk so briskly that Henry had to do a little jog to catch up with her. They reached the booth and Megan waved at the guard, who was so engrossed in his argument about whose turn it was to fill the car with petrol that he didn't even look at either of them. He lifted his hand at Megan and she walked past. Henry did the same, lifting his hand at the man, and he nodded at him. Within seconds, Megan had the door to the outside world open and held it for Henry to walk through. He grinned and then bent and kissed her on the cheek. Taking a deep breath, he realised this was what freedom smelt like.

Megan scurried towards a small black Ford Ka that was parked nearby, pulling the keys from her pocket. 'There's one more guard to get past,' she said, 'but it's fine; they never give the staff cars a second glance and there's no siren sounding so they won't have a reason to.'

They got in the car and Megan reversed out of her parking space. Up to now she'd done really well but Henry found it irritating that she hadn't had the forethought to park her car facing the right way in case they had to rush. She stuck to the speed limit and he tried to push himself as far down in the seat as possible. He could see the guard and he hoped this one would be just as distracted as the last. As Megan stopped at the barrier she waved at the guard, who waved back and pressed a button to lift the metal barrier up. Henry couldn't quite believe it; this place housed some of England's finest monsters yet the security was appalling. He would sack every single one of them and hire people who were so desperate for a job they would actually do what they were supposed to, and then he laughed.

Megan looked across at him with a huge smile on her face. 'What did I tell you? Now, let's get some distance between ourselves and this place before they realise. We've got another twenty minutes before Nurse Happy goes back to the ward and wonders where I've disappeared to. If she thinks I'm in the staff bathroom that would give us another ten minutes. Didn't I tell you to have a little faith?'

'Yes, you did, Megan; I'm impressed and extremely thankful. What about the car? They will know this is your car, and we'll end up being put on the ANPR cameras. The minute we pass through one it will recognise the number plate and we'll be surrounded by traffic police in the blink of an eye.'

'I have another car that's registered in another name waiting for us in the car park of a disused warehouse. We'll ditch this one and take the other one; by the time they find this we'll be long gone and they won't know what car we're in.'

Henry nodded. 'You certainly aren't your average girl at all. I approve one hundred per cent.'

She smiled, proud that she had pleased Henry but even prouder that she had just changed the entire course of her life in less than an hour.

1782

Marcus King was sitting in his chair by the fire, the pewter tankard with the last few drops of ale he'd been drinking all night dangling from his hand as his eyes began to close. He had been busy the last few weeks, helping Joss on the farm now that he had no one but himself. Marcus had spent the last four days helping to harvest the hay and it was heavy work. His head nodded and a gentle snore came from his mouth. The room was dark, the candle almost burnt out. The fire had died down but it was a mild night, and he'd no energy to go out for more wood.

There was a sharp scratch as something moved along the window, quiet at first, but then it grew louder. The noise seeped into his unconscious mind until the tankard clattered to the floor and he jolted upright, his eyes opened, and for a second he was disorientated. Unsteady on his feet, he pulled himself up, about to go upstairs to bed, when the noise started again; this time it was on the window right next to his chair. It sounded as if something sharp was being dragged against the glass and he felt the hairs on his arms stand on end. He turned to look out of the window and see which silly bugger was outside playing games, but it was dark outside and he couldn't see anyone. He stepped closer, pressing his nose against the glass, but drew back and rubbed his nose. The glass was white. There was a layer of frost across it. Marcus shook his head with disbelief. How could that be? It was the middle of August. He reached out a finger to touch the windowpane and heard a giggle come from somewhere in the room behind him. He swung around. He had lived on his own for as long as he could remember. He had never married; there should be no one else in the small cottage except for him.

A loud screech on the window next to him made him jump back as he watched claw marks appear in the frost and the noise was horrific, so loud he wanted to cover his ears with both of his hands to block it out. The sound filled the whole room. He rubbed his eyes, not wanting to believe what was happening, hoping he was still asleep and this was all some nightmare. He didn't understand what could be happening; none of it made any sense.

The only book he possessed was a Bible and it was always on display on the kitchen table. It began to shake and then moved of its own accord, slowly across the surface of his kitchen table, and his heart raced as fear took over his body. The book reached the edge of the table, where it hung, suspended in mid-air, balancing on nothing, and then it dropped to the floor with a loud thud, its pages opened onto Exodus 22:18. He picked the candle up from the windowsill. Beyond terrified, he walked across to see where it had landed and the words jumped out at him: 'Thou shalt not suffer a witch to live'. Fear ran through his veins and he knew exactly who it was that was playing games with him. A warm trickle of urine ran down his leg.

'Who's there? Get out of my house at once. I never invited you in so you have no right to be in here. Leave this minute!'

He stood where he was and listened for any noise but there was none, then he walked across the room to the staircase to listen and was greeted by silence. Thank the good Lord, he had told her to leave and she had. Marcus didn't believe in anything other than hard work and good food washed down with a pitcher of ale, but a sliver of unease crept through his mind: *why were you so adamant that Betsy Baker was a witch if you don't believe in anything supernatural?* He convinced himself that it had all been some bizarre dream and laughed. Shaking his head at his foolishness, he walked up the stairs to his bed. He could even have a bit of heatstroke after working out in the fields in this burning heat. What he needed was to lay his weary body down and get a good night's sleep.

As he reached the step second from the top the temperature dropped so drastically he shivered and felt his teeth begin to chatter. A high-pitched giggle in his ear made the tiny hairs stand on end and a fear like nothing he had ever known lodged itself in the base of his throat. He wanted to scream but he couldn't make a sound. He looked up to see Betsy Baker standing on the step above him. She was so white that she glowed. Around her neck was an angry red and blue ring where the rope he had used to hang her had bit into her soft white flesh until it had choked her to death. She lifted a finger, which had a long pointed nail at the end of it.

'I told you I was no witch but I struck a deal with the Devil and here I am. I also told you I would come back to get you and that was the truth, Marcus King. You're not so big and brave now it's just me and thee, are you? What's the matter – has the cat got your tongue?'

Marcus couldn't speak if he'd wanted to. His brain was still registering the fact that the woman he'd insisted on hanging and then helped to bury with his own two hands was standing in front of his very eyes.

She leant forward and with both of her hands shoved his chest as hard as she could. Marcus felt his chest freeze where her hands touched his skin and his whole body go backwards. He toppled, head over heels, down the steep stairs until he hit the bottom and his neck snapped.

Betsy smiled to herself then nodded her approval as she disappeared, leaving his body to be found by one of his friends, who had no doubt helped to kill her. She left the Bible open as a warning to whoever had the unfortunate job of finding him. Let them know she had meant every word spoken before they'd killed her and that she would not rest until they were all as dead as she was.

Chapter 15

Will opened his eyes and looked around the dark room. He didn't have a clue where he was and for a few seconds he wondered if he was going to find a naked Amelia lying next to him. He felt his stomach lurch with déjà vu from the last time he'd felt like this, waking up next to a nearly naked Laura and almost ruining his whole life, but then he tried to get up and realised that he couldn't move his arms or legs freely; they were restricted.

His eyes adjusting to the dark, he could make out a small room that smelt of damp. He was in a cellar and that was when he really lost it. He tried to pull his arms and legs as much as he could. The last time he'd woken up in a cellar, a serial killer had been trying to kill Annie in front of his very eyes. What if he was still there and he'd dreamt the last two years of his life whilst he'd been unconscious? Struggling to breathe, he looked around to see if he could make out Annie's shape in the darkness. He looked left and right but all he could make out was a chair in the corner and some boxes.

He racked his brain: where the fuck was he? He pulled his arms some more but the rope bit into his skin and then it all came back to him. He remembered leaving Annie at the hospital last night to help Amelia with her car. He'd bent down to have a look at the engine and that was the last thing he knew about. He felt some weird relief that Henry Smith wasn't going to walk in carrying the old long-bladed knife he favoured to cut his victims' throats. Annie had managed to save them both from him but only just. If Henry had had his way they would both be dead in the cellar of the desolate Abbey Wood mansion. Along with Jenna White and God knows who else's remains. But why the hell had Amelia decided to knock him out and bring him here? It didn't make any sense.

His throat was parched and he couldn't remember the last time he'd had a drink. He coughed. A hole in the ceiling appeared as a trapdoor was flung open and light flooded the small space. He scrunched his eyes up; they had just been getting used to the gloom. A shadowy figure appeared at the top. Whoever it was came down the stairs, then stopped at the bottom, pulling a chain and lighting up the single bulb that was hanging from a cord in the ceiling just above Will's head. The glare was harsh against his sensitive eyes but he blinked a couple of times and they adjusted. There was a man standing in front of him who he'd never seen before in his life. He stepped forward.

'I'm really sorry about this, mate. I don't think you'll be here long. As soon as she gets what she wants we'll be off and leave you to it. Do you want a drink, something to eat?'

Will had heard it all now. He didn't understand exactly what the man, who was in his early twenties with collar-length brown hair and a pair of sunglasses on his head, was saying.

'I'd like a drink of water, please.' Will didn't want to be rude and piss him off.

'Yeah, no problem, mate. I'll get you a bottle and then you can help yourself. Are you hungry? It's just she's not in at the minute so I can sort you out a bite to eat before she comes back and sees her arse. Right moody cow she's been lately.'

Will nodded, finding it hard to believe. Had he been kidnapped by Amelia and her pissed-off boyfriend?

The lad disappeared upstairs but came down minutes later with a supermarket sandwich and a bottle of water with a sports cap. He unwrapped the sandwich and walked towards Will, handing him one.

'Can you manage it yourself?'

Will took the sandwich. He could just reach his mouth with his hand so he could take a bite. He nodded, not realising how hungry he was until he'd smelt the ham and pickle just before he bit into it. He ate it in two bites and was passed the second half. When he'd eaten that he took a long gulp of the water.

'Thank you. Can you tell me why I'm here?'

The man nodded. 'Yeah, I really am sorry about this. She reckons she's your half-sister and is entitled to some of the money your old man has tucked away in the bank. I told her it was a stupid idea but she doesn't listen when she gets like that. It's easier to go along with her, only I didn't realise she was actually going to …'

He paused and Will nodded in encouragement.

'Well, I didn't realise she was going to go through with it. I mean, kidnapping is a serious offence. So is your old man worth a lot of money then or is she getting her knickers in a twist over nothing?'

Will thought that, despite the fact that this bloke was holding him hostage, he was actually all right, although he was comparing him to Henry Smith.

'To be honest, it's not something I've ever really thought about. I work and make my own money. I don't rely on my dad to support me; I never have. I suppose he must have a fair bit because he has a nice house and a boat. Look, what did you mean when you said that she thinks she's my half-sister? Who are we talking about – Amelia?'

A gust of wind made the front door slam shut.

'Shit … she's here; sorry, I'll tell you next time.'

He turned and walked back up the steps as another figure blocked out the light then stepped aside to let him out. The trapdoor slammed shut and Will heard a bolt being slid across it. A woman was shouting and he heard the man who had just been down there telling her to stop freaking out. There was a lot of stomping around and Will looked around to see if there was any way he could make his escape.

* * *

It was forty-five minutes before Nurse Reed discovered that her colleague Megan was no longer on the ward. She'd come back up after having a much longer coffee break than she should have because she'd gone across to the other side of the hospital to try and find out exactly who the special visitor was. She'd talked to one of the nurses on that ward and had been surprised to see it wasn't some crackpot politician but a member of the royal family. When she'd finally looked at her watch and realised how long she'd been she had scurried back, ready to grovel to Megan and let her have just as long a break as she'd had.

When she got there and couldn't find Megan anywhere she assumed she was in the toilet, but after fifteen minutes she began to feel uneasy. That was when she started checking on the prisoners in their rooms to make sure everything was OK. She left Henry Smith's room until last; there was something about the man that made the hair on the back of her neck stand on end and her skin crawl. Megan seemed to have an unhealthy fascination with him and a couple of times she'd thought about mentioning it to the ward manager but hadn't. Megan had talked about Henry's crimes a lot, yet she never seemed to comment on the other prisoners' backgrounds – and some of theirs were much worse than Smith's, if there was such a thing, but there was a notorious child killer on the ward who some people found morbidly fascinating.

She marched to Henry's room and peered through the small window. There was no sign of Henry but he could be in the bathroom. She would check back in five minutes but that still didn't explain where Megan was. No one was allowed to leave the ward unattended; it was instant dismissal. All the other prisoners were either zoned out in their beds or chairs. She went and checked the toilets, television room, laundry room and every other room, nook and cranny she could think of. She sat down on the chair behind the nurses' station and took out her phone; she didn't even have Megan's mobile number.

By this time she was feeling as if she wanted to throw up the piece of coffee and walnut cake along with the large latte she'd consumed down in the staff canteen. She didn't know what to do, not wanting to get either of them into trouble, but if Megan didn't come back soon she would have no choice but to alert staff. She stood up and went back to check on Smith. His room was still empty and this time she felt her lungs close up, making it hard to breathe. She lifted the keys from her pocket and, with hands that were shaking, she inserted one into the lock and opened the door. There was no noise coming from the bathroom, no running water or the sound of the toilet flushing. She walked towards it and stood outside the door.

'Henry, are you in there?'

Silence greeted her and she reached out and knocked on the door. Images of a very dead Megan lying on the bathroom floor with a blood-soaked Henry standing above her made her feel sick to the core. She reached out and pushed the door open. The bathroom was empty. She felt relieved that there was no dead Megan but then the realisation that there was no Henry either hit her hard and she felt her knees tremble. She spun around in case he was standing behind her but the room was still empty. It was then that she turned and ran to the nurses' station to hit the panic button. She slammed her fist down onto it hard but there was no noise. She did it again and again. Picking up the phone, she rang security.

'Code Red Ward Nine.'

* * *

They had swapped cars without incident and Megan had taken all the back roads, avoiding motorways until they were almost at the Cumbrian border. Henry had offered to drive but Megan declined.

'I didn't put you on the insurance, Henry, for obvious reasons. If we were to get stopped it would look very suspicious and the police would end up seizing the car and if they did a computer check on you it would be game over. It happened to my ex-boyfriend. They took his car off him and left him on the side of the road miles from anywhere. We'll take a break in a minute, if you don't mind, though. I just need something to eat and a cold drink; I was too nervous to eat breakfast this morning. How long is it from here to your caravan?'

'About an hour, but there's no rush – we've got all day. You've surpassed yourself, Megan; take a break.'

She pulled over at the next lay-by and reached into the back of the car, rooting around in one of the carrier bags. She pulled out a sandwich and offered it to Henry, who declined. He didn't tell her but his stomach was churning with nerves. It had all gone to plan and things didn't normally go so smoothly. He wouldn't be able to settle until they were safely inside the caravan on the far end of Walney, safe from prying eyes. He put his head back and closed his eyes, waiting for his partner in crime to finish chewing her egg mayo roll which, incidentally, was stinking the car out. Henry could let it go this time because she had done so well but he wouldn't put up with her eating anything that reminded him of his mother's Sunday teas that he'd suffered all his life until the day he had killed her. He would be telling her egg sandwiches were a definite no. Eventually, Megan wiped her hands on her trousers and started the engine again. They were soon on their way.

After another twenty minutes Henry began to direct Megan. Although Barrow-in-Furness wasn't exactly hard to find and it was miles from the motorway, it was his home and where Henry belonged. It was where he had found the crumbling mansion in the woods and the secret room in the cellar that had once belonged to a much more famous killer than Henry, but it had been his secret and the only other person who had known about it was Police Officer Annie Graham. From what he had gathered, she hadn't told anyone about that room either, which had puzzled him because if she had gone public with the knowledge that she knew who Jack the Ripper's true identity was and could prove it, she would have become richer than most people dream of, but she hadn't breathed a word about it. He would ask her why when he finally had her to himself.

That room had been where he'd killed his first victim and where he'd tried to kill Ms Graham, until he had been thwarted by her lover, but Henry had managed to injure him sufficiently that he could not fight to save her life. In the end it had been Annie against Henry and last time she had won, putting up an excellent fight. This time she wouldn't. He would bide his time until he was strong enough, both mentally and physically, for the challenge.

They drove along the bypass until they reached the outskirts of Ulverston. Megan laughed at the monument on the top of the steep hill overlooking the town that could pass as a lighthouse.

'What is that – oh, no, you know what it looks like, don't you?'

'What do you think it looks like, Megan?'

She giggled and shook her head. 'Sorry, I have a filthy mind sometimes. It's nice. A bit of a strange place to put a lighthouse, but still, it's different.'

Henry bit his tongue. He hated ignorance and he had to remind himself that she was half his age. She carried on driving through the town and towards Dalton, then Barrow. Henry told her to take the road that led through the industrial estate so they could head straight for Walney Island and the caravan site. He smiled at the sights. He had missed this place. They passed Asda and carried on to the roundabout, which would take them past all the fast food restaurants. Henry pointed them out to her, even though she couldn't miss the bright neon signs offering their greasy wares.

'I suppose you should remember how to get here. Isn't that the crap that all you youngsters live off?'

She laughed. 'Don't tell me you don't like a greasy meal after a heavy session the night before? Do you drink, Henry? I totally forgot that you've been teetotal since you've been lodging with us.'

'I don't really know. I mean, I do drink but I haven't missed it. I could always take it or leave it. I quite fancy a glass of something strong, though, once we get settled. In fact there's a shop on the way to the caravan. Do you want to nip in and get a bottle of something to celebrate our escape to freedom with?'

'No need, I came prepared. I have a bottle of Irish cream liqueur and a bottle of whisky.'

Henry nodded his approval. He directed her to take the second exit off the roundabout, which led onto Jubilee Bridge and Walney Island. Then she turned left and followed the road until he told her to turn off onto the road that would literally lead them to the very pinnacle of the island and the caravan site. They passed fields full of horses, a pub and then a field that had almost every animal known to man in it: there were alpacas, birds of every description, goats and rabbits. Megan slowed down to stare at them all. There was a woman in the field with a goose tucked under one arm, and she waved at them. Megan grinned and waved back then carried on driving.

'Did you see all those animals? I love animals, especially birds. There's something so beautiful about them.'

Henry nodded. He couldn't miss them. He just wanted to get inside the caravan, stretch his legs and have a glass of whisky. Finally, she reached the entrance to the site and looked at him.

'Now where? This place is huge.'

If his memory served him right, it was one of the newer caravans at the back of the site. He'd brought his mother over here a couple of times to visit. He pointed at the one and she parked the car, both of them relieved to be able to get out and stretch their legs. They walked towards it and Henry was thankful there was no one around to see them and think it was funny that the man with the cap and the hood up, even though it was particularly warm, was feeling under the caravan steps for a key. His fingers brushed the tape that was holding it to the metal step and he peeled it away and waved it at Megan, who was busy getting the bags from the car. He opened the door and was hit by a blast of warm air. It was stuffy inside but it would soon air out if they left the door and windows open for a bit. The static caravan was a good size and had two bedrooms, which was fine.

Megan giggled like a kid. 'I love caravans. They remind me of when I was younger and we used to go on holiday to Blackpool or Scarborough with the whole family. It was cramped and we did nothing but argue and fight but I loved it.'

He stood at the door and took the bags from her as she passed them to him.

'We have enough supplies for a few days. We can lie low and see how much news coverage there is about us both before deciding what we're going to do.'

She came inside and he pushed the door to, not wanting to shut it completely until it wasn't as stuffy. He opened a cupboard and took two glasses out of it, rinsing them under the tap. Megan passed him the bottle of whisky and he poured it into them.

'Congratulations, Megan, and thank you. Here's to us, the killer and his brilliant nurse out on the run.'

He clinked his glass against hers and then tipped his head back and downed it in one. The fire rolled down his throat, making him cough and splutter. Then he opened his eyes and smiled. 'Here's to freedom.'

Megan sipped slowly at hers. 'Yes, here's to a whole new chapter in both of our lives. Henry and Megan, what a team.'

She turned around and put the food away that she had brought. Henry felt bad; he hadn't contributed money towards any of this. He couldn't access his money. He had a hefty chunk in the local building society but the minute he touched it they would know.

He would wait until he had done what he had to do and then go in and withdraw it before leaving this town for good.

He opened one of the curtains just enough that he could sit and watch the sea as the tide came in. He had missed the simple things in life the most and it had taught him that you only had to live simply to enjoy your life. Megan went into the small bathroom with a bag of toiletries and he put his feet up and watched the view. This was what it felt like to be free. He owed it all to her so he wouldn't be killing her after all, unless she began to drive him mad and then he might have to out of necessity, but until then it would be nice to have her company.

He had no idea how long he had been watching the tide but when Megan came out of the small shower room her blonde and fuchsia hair had been replaced with dark brown and he did a double take. She looked totally different, with only a towel wrapped around her naked body, and he had to look away as his cheeks burned.

'Before you say anything, I hate it as well but my blonde and pink hair was too distinctive. What a bloody nightmare, trying to dye your hair in a bathroom where your elbows hit the walls every time you move. It made your bathroom look like one at a luxury hotel. Still, it's an adventure and I love it, even if I do get claustrophobia every time I need a pee.'

'I think you suit it; makes you look older.'

Megan laughed. 'Henry, would you like me to get dressed? I'm sorry, I forgot you haven't – you know – for a long time.'

He was still staring out of the window and not looking at her. 'I'm OK, thank you; it's just a bit of a shock. I'm not that used to living with women … well, not anyone as young as you. I know it's a whole different culture these days, but I would appreciate it if you could keep some clothes on when we're together.'

'No problem.'

She disappeared into one of the bedrooms and came back out wearing a pair of pyjamas that were covered in pink rabbits. Henry nodded his approval and had to stop himself from wondering if she was naked underneath; it was totally inappropriate. He wanted them to be on an even keel. It would get messy if they started anything other than being friends. If they fell out he knew there was nothing like a scorned woman for getting revenge but it didn't mean that he couldn't enjoy the view. She was pretty in an unconventional way so for now he would be quite happy to enjoy her company and the occasional glimpses of her forbidden flesh.

Chapter 16

Kav finished his coffee and put the delicate mug down on the kitchen table. 'I think that we should get back to the station now, if that's OK with you, Annie. There's a lot of stuff we can be helping with but I don't want to be stuck in Windermere doing it. I'd rather utilise my own staff.'

'Thank you, for everything. Yes, of course you need to get back. Sorry, I'm not thinking straight. I'll stay here and you know where I am if you want me. I don't think Amelia can be that far away from here. She wouldn't drive miles to work every day if she didn't have to. So I'm nearer to Will here than I would be in Barrow.'

Kav nodded, relieved she was going to be stopping with Will's parents, who could keep an eye on her, because she looked dreadful and he was worried about her.

Jake stood up and hugged Annie, squeezing her tight. 'If we hear anything I'll let you know, I promise. Do you think you should have a lie-down, Annie? Because you look worn out and you don't want to end up back in hospital.'

'I will, thanks, Jake.'

She walked them to the door, too exhausted to go down the steps and walk them to the police car. She waited until they both got in and then waved them goodbye. Tears fell down her cheeks and she let out a sob that racked her whole body. What a mess this was. She sat down on the top step and buried her head in her arms. A warm hand touched her shoulder and she turned to see Tom.

'I'm sorry, Annie, I really am.'

Wiping her tears with her sleeve, she smiled. 'It's not your fault; it really isn't.'

He sat down next to her so that he could hold her hand. 'You're too kind, but if I hadn't had an affair all those years ago this would never have happened. I used to watch Will go from one relationship to another and it broke my heart. I wanted to tell him that he would never be happy living like that, but how could I? He'd want to know how come I was the expert all of a sudden.'

'You can't blame yourself. How were you to know that there was a daughter out there who knew about you? If it's anyone's fault it's her mother's for not telling you all those years ago. I'm pretty sure you would have been in the doghouse but not for long. What if Amelia – if that's even her name – isn't your daughter and it's just a lie that she was told from an early age? Would her mother really not contact you and tell you? Surely she'd have wanted money from you?'

'Back then I didn't have much money; the business was only just beginning to take off. I worked day and night to turn it into the success it was before I sold it. So I had a little bit of money but not a lot because I kept investing most of it back into the business. It was years later that I was finally able to sit back and reap the rewards and by that time Elizabeth had died and it was just me and Will. I was so lucky when Lily came along. She didn't give a damn about money. In fact she thought I was the gardener here and was more than happy enough to go out with me so I knew that she was the one. I meant what I said to those detectives; I would give this all up in an instant to know that Will was safe and back in your arms.'

His arm went around her shoulder and he pulled her close

to him. Annie leant her head against him, trying her best not to cry onto his checked shirt. They stayed like that until Lily came looking for them. She nodded at Tom and smiled then went back inside.

Annie was the one to pull away first. 'Sorry, I never cry but since I met Will I've turned into a right softie. In fact I never used to get upset about much. I'd bottle it all up and keep it inside. Now I'm a gibbering wreck. I'm also really tired. Would you mind if I went for a lie-down?'

'I should think so; after everything you've been through, no wonder you're an emotional wreck. Yes, I was going to suggest you have a rest. Even if you can't sleep, it might make you feel a bit better. How are you feeling physically? Lily phoned my doctor to come and give me a once-over. I'd like him to give you a check-up because I know that you didn't get discharged from the hospital this morning. The staff nurse I spoke to when I phoned told me that you practically ripped the drip out of your arm and left in a hospital gown and bare feet.'

Tom arched one eyebrow at her but he grinned at the same time.

'Ah, you heard about that. Do you know the security guard thought I'd escaped from the mental health unit and was going to take me back? I did look a state but I think I'm OK.'

'My son is incredibly lucky to have found you, Annie. You are both made of the same tough stuff. Please put an old man's mind at rest and let the doctor take a look. Then I won't mind so much when you go rushing off to rescue Will.'

She laughed and stood up, holding out a hand to pull Tom up. 'If it makes you feel any better, I will.'

'Good, now go and have a rest or a bath or whatever it is you need. Lily has plenty of clothes that would keep a women's refuge going for a year.'

'I'm good, thanks. I left some stuff here the last time we stayed.'

She waited for Tom to go back inside and then she followed

and shut the door behind her. She went upstairs to the guest room that was Will's old bedroom and he went off to find Lily.

Inside the bedroom that Annie and Will used whenever they stayed over, Annie slipped off her shoes and threw herself onto the bed, sinking down into the mattress. She couldn't possibly sleep but she was so tired and her chest ached. She didn't know if that was because of the operation to repair her punctured lung or whether it was aching for Will. Her head was hurting and her eyes wanted to shut tight and block out the nightmare.

Rolling over onto Will's side of the bed, she curled up into a ball and concentrated really hard to see if there were any of her spirit friends around that could maybe help and give her a clue to where he was being held. She emptied her mind and tried to think of nothing, which was hard because an image of Will was always there, hovering in the corner of her mind. She breathed deeply, concentrating on asking for help. Occasionally, Sophie, the nine-year-old girl she'd helped escape from the Shadow Man last year, would come and say hello but not very often. Now she was with her mum she wasn't earthbound like before.

Annie tried to summon her. For a nine-year-old girl she was very wise and knew a lot about everything, but she couldn't quite reach her. It was as if something was blocking Annie from connecting with anyone. She felt herself drifting off, unable to stop herself, and she let her whole body relax.

The sound of fingernails being scraped along a glass windowpane made Annie open her eyes. She was unsure where she was but it was dark and very cold. The room was pitch-black and the noise made her shudder. The bed felt hard; there was no way this was the same mattress that she had first lain down on. There was a blanket wrapped around her but it was rough and not the goose-down duvet she had pulled over her not that long ago.

Annie's heart raced. She knew it was a dream but all the same she was scared. Sitting up, she waited whilst her eyes adjusted to the gloom. Movement in one corner made the hair on the back of her neck stand on end. There was someone in the room with her and she had no idea who it was or where they were. Annie squinted, focusing on the corner, and watched, terrified, as her eyes fixed on the outline of the woman she'd seen standing in the middle of the road before her accident. Her head was bent forward so her long dark hair hung over her face. The woman in the corner was dressed in a long white cotton gown and had bare feet. The gown was tattered and torn as if she'd been running through brambles and when Annie looked at her feet she could see the scratches and bruises that covered them.

'Who are you?'

The woman didn't answer but lifted her head up until the hair fell away and Annie could see the white face and crystal-blue eyes. She stared straight at Annie, not breaking her gaze, and Annie, for the first time in months, felt threatened, that her life might be in danger. Whoever this woman was, she didn't want to pass a message on to her family because, judging by what she was wearing, her family had probably all died at least two hundred years ago. Annie didn't break her gaze, too afraid to be the one to look away first. She had to let her know that she wasn't going to be intimidated by her, even if her insides had turned to slush.

'I asked you who you are. And what do you want?'

The woman grinned at her. Her skin, stretching over her teeth, looked as if it was about to crack open and fester.

'Who am I? I should be asking you the same question. What right have you to come in and wreck my house? It doesn't belong to you; it belongs to me, just like it always has.'

'Your house? I hate to disappoint you, but it was your house a long time ago. It isn't any more and it's time that you left it and moved into the light. Why are you still here and what are you doing trying to scare everyone who goes inside?'

'Let me tell you, there is no light for me. They would not have me in the light; that is not the place for women who like to kill for pleasure. Are you worried about your man? Do you know where they have taken him?'

Annie shook her head.

'No, I thought not.'

'Please, if you know where he is, tell me.'

'Why should I tell you anything? I quite like your man, though; he reminds me of my Joss, although I haven't seen him for a very long time.'

From somewhere came the sound of knocking on the door. Annie turned to see where the door was and the woman disappeared. Annie felt as if she were falling through the blackness towards the knocking and landed onto the soft mattress that she'd first lain down on. The knocking on the bedroom door got louder and she heard Lily calling her name. She had to close her eyes. The room was so light compared to the one she'd just been in.

'Come in.'

Lily ushered the doctor in, who smiled at her. 'Officer Graham, I'm glad to see you. I heard about your accident and I've been worried. It's nice to see you all in one piece.'

Annie smiled back. 'It's nice to see you, Phil. It makes a change to be needing your assistance instead of meeting over some poor unfortunate dead body.'

'It does indeed. Funny how we're always on shift when the good people of Windermere decide to die. Joking aside, how are you? Lily has told me everything and how you discharged yourself from the hospital.'

Lily grimaced and mouthed 'sorry' to Annie then turned to leave the room, closing the door behind her.

'I have to say I've been better. I'm worried sick about Will and I'm tired, and my head and chest are hurting but I'm alive so I shouldn't be complaining.'

He walked over towards her. 'Yes, amazingly, you are alive but if you don't start looking after yourself a lot better I have no idea how long for.' He arched his eyebrows at her and pulled a chair from the corner of the room towards her, and then he sat down.

'I want to check your blood pressure, your head and some other bits and pieces; is that OK?'

Annie nodded, knowing fine well it had to be OK because she didn't want to collapse before they'd found Will. She answered all of the doctor's questions, nodding and holding out her arm for him to wrap the bright blue cuff around. Twenty minutes later, after she had answered his questions and followed his fingers with her eyes, he declared her alive but told her to take it easy. No work for a while and plenty of rest. She had agreed with him. She wouldn't be going to work until they had found Will and when they did she didn't know if she wanted to go back. She was fed up with all the drama and needed a break. She stood up to see him out.

'Don't worry, I'll see myself out. You seriously need some sleep. You should really still be in the hospital. Look after yourself, Annie, because you only get one shot at this whole life thing and if you don't take care of you, who will?'

He closed the door behind him. Annie picked up the phone from the bedside table and rang Jake.

'Hey, tell me something good. Have you found Will? Am I hallucinating this whole shitty mess?'

'Ah, I wish that you were … Sorry to be the bearer of bad news, but no, we've only just got back to the station. There was an accident on the A590. The good news is Kav is on a mission and the way he's going, fingers crossed, Will should be home by teatime. He's been on the phone to the serious crime squad up at headquarters and two of them are on their way down as we speak to come and see Tom and Lily. Apparently they are shit-hot.'

'Really, that's great. Please tell Kav thanks. I don't know what to do with myself, Jake. I feel like a spare part and I want to be involved. I hate it, not being able to help.'

'I know you do, flower, but trust me, there's nothing you can do. If we find anything, you know I'll be in touch. What did the men in black say?'

'Not a lot. I wish you were still here.'

'Do you want me to come back? Because I will. I would give anything to be in that house. It's amazing. They must be minted and I mean seriously minted.'

Annie chuckled. 'Yes, I suppose they are. I've never really thought about it since I got over my initial shock, but I told you, didn't I, that I met them through work and didn't even know they were related to Will.'

'Yes, you did, and he never told anyone either. You're both a pair of dark horses. I'll ring you as soon as we know something. Bye.'

'Bye.'

She put the phone down and threw herself back onto the bed. This time she didn't close her eyes, too afraid of the woman from her dreams. What did she want with her? She'd already almost killed her once. It had been the vision of her in the road that had made her swerve and lose control of her car. Annie didn't want to admit to herself that she found the dead woman disturbing; hell, that wasn't the right word. What she found her was terrifying but she couldn't admit that out loud; she didn't want her to know. As if she had the time to be haunted by a scary woman from a few hundred years ago when Will had been kidnapped.

She tried to remember if there was a time when her life had been simple but couldn't, unless she counted being the chubby kid in junior school with the frizzy black curly hair, and that had been a nightmare because of one boy who'd made her life a misery until one day she'd really had enough and punched him so hard in the face he'd got a black eye. Her life was turning into a living nightmare and she was fed up with it all.

Chapter 17

Henry opened his eyes and for a moment had no idea where he was, then he heard a seagull's loud cry and remembered. Although his room at the secure hospital was much bigger than the bedroom he was in now he was happy enough to be lying in a cramped single bed with the sound of the waves crashing against the shore to lull him to sleep.

There had been no coverage in the local paper the last two nights except for a small side column about his escape. The police obviously didn't think he was stupid enough to return back home; instead they would be thinking he was heading for somewhere he could remain anonymous, maybe London or Birmingham, one of the big cities. They probably didn't want to panic the locals either, but he knew the police here would be on high alert and he would be on the top of their wanted list. They would all be on the lookout for him so it was highly unlikely he'd be leaving this caravan for a few weeks yet to venture anywhere. Never underestimate your opponent, and both Annie Graham and Will Ashworth had been truly worthy opponents.

He took out the cheap pay-as-you-go phone that Megan had given to him yesterday and typed in 101. A voice on the other end informed him he was being transferred to Cumbria Police.

His palms were sweating and his pulse raced. Finally, a voice on the other end asked if they could help.

'Yes, I think so. I need to speak to PC Annie Graham. Could you tell me when she's next on duty?'

There was a slight pause as the call handler began typing on the other end. 'I'm sorry, according to the duties she's not in work for the moment. She's off sick. Would you like to speak to another member of the community team?'

'No, it's OK, thank you. It's something that only she can deal with.'

Henry ended the call and grinned to himself, hoping that whatever was wrong with her wasn't serious. He could hear Megan moving around in the kitchen and smiled. She was sweet and a very good cook. She had promised to look after him and she was doing exactly that. The smell of frying bacon hit his nostrils and his stomach rumbled. He'd had no appetite in the hospital but here everything tasted so good.

He got out of the bed and caught sight of his reflection in the mirror. He had lost weight but he had no muscles and looked like your average middle-aged man. His scalp and face were a mess but Megan had brought some special oil with her that was supposed to help heal scars and she tenderly rubbed it into them, never flinching, at least three times a day. Henry had never been vain but it did upset him to see one side of his face so puckered up. Megan had informed him that it made him look like a hardened criminal and he'd laughed at her. He certainly didn't look like a male model. He pulled a T-shirt on and a pair of jogging pants. They were extremely comfy. That was another thing to thank her for, his introduction to modern-day sports clothing.

Opening his bedroom door, he stood and watched her moving around. She was very graceful. She was only wearing a strappy vest top and the shortest of shorts and he admired the view very much from behind.

She turned around and squealed. 'Jesus, Henry, you gave me a fright.'

'Sorry, Megan, I didn't mean to.'

'I'll forgive you this time.'

Then she turned around, picked up the frying pan and arranged the bacon onto the slices of freshly sliced buttered bread. She handed him a plate and a mug of coffee.

'So what do you want to do today? Should we go for a little drive around, or a walk so you can get some fresh air?'

He pointed to his mouth as he chewed and she smiled.

'Sorry.'

Henry swallowed the mouthful of his sandwich. 'Don't be daft – it's fine. You know you don't need to be so nice to me all the time. I can take a bit of shit. God knows I put up with my mother's griping for long enough.'

'I wouldn't dream of griping at you. I want you to be happy, not miserable. I don't want you regretting escaping with me. We may not have much at the moment but we have our freedom and each other.'

Henry paused. 'Megan, if you're worried that I'll kill you when you start to get on my nerves then please don't. I need you more than you could ever know. How would I survive if you weren't around? I'm eternally grateful to you for everything and one day I will repay your kindness.'

Henry wasn't sure but he thought he saw her whole body relax as if a great weight had been lifted off her shoulders. He put his plate down and walked over to hug her, pulling her close. His fingers brushed her long fringe, tucking it behind her ear.

'You, Megan, are the best thing that's ever happened to me and I promise you I won't forget that. If there ever comes a time where I think I may be losing control you must leave, take the car and drive as far away as possible from here. Do you understand?'

'Yes, Henry, I do.'

She squeezed him back. He wanted nothing more than to pick her up and take her into her bedroom with the queen-size bed but he knew that he couldn't. Instead, he pulled away from her and picked his sandwich up.

'I don't know how I would actually survive without you, but I'm sure I would manage. Can you live off seaweed?'

He turned away so she couldn't see the erection that was poking through the front of his pants.

'Henry, what happened to your mother?'

'She died, Megan. She was old.'

He wasn't sure if this was a trick question because he would have thought that Megan knew exactly what had happened to her, but he decided it was best not to tell her that he'd strangled her and put her body into the chest freezer.

They both sat at the small table and finished their breakfast. Megan went to get dressed and returned five minutes later. She looked so young, her face fresh, with not a scrap of the heavy make-up she used to wear back at the hospital. In fact she looked like a completely different person, which was just as well considering they were both at the top of England's Most Wanted list.

'I'm just nipping to get some papers, see if there's anything about us in them. I'm surprised there hasn't been up until now.'

'Ah, I know why; they don't want the scandal of having one of the country's most important visitors at the hospital whilst a serial killer escapes, but I can imagine that the story will have broken this morning. There is no way they can contain it much longer. If the local paper had a small byline in it then the nationals will be all over it. You will have your fifteen minutes of fame, Megan. How do you feel about that? Do you regret throwing your life away for a monster?'

She looked at him. 'No, Henry, not for one minute. I worship the ground that you walk on and I want to be just like you.'

With that, she opened the caravan door and ran down the steps, letting it slam shut behind her. He watched her through the small window as she walked towards the clubhouse where she had left the car and then drove away without so much as a glance back.

* * *

Kav, who had been drumming his nails on his desk for the last thirty minutes, looked as if he was ready to commit a murder. He had sent everyone who had been hanging around the parade room trying to look busy whilst waiting for some gossip out on foot patrol, except Jake, who was sitting opposite him, picking at the skin around his thumbnail. Kav picked up the phone and rang Detective Nick Tyler, who answered on the first ring.

'What have you got, Nick?'

'We have an address for an Amelia Watts and task force are on their way as we speak but I'm not holding my breath. I seriously don't think she would be so stupid as to put her real address down on her employment form if she had been planning to kidnap a police officer. I've requested a cell site analysis on Will's phone and that's being looked into as we speak but even though it's been rushed through you and me both know how long it takes and again it's tenuous.'

'Why?'

'Because in all probability they would have got rid of his phone straight away. They aren't going to leave it with him so he can phone a friend to come and help him.'

'Bollocks. Anything else you can do? Anything we can do?'

'I'm afraid not; we're doing everything at this end. It's going to be a case of waiting for her to get in touch again with details of the drop. I'll be in touch as soon as I know anything, Kav, I promise.'

'I know you will, son, because if you don't I'll come and find you and plant my size-eleven boots up your arse.'

'Now there's an experience I'd rather not have.'

Kav put the phone down.

1782

Joss was working in the fields. He was hot and sweaty and wanted nothing more than to sit down in a cold bath and freshen up. Then he was going to the village pub for a cold drink of ale to numb the pain inside his chest. It had been four weeks now since his boys and family had been killed and Betsy had been hanged from his front porch.

He was in the process of moving into his parents' farmhouse because he could not bear to live in his house. It was full of despair and when he lay alone in the bed at night he could hear noises from other parts of the house. One night he had dreamt that his boys were in their room, playing with their toys, and he had run to them and held them tight. Tears falling down his cheeks, he could smell the soap in their hair. Then a high-pitched noise of something being scraped along the glass had woken him and he'd found himself clutching a pillow that was damp from his tears. Lighting the candle by the bed, he'd shouted, 'Who's there?' But there was no reply, only dead silence.

Joss had forced himself from his bed, the room so cold he had shivered so hard he'd almost dropped the candle to the floor. He'd gone from room to room, checking to see if there was anyone in the house with him, but there hadn't been. The rest of the house had been much warmer than his room and he'd gone to sleep in his sons' room, making himself feel as close to them as possible. He didn't believe in ghosts or witches or such like but he had felt disturbed at the dream and the noises.

He wiped his brow with his sleeve and was about to jump up onto the horse and cart that he'd laden with hay, when he saw a figure in the distance running towards him. Whoever it was had their arms in the air as they waved them frantically at him. Joss stood his ground and crossed his arms over his chest, wondering what the hell was going on. As the figure got closer he could see it was Seth. His face was red and he was panting. As he reached Joss he doubled over to catch his breath.

'Now, then, Seth, what has you so excited that you almost gave yourself a heart attack running all this way in the sun?'

'Marcus …' Seth shook his head and took some deep breaths.

'Calm yourself down, lad; whatever it is can wait. No need to go getting all worked up over it.'

'It's Marcus … he's dead. Fell down the stairs and broke his neck, by the look of it.'

'How do you know this?'

'Because I saw him; I was supposed to go and help him this morning. He said in the tavern last night he had a job I could help him with and he'd pay me. Well, I was on time, not a minute late; you know how he hates it when you're late. I hammered on his door but there was no answer so I hammered again. Then I peered through the windows and could just see him lying on the floor at the foot of the stairs. So I ran around to the back door, thinking he was drunk. I kicked it open then I went inside and shouted his name but he didn't answer. He didn't even groan or tell me to go away like he does when he gets in that state. So I walked across to him and kicked him with my shoe, not hard like, just sort of nudged him, but he felt as stiff as a board. I bent down and looked at his head, which was lying at a funny angle to his body, and it's then that I realised he was dead. His face was white and his lips were blue, his eyes were wide open, staring at something, but he wasn't breathing. Joss, his face was horrible. I've never seen a grown man with such a look of terror on his face. He was staring at a book that had fallen to the floor. I looked at it myself and it was the Bible. What page do you think it was left open at?'

Joss couldn't speak; the words wouldn't come out.

'Joss, it was on the page that said, "Thou shalt not suffer a witch to live". His house was so cold, he was cold and he looked scared. Do you think it was Betsy Baker? She said she would come back for each and every one of us. It would make sense she would kill Marcus first; he was the one who wanted to hang her more than any of the rest of us.'

'Don't be daft, Seth. Betsy's dead. We killed her with our own hands and buried her in my garden. How could she come back and kill him?'

'I don't know, Joss, but I'm scared. I don't want to die of terror like that … He looks horrible.'

'Marcus always looks horrible. I bet he was drunk and fell down the stairs of his own doing. I would look scared if I was falling to my death and I think you would, Seth. Who is there now?'

'Dr Johnson and the priest when I left to come and tell you.'

Joss jumped up onto the cart and held his hand out for Seth. 'Come on, let's go and see what the good doctor has to say about it all. Seth, you do know you mustn't tell anyone about what happened to Betsy, don't you? You could get the rest of us hanged for what we did.'

'I know, Joss, I'm not a fool, but I really am scared. To tell the truth, I've been scared since the day it happened. I go to bed and think about Betsy's face as she was choking to death and I dream about her, and then I wake up and think about her. Only time I forget is when I'm working for you or at the inn.'

Joss agreed with Seth. He was the same – he couldn't get her out of his head. When he closed his eyes to picture his beloved children it was always Betsy's face that appeared. He turned the horse and cart around and headed towards the village. He had to see for himself or he'd lose another full night's sleep.

He stopped at the trough and jumped down to tie the reins to the metal bar so the horse wouldn't wander off. Seth jumped down and they both began the short walk to Marcus King's house. There was quite a crowd outside and the builder who doubled as the undertaker had already arrived with his wooden handcart to take Marcus away until they could bury him. Seth stayed where he was, his hands clasped together and his lips moving in silent prayer.

Dr Johnson was coming out of the front door and Joss pushed his way through the crowd of people to reach him. The doctor nodded at him and when he turned to go back inside, Joss followed. He retched at the repugnant smell, which was beginning to fill the room. He walked across to where Marcus was lying in a heap, his white face tinged green. His terrified eyes were staring at something that only he could see.

Joss turned towards the doctor. 'Did he die of a broken neck or fright? Because to me he looks scared to death and I want to know if I'm going to die of anything similar and so does Seth.'

'What do you mean, Joss? The man clearly died from falling down the stairs. Why would he die of fright?'

'You know as well as I do. Because of …' Joss looked around to make sure no one was in hearing distance '… because of what we did to Betsy Baker. She said she was coming back for all of us, one by one. Marcus was the one shouting the loudest. He was the one who put the rope around her neck and pulled it tight, so it would make sense she would come for him first.'

'Now, I don't know where you're getting this from, Joss, and I think perhaps you've suffered so much misery the last few months you know nothing but sadness. But come on, man, a dead woman cannot come back and kill a fully grown man. Especially not one as big as Marcus King. Do you know what you're saying? Do you realise how much strength she would need to push that big lump down the stairs?'

'Believe what you will, Doctor, but I'm telling you now we all need to watch our backs. Or she will catch us off guard, then we'll all be done for and end up looking like that.'

Joss pointed at his friend's corpse then turned and left, crossing himself as he went out of the house and back to the cart and Seth, who was almost the same colour as Marcus.

'Well, then, Joss, was it bad? What did you think he looked like – just as I'd said? What did the doctor say?'

Joss took a moment. He didn't want to scare Seth too much

but he needed to know the truth, otherwise he would be left open to – *open to what?* he asked himself.

'Bad, he looked bad. You were right; he looked as if he died of fright. His eyes were locked open and I don't know what the last thing was he saw but it wasn't an angel of mercy from the good Lord. I've never seen a man look so horrified.'

Seth buried his head in his hands and sobbed quietly. Joss untied the horse and got back on the cart, taking them back to his parents' farmhouse. Neither of them spoke a word to each other. He stopped outside and unfastened the horse from the cart. After leading it to the nearest field, he opened the gate and watched it run for a while. It dropped to the ground and rolled in the grass, relieved to be free once more. Joss wished his life was so simple. He turned and marched back to Seth.

'Come on inside; we'll have something to drink and then we need to talk this through like men. We should tell the others to come as well and see if they have anything they would like to tell us.'

No sooner had he finished speaking than he turned to see a group of men walking down the lane towards him and he nodded to himself. They already knew. The only man missing was Dr Johnson but he was busy. Joss had a feeling that as soon as he finished with Marcus King's body he too would be on his way here. Six grown men and every single one of them looked scared of their own shadow. He waited for them to reach his gate.

'So I see you have all been thinking the same as me and Seth here. Marcus King is dead and who do you think may be next? We need to go inside and talk about this like men.'

There was a group murmur and Joss led the way into his parents' huge kitchen. They all took seats around the pine table that filled the middle of the room, the table where his mother would feed all the men who helped out during hay time. He had seen up to fifteen grown men seated around this table laughing, eating and drinking ale. He had never seen a group of men with faces so solemn and he felt responsible for it all. If he'd never fallen for her – it pained him to say her name – none of this would have happened. He would be sitting here with his family, not a group of strangers worrying about a woman they had killed coming back for her revenge.

Chapter 18

The caravan door opened and Henry, who was dozing off, jumped up and, not for the first time, wondered where he was but then Megan breezed in with some daily papers stuffed under her arms and a carrier bag full of groceries.

'I've been thinking, Henry.'

'Yes, Megan?'

'Well, you know how you're a bit of a legend?'

'Yes …'

'I wouldn't mind being a bit of a legend myself.'

'You already are, Megan. The police are going to be searching for your body and when they finally convince themselves that sweet little Megan wasn't forced to help Henry Smith escape they will realise that sweet little Megan is one dangerous woman. You will forever be known as the nurse who threw her life away to help a serial killer.'

'I know that, Henry, and it's all very good but …'

'But what?'

'I want to be known as Nurse Megan who turned from a saint to a sinner. I don't just want to be the bit on the side who helped you to escape.'

Henry began to laugh, really laugh. He hadn't chuckled so long in years and Megan threw a newspaper at his head.

'I'm serious; stop laughing. I want to be just like you.'

Henry managed to contain himself and wiped the tears from the corners of his eyes. 'Why, Megan? What's so good about being labelled a serial killer?'

'There's something inside me that I'm finding harder and harder to control; it's like a red mist. Every time someone pisses me off I want to stab them and not just once … I want to stab and cut them over and over. Now I'm going to make us a coffee and I want you to tell me exactly how it was before you killed Jenna White; I want to know how you felt. What you did and how you felt when it was done. I need to know everything.'

Henry sat up straight. This sounded all too familiar because it was exactly how he'd felt in the hours before he would go and kill. It was bizarre that he had met Megan, who felt exactly the same. He had never really believed in fate but he was beginning to think that they had been destined to meet. Look at the other infamous couples who killed: Brady and Hindley, Bonnie and Clyde, the Wests; there was some strange chemistry between them, just like Henry and Megan. There was no denying it would be extremely difficult – they were both in the public domain now – but he thought that it might be possible.

'I need to think about it, I mean really think about it. What you're asking is a big, big thing. We'll both be taking a huge risk and it would take some serious planning on our part to ensure we didn't get caught straight away.'

Megan smiled and walked back down the caravan to the small kitchen, where she filled the kettle and put away the bread and biscuits she'd just bought. Henry watched her a little bit in awe and even more worried that she might be too hard to control. He didn't want to jeopardise his revenge on Annie Graham and he didn't really want to share it with Megan either, but Annie had proved herself once over and if he had some help she wouldn't be able to do anything to escape the next time, but the deal would be that Annie was his – she always had been and always would be – and he wouldn't settle until he'd slit her throat and held her in his arms while she bled to death.

He knew that once she was dead he would kill himself. He would not go back to the mental hospital and his life would have no value once she was dead. He wanted to kill Will first but his would be a swift kill; he supposed he could let Megan have him because it would be Annie that he spent his time on. He would finally get his finale but until then he had to think of a way to keep Megan happy, otherwise she might go off the rails before he got the chance and that would be dangerous for them both.

* * *

Will had managed to rub the skin on his wrists until it was red and chafed, trying to get out of the rope that was tying him to the metal rings on the wall. He had heard a lot of shouting and arguing upstairs hours ago when Amelia had first come home and then it had gone quiet. He'd dozed off a couple of times, all the exhaustion and worry from the last few days catching up with him. He wasn't scared of Amelia even though her boyfriend clearly was, judging by what he'd said, but he was really pissed off with her. In fact, he didn't think he would have a problem smacking her a couple of times if he had to and Will didn't hit women full stop. But she had taken him away from Annie and his family when they needed him the most and he couldn't let that go. Annie would be so worried about him and he knew that by now she would have discharged herself from the hospital when she should be there taking it easy.

He couldn't believe that his dad had another child and had never mentioned it to anyone ever. Then Will wondered if his mum had known. She would have been heartbroken to know that Tom had cheated on her and got someone else pregnant when she was told not to have any more children. He was angry with his dad but not enough that he'd never speak to him again, but he wanted to know what had happened for them all to end up in this mess. Will had never relied on his dad's money for anything, yet here he was, tied up in a cold damp cellar because he had some long-lost psychotic half-sister who did want money.

There was the sound of a bolt being slid across and a shadowy figure came down the stairs. The bare bulb illuminated the room, making him squeeze his eyes shut. He had become accustomed to the dark and the light hurt his eyes.

'So if you behave and do what you're told you should be a free man in two days. Daddy is busy as we speak, getting his cash together, getting my cash together. Then we'll let you get back to your life.'

Will had to bite his tongue to stop him trying to lunge for her. He nodded.

'Are you hungry, thirsty? I don't want you going home malnourished.'

He shook his head. He would rather die of starvation than ask her for anything.

'Suit yourself but there's no need to be a martyr.'

She turned and walked back up. She tugged on the string and the room was black once more. Will opened his eyes. He preferred the dark to being dazzled. The trapdoor slammed shut and the noise echoed around the small room. He knew what she looked like; they all knew what she looked like. His dad, Lily, Annie – he wasn't pinning his hopes on her letting him out of here unharmed. If she went by what the majority of kidnappers did when the victims could identify them, she would more than likely kill him and do a runner. Well, she could go and get fucked. He wasn't going to die because she was jealous and thought that he should. He looked around for something to use to rub the rope against but it was hopeless; the only other chance he had was if he could convince her boyfriend to let him go. He didn't seem like the brightest of blokes, especially getting mixed up in this.

Will closed his eyes and felt his head begin to nod to one side. Considering his circumstances, he was sleeping like a baby.

* * *

Luke was playing on his Xbox but keeping a close eye on Amelia. He was fed up with the stupid bitch and wished he'd never moved here with her. They were in a serious world of shit and she didn't get it; she honestly thought that once they'd got the money they would be out of here and away. Never mind the fact that Bill, Will, whatever his name was, had seen both their faces and would be able to identify them in a line-up from a hundred miles away. He had no idea what he was going to do but he wasn't going with her. He thought about phoning the police himself. He could ring from the iPhone he'd kept in the car. He'd turned it off and then lifted the carpet up in the boot and put it inside the spokes of the spare wheel. He could tell them where they were and grass her up, then he could hop on a train and go anywhere as long as it was as far away from the English Lake District as possible.

The more he thought about it, the better it sounded. Of course she would flip but he didn't care; he didn't want to spend his life with her – she would probably tie him in the cellar and leave him for dead if he pissed her off.

Amelia walked past and patted him on the head. 'Have you been a good boy today, Luke? Sorry about earlier; it's just that I don't want you talking to him and getting all friendly. Next thing I know, you'll both be sitting on the sofa drinking cans of lager and discussing who will win the Champions League.'

Luke grunted some form of reply at her; the less he said the better.

She slapped him across the face, the shock making him jump off the sofa and throw the control pad on the floor.

'Ouch … what did you do that for?'

'Because you weren't paying attention – when I talk, you listen, not ignore me. Who do you think you are?'

'Sorry, you're right. I didn't mean to ignore you.'

Inside he was so angry he felt like wrapping his hands around her neck and choking the life out of her but he didn't; instead, he followed her up to bed like the good boy that he was.

Chapter 19

Annie slept all night, no dreams; in fact she didn't remember falling asleep. The en-suite bathroom light was still on and she felt guilty for not turning it off but she hadn't wanted to be alone in the dark in case the scary woman paid a visit. She got up, showered, dressed and ran downstairs to a deserted kitchen. She had expected Lily or Tom to be up but guessed both of them had probably not slept too well and were catching up. Starving, she opened the cupboards until she found a box of porridge oats and microwaved some. Picking up the phone on the wall next to the breakfast bar, she rang Jake, who answered just before she was going to put it down.

'Morning.'

'Oh, it's you. I thought it was some PPI crap or something.'

'Cheers, don't sound so happy. Have you heard anything at all?'

'Not a peep but I've just finished speaking to Kav. We're going to be coming up to see you soon and then go to see Nick and his team. Oh, for some reason your builders have rung the station asking to get a message to you. Apparently they need to speak to you as soon as you can; there's a problem with the house.'

'That's all I need. I'll ring them and, if I need to, can you drive me there after lunch?'

'Of course – have to go but I'll see you soon.'

He ended the call and Annie put the phone down, worried about what the builders wanted. Deep down, she knew what it was but didn't want to think about it right now. It was something to do with the woman … girl … ghost. She got her porridge out of the microwave and left it on the side to cool while she went into the study to borrow Tom's computer. She needed to do some digging and find out exactly who the dead woman was and what it was she wanted from Annie.

She sank down into the soft leather desk chair and sighed. She could sit here all day and work. The computer loaded and she typed 'Hawkshead village in the 1700s' into the search bar and hit enter, waiting to see what it would bring up. Before long, the pages began to load. There were diary entries, parish records that had been updated by computer. At the very bottom was a list of deaths in the village that happened in 1782. There was one suspected death by arsenic poisoning and four confirmed deaths by arsenic poisoning. Alarm bells rang in Annie's brain as she clicked on it and waited for it to load.

The photocopied handwriting filled the screen and she read the list of names and dates. There was a Gladys Baker, survived by her daughter Betsy Baker, and as she read the name Annie felt the room begin to spin. She knew that Betsy was the woman who had been trying to scare her half to death and caused her accident.

As she read further down her hand flew to her mouth: two of the victims were boys, both aged nine: Arthur and Cuthbert Brown, survived by their father, Joss Brown. If Betsy Baker had poisoned so many people, no wonder they had been chasing her through the woods until they had caught up with her. Annie didn't agree with them taking the law into their own hands and killing Betsy, but she now knew what the dreams were about. She needed to go to the house and put Betsy Baker to rest, once and for all. Annie had a feeling that they wouldn't have buried her in the church or given her a proper funeral and suspected that somewhere in the grounds of her new home was an unmarked grave containing Betsy's remains. Jake would go mental but she had no choice; until she did this there was no way they would be able to settle in their dream home.

Annie googled the phone number for her friend Father John, who was the priest at St Mary's in Bowness. It had been a while since she'd spoken to him but he would know what to do and give her some good advice. Tom had an old-fashioned phone on his desk with a proper dial and it felt strange putting her finger in the dial and waiting for it to turn around. Finally it began to ring John's number and she grinned when she heard his voice on the other end.

'Hello, Father John speaking.'

'Hi, it's Annie.'

'Annie, how lovely to hear your voice. How are you and how are those wedding plans coming along? I've had my best dress sent off to be dry-cleaned just for the occasion.'

'I'm not too good, to be honest, John. I don't know where to start, really.'

'Well, I suggest that you start at the beginning, because I have all day for you.'

Annie blinked back her tears and relayed everything that had happened in the last few weeks to him. She knew that he wouldn't tell anyone about Will or anything else that was happening.

'Oh, dear Lord, Annie, you poor thing. How are you coping? Do you need me to come and see you? Because I'm on my way.'

'I've been better but I've also been a lot worse. I would love to see you, John. That's if you have nothing more pressing to do.'

'You mean apart from sitting Mrs Bexley and Miss Smithson down and banging their heads together! I've been waiting for an excuse to come along to put this meeting off; it's great to know that the old guy actually listens in to my prayers now and again. In fact, you could return the favour once everything is sorted out and come and do the mediation between the pair of them.

Who would have thought cake baking could turn into such a deadly battle of wits?'

'I'll do anything for you. I'm at Tom and Lily's house; they needed someone to stay and be the liaison although I don't know an awful lot. I'm relying on Jake to pass everything on but I know the police are doing the best they can.'

'I'll be there soon. Do you want normal attire or the full monty?'

'Normal will be fine. I don't want to freak Tom out.'

'Leave it with me.'

The line went dead and Annie thought back to the first time she'd met him. She'd been admiring the beautiful roses in the presbytery front garden and had thought he was the gardener in his shorts and faded rock-and-roll T-shirt. They had worked together to get rid of a Shadow Man who had claimed the soul of nine-year-old Sophie and between them they had managed to banish him to the shadows for good; at least Annie hoped it was for good. Now she needed his help to send Betsy Baker to the other side because, by all accounts, she was very much grounded on this side and not very happy.

Annie forced herself to get out of the chair and to go back to eat her breakfast, wondering if that bitch Amelia was feeding Will and taking care of him. A vision of him, alone in a damp dark cellar, flashed across her eyes and she felt her heart skip a beat. Closing her eyes to concentrate, she could make out Will's familiar figure on a bed but it was too dark to see anything else. An icy-cold, tiny hand slipped into hers, breaking her concentration. Annie looked down to see Sophie and smiled.

'Will is OK, Annie. The man who helped the woman to take him is scared and wants to let him go.'

'Thank you, Sophie, but how do you know this?'

'Because I whispered in his ear that he should, over and over again, and he agreed with me.'

'You are amazing. I love you, Sophie.'

'So don't worry about Will; he is going to be coming home before you know it, but I'm really scared for you, Annie. I think you are in a lot more danger than Will.'

Annie felt a cold shard of fear lodge itself in the base of her spine and she wasn't sure if she wanted to hear what Sophie was about to tell her.

'Why?'

Sophie beckoned for her to lean towards her so she could whisper in her ear. Annie did so and shivered as the little girl's cold lips pressed against her ear, but she didn't pull away.

'That woman is horrible; she scares me and she watches you all the time.'

'Do you mean Betsy Baker?'

Sophie nodded. 'She's mean and very angry. I think she will do something really bad if you don't get rid of her.'

'Do you know why she's so mad with me – why she doesn't like me?'

'Because your great-grandad was a distant relation to a man called Joss. Your cottage belonged to Joss and he was there when the other men did something horrible to her.'

Annie nodded. It all made a lot more sense. There was a reason she had fallen so in love with Apple Tree Cottage; she was meant to be there. Maybe it was her destiny to put Betsy Baker to rest, once and for all.

'Thank you, Sophie.'

Annie looked around for her ghostly friend but she'd disappeared as quickly as she'd come.

She looked at the grandfather clock in the hall. It had been twenty minutes since she'd spoken to Jake; hopefully by the time she'd eaten and washed the bowl they would be pulling up outside the front door.

* * *

Megan was always up before Henry. He'd asked her why she never stayed in bed and her reply had astounded him. She'd told him that life was too short to spend it wallowing in bed sleeping.

'Why dance in the dark when you could run in the sun?'

He agreed with her to a certain extent but there was nothing worth jumping out of bed for at the moment; there was no job, no agenda, nothing except for the two of them. He went into the kitchen-diner and sat down at the small table. There were two daily papers spread out on the small plastic-coated table with both their pictures filling the front pages. The headline on one was: 'Where is Britain's most dangerous serial killer and his nurse?' So the police had checked the security cameras and realised that Megan had been a willing accomplice in his escape. He wondered how she would be feeling at seeing her face plastered all over the nationals like this. Her blonde hair with the fuchsia-pink streak dominated the photos. Thank goodness she'd had the foresight to dye it brown or there would be armed police with machine guns surrounding the caravan and ready to storm it within minutes.

He wondered where she was. Maybe she'd changed her mind and gone to the nearest telephone box to call Crimestoppers and turn him in. He stood and turned the gas on, filling the kettle. He might as well make the most of his freedom; it wasn't as if he could go anywhere. He had nowhere else to go and if she turned up with the police he would deal with it then. There was no point in worrying about it.

He opened the cutlery drawer and took the sharpest knife out. He would keep this close in case he needed to use it. There was nothing he could do now; it was out there. He would only be able to leave after dark, not that he'd gone out much; Megan was quite happy to do the running around. The kettle whistled and he poured the boiling water over the teabag, then he popped two slices of bread into the toaster. He enjoyed having Megan around but he much preferred his own company; it could be quite a challenge engaging in conversation with her. If she was feeling happy it was the latest gossip from the soap operas but if she was feeling down all she wanted to talk about was death and killing people. It hadn't been something that Henry had really thought about before he'd done it; well, not to the extent that Megan talked about it – she was quite obsessed with the whole idea of killing someone.

Last night she had said that she wanted to kill women who looked like the bullies who had made her life hell at school. Women with long hair – it didn't matter what colour as long as it was really long and they loved it, and by loving it she meant that they did nothing but play around with it. She wanted to abduct them, take them somewhere to a cellar or an empty room in a disused house and tie them up. She wanted to take a pair of sharp scissors and cut their long hair off until it was in a pile on the floor. Henry had listened to this, quite fascinated by her desire to take a person and then take away everything from them that had defined them. She was going to gag them and wasn't sure how she would kill them, but after looking at various methods she was quite keen to try garrotting them. It was something she thought she could manage on her own, given the right tools.

Fuck, Henry had been so freaked out by the conversation he had excused himself and retired to bed to be alone with his thoughts. She was definitely on a par with some of the most depraved killers he'd heard of, but of course he couldn't criticise her because he had done something very, very similar. It was just strange to look at her pretty face and hear those words spoken from her mouth. They would be calling her the Angel of Death once it all broke out. Megan had been quite clear that she didn't want to spend ages setting up blind dates or meetings with her victims but she would take extra care when out and about and if she saw someone who matched her profile then she would follow them home and figure out how and when they could abduct them.

He ate his toast and sipped his tea whilst reading the articles in both papers. They were very similar, apart from one that said the people of his home town were on high alert in case he returned there. Too late, he'd been here three, maybe four days now; it was hard to keep count, and no one at the caravan park looked remotely as if they were on high alert. Caravan doors were propped open from morning until night; there were kids running around everywhere, playing football and having water fights. He didn't mind the football but the incessant screeching when they blasted each other with water from the neon-coloured submachine guns was unbearable. In his day the best you could get was an empty washing-up liquid bottle and if you were really lucky a brightly coloured, see-through plastic water pistol, but Henry had to make do with the bottle. Not that he'd had many water fights; he hadn't had a lot of friends when he was a child. As his mother had always told him, 'You're such a loner, Henry Smith. Go out and make some friends.'

His fists curled up involuntarily at the thought of her. To this day he didn't regret killing her. At the time he'd felt sad that it had come to such a terrible decision but once he'd got over the initial guilt he'd found it didn't bother him at all. How could you miss someone who'd dominated your whole life until the day you finally liberated yourself?

1782

The noise was horrendous. The men were all talking at once, their voices getting louder and louder. Joss picked up a pan from the stove and banged it down onto the table so hard that they all jumped and stopped talking.

'Jesus, will you all listen to yourselves? None of this is even possible. How can a woman, a dead woman, cause so much panic? We are all grown men and very much alive, unless you carry on like this and you will all scare yourselves to death, which is exactly what could have happened to Marcus. He liked to drink, did Marcus, and we all know that. How did we all meet?'

There was a murmur from everyone, agreeing with Joss.

'You're right, Joss; he did like to drink and did the doctor not say he died from falling down the stairs? Broke his neck, he did, but how? He didn't have enough ale in his house or empty bottles to get that drunk he couldn't walk straight. And I saw the look on his face when they carried his body out – terrified, he was. A mask of fear he was wearing when his heart stopped beating.'

Joss nodded. He agreed with Samuel to a certain extent but the problem was that now they were all scared.

'Look, why don't we stick together? Those of you who are lucky enough not to be married can stay here with me. Those of you with wives make sure you're never left alone long enough for anything to happen. I can't believe I'm saying this, but if we stick together she won't be able to hurt us all. That's if it even was her; we might just be worrying over nothing. If after a couple of days nothing happens then we'll put it down to Marcus's bad luck and his inability to hold his beer.'

No one answered but Seth looked relieved; in fact, when Joss looked at each of them in turn they were all wearing the same expression of relief.

'I suggest you go home and get anything you might need for the next few days then lock up your houses and come back here. Bring some food as well because I have no idea how much food is in the pantry.'

The heavy atmosphere in the room had eased. It was not the answer to the problem but at least it was a temporary solution. He stood with his back to them all as they began to move around and leave to go and get whatever they needed. His brain felt as though it was too heavy for his head to hold up and he prayed for some kind of answer to the problem as soon as possible. The men all shuffled out of the door except Seth. Joss dropped onto a chair opposite him.

'We need to speak to Father Sawyer, ask him if there is something we should have done with her body. I don't think we can exactly ask him to bury her in the church grounds, but I think there might be something we could have done that would stop all of this.'

Seth nodded and for the first time in days the frown lifted from his brow. 'That's a grand idea; maybe he could come and bless her grave. I think he already knows something went on because he was fishing around at the inn two nights ago. If we swear him to secrecy he will have to keep it to himself. Priests aren't allowed to break confession, are they?'

'I don't think so, Seth, but we don't really have much choice, do we? As I can't think of anything else that we can do.' Joss stood up. 'Come on, let's go and find the priest and see if he can help.'

Seth followed him and they began the short walk back to the village and the church, which was on the hill overlooking it. They climbed the steep stone steps and walked up the path to the church. Seth lingered behind Joss, uncomfortable; he really hated churches.

Joss hoped that when he reached the church doors God wouldn't decide to strike him down dead; then again, if he died it would be the end of this nightmare. He twisted the iron ring on the door and it swung inwards. There was a strong draught of cold air, which blasted Joss and he shivered. Seth tripped over the step and fell into him, pushing him forward. He missed his step and clattered through the internal door into the church. The priest spun around to see who or what had made such an entrance. His face visibly relaxed at the sight of Joss and a very red-faced Seth.

'Sorry, I missed my step.'

'Happens a lot that – as long as you didn't hurt yourself.'

'No, I didn't. Thanks.'

Joss smiled at him. He hadn't been inside the actual church in a while. Not since his wife had died and he had lost all faith in the good Lord. He made an exception for funerals, suffering through a church service to show his respect to the dearly departed.

'What brings you two here on such a fine day? I'd have thought you would be out working the land, Joss?'

'I should be, no doubt about it, but I have a problem. Well, we have a problem; there are a few of us but they are too afraid to speak about it.'

The priest nodded. 'Would this have something to do with the sudden disappearance of one Betsy Baker and the demise of your entire family?'

Joss bowed his head. 'Yes, Father, it does.'

'I wondered when one of you would be forced to come and see me. I suppose Marcus dying in such a manner has put the fear of God or the Devil into you all, has it? I know what you all did. I'm the first person someone comes to see if they need to confess their sins. You all honestly didn't believe that every one of you would carry your secret to the grave and not tell another soul?'

Seth let out a sob and pushed the sleeve of his jacket into his mouth to stop him from crying out his admission of guilt. Joss patted the lad's shoulder and turned to face the priest.

'I suppose not; so you know about Betsy then. You know that it was her who poisoned my boys, my parents and then planned to murder me. You know that we chased her through the woods with hunting dogs and dragged her back to my house to hang her and bury her in the garden.'

The weight of confessing lifted from Joss's shoulders and he felt much better; so be it if the priest decided to tell the authorities. If Joss was hanged at least he would be reunited with his family; he didn't care about living or dying any longer.

'I do. I know every single detail but do not fear, for they were passed to me in a confession and we all know that they are sacred and can never be broken. Your secret is safe with me and if it's forgiveness that you want then I forgive you. If she had done the same to my family I would want to see her hanged until she breathed no more, priest or no priest. So what have you come to see me for?'

It was Seth who spoke next. 'She's come back for us all; she said she would and she has.'

The church door flew open, hitting the wall with such force a chunk of limestone fell to the floor. The colour drained from Seth's face and Joss felt a cold shiver run down his back. The priest looked at them both, fear etched across his face. He walked briskly down to the huge wooden door to close it.

Seth stood so close to Joss that he couldn't have moved fast if he needed to and whispered into his ear, 'She's here. She knows we're talking about her. What are we going to do?'

From somewhere behind them came an ear-splitting sound of sharp nails being dragged across a pane of glass, the sound amplifying around the eaves of the church. Seth lifted both his hands to his ears; the noise actually hurt his brain it was so loud. The priest was trying to shut the door but it wouldn't move, and his face turned crimson with the effort. Joss ran to help him, followed by Seth, who didn't want to be left on his own near to where that awful sound was emanating. All three of them put their shoulders in and pushed at the door with all their might. The priest prayed out loud and the door moved an inch so they shoved it even harder and managed to move it slowly back so they could close it. The force behind it on the other side was huge and Joss was too scared to think about how something invisible could be so strong.

With one last push the door slammed shut and the priest took the key from his pocket. He inserted it into the lock and turned it until it clicked and the door was locked. All three of them sighed; they leant with their backs against the door while they waited for their breathing to return to normal. Something threw itself against the door and the whole thing shook; the wood felt as if it was being pushed through. Terror made them turn around and Seth pulled Joss away from it. The priest shouted at the door in

Latin as the wood bulged into the church. Joss was scared it was going to break and splinter towards them. As the priest shouted louder the door became flat once more and the noise stopped. The atmosphere, which had been heavy moments ago, returned to one of peace and serenity.

Father Sawyer turned to them. 'You need to show me where you buried her. Did you give her a proper burial? Because if not we have to dig her up and at least bless the grave. Did you place a cross on her chest, sprinkle her with holy water; was she properly laid out?'

'No, Father, we did none of that; we were so guilt-stricken and afraid for ourselves at what we had just done that we threw her into a hole in the ground and buried her.'

'There is no way we can move her body into consecrated ground now – it will be rotten – but if I bless her and we do what I've just said I might be able to contain her spirit. I can't say if it will work but it's better to at least try than all die of terror.'

Joss nodded. 'When shall we do it?'

'I'm afraid we have no choice; we must do it now before she becomes too powerful for me to fight. Now, kneel down at the altar. I'm going to bless your sins and forgive you both. Then I'm going to baptise the pair of you because I have no idea whether your parents did or not and it won't hurt to do it again, and then we are going to go and do the same to the remains of Betsy Baker and ask God to take her in, away from the forces of evil so that she may rest in peace.'

Chapter 20

Jake knocked on the front door as Father John pulled into the drive behind him. He turned and grinned, saluting the priest, who saluted back.

'Good morning, Father, long time no see. I hope you're here on a nice visit and not some scary shit that will turn my hair grey.'

'Morning, Jake. Now what makes you think that? I'm here to check on our special friend Annie and see how she is.'

'She's special all right.'

The door opened and Annie poked Jake in the ribs. 'I heard that, cheeky.'

Jake walked in, rubbing his side, and Father John opened his arms and grinned at Annie. She fell into them and he wrapped them around her. There was something safe about being hugged by a man of God, well, this one, anyway; he was such a good person through and through.

'Have you heard anything about our William?'

Annie shook her head. She had never called him William once and it sounded strange; she much preferred Will.

'Nothing, but I have it on good authority that Will is going to be set free anyway and, if not, then by tomorrow Tom will have the money ready by lunchtime to do the drop.'

John nodded. 'I see and then they will let him go. Is that right?'

'I hope so; that's what they said.'

'Is there anything I can do? Maybe I could take the money? They won't feel threatened by a priest. That way, you're not putting yourself or Mr and Mrs Ashworth at risk.'

'That's very kind of you, John, but I couldn't ask you to do that. I want to take the money. I want to be there.'

Jake looked at her. 'And we all know why that is, but you can't beat her up, Annie. As much as you want to batter her, you'll lose your job and she might have a knife or a gun. We don't know how dangerous she is.'

'I don't care about my job, Jake. I care about getting Will back safe and sound and then hunting her down and bringing her to justice, one way or another.'

Jake shook his head. 'You're a pain in the arse.'

'I know.'

John laughed. 'Annie, Annie, Annie, you don't change one little bit and that's why we love you.'

She led them into the kitchen and they all sat down at the table.

'John, I have a big favour to ask you, which doesn't concern Will … Well, not at this moment in time, but if we don't sort it out very soon it could well do.'

'Ask away; I told you I'd do anything to help you.'

'Anything?'

'Yes, anything.'

'I think my new house is haunted. No, I don't think, I know that it's haunted. By a woman called Betsy Baker who lived there back in 1782, before she died.'

She gave him a chance to digest the information, which didn't take very long.

'How do you know that it's haunted? A lot of old houses have draughts and creak in the night.'

'This is more than that; I've been having nightmares and visions. I keep seeing a woman dressed in a white gown running through the woods near the cottage being chased by a group of men with dogs, only I kept waking before they caught up with her. Last week I was driving home from the cottage and I caught a glimpse of a flash of white running through the trees; as I rounded the bend she was standing in the middle of the road and I had to swerve to avoid hitting her. I went off the road, crashing my car into a tree and ended up in a coma in hospital for a few days.

'Whilst I was unconscious, the dream carried on, only this time it went to the end. She'd poisoned an entire family and the men caught up with her. They dragged her back to the cottage and hanged her from the beams of the front porch. Only I felt as if it was me they were hanging; I could feel them dragging me. Their hands were rough and then they looped the rope around my neck. I could feel myself being lifted from the ground and choked. That was when I came out of my coma. The builders are refusing to work in the cottage. They keep finding their tools missing; one of them was strangled by something invisible and someone keeps breathing icy-cold air down their necks. There is a terrible sound of nails being scraped along glass whenever one of them is in there on their own; I've heard it myself when I've been there.'

Jake gulped. 'I heard it too, the last time I was there with you and Alex, only I didn't want to say anything in case you thought I was losing it.'

'See, I knew you had seen something. You were acting so strange even Alex thought you'd flipped. Why didn't you just say?'

'Because I didn't want to put you off living in your dream house, Annie. I didn't want to be the one to tell you. I thought with you being psychic you'd pick up on it and get it sorted out yourself.'

'Ah, then we have a bit of a problem. I've never heard of Betsy Baker ... Who did she kill?'

'I think she poisoned her mother, her boyfriend's children and his parents, with arsenic by the sound of it. There is no official record of her being hanged, from what I can find, but I trust my instincts enough to know that what I saw was an action replay and it wasn't very nice. What can we do, John?'

'I think we need to see if we can find a grave in your garden and see if Betsy Baker is buried in it and then we need to report it to the police and let them take over.'

'That would take months – years, knowing what our police are like. Technically, me and Jake are the police; if we find her grave and it's a really old skeleton, can we not transfer her to a quiet patch in the church grounds and give her a proper send-off? I want to move into my house after the wedding and I won't be able to if we notify the authorities; they'll want to dig everything up.'

John shrugged. 'Your call, Officer Graham, but if we find any evidence that she hasn't been in the ground for at least two hundred years then we report it. I'm too old to argue with you and I want to help.'

Jake looked at them both. 'I don't know about this; if there's a body in there we should do the right thing, Annie.'

'Jake, it's not going to be a body as such, is it? If I'm right, she's been buried there since 1782 and nobody missed her then. If we don't give her a proper burial, she'll be grounded in my house forever and I'll never get rid of her and, besides, it's not as if she was an upstanding pillar of the community. She killed at least five people, possibly more. She tried to kill me. She wasn't a very nice person.'

He shrugged his shoulders. 'I suppose so. Trust you, Annie – only you could buy a house that's being haunted by Cumbria's first female serial killer. You couldn't get one that was haunted by a tabby cat or a friendly dog?'

'No, Jake, you know that's not my style.'

'I know it isn't but I wish to Christ it was. Sorry, Father.'

John smiled. 'You're forgiven, my son. When shall we do this? If I'm to dig a grave in the churchyard without any of my nosy parishioners catching me I'll have to do it when it's getting dark. How about if I get it prepared tonight and we move her tomorrow?

She will need to go straight from one grave to the next and you'll have to transport her in a specially blessed container of some kind. You can't just shove her into a cardboard box and hope for the best. If she's haunting you, Annie, she must have quite some spiritual power.'

'I've got a plastic under-bed storage container. Can you bless that if I bring it to the church with me in the morning? We could put a cross inside and sprinkle it with holy water.'

'What about some garlic and a wooden stake to drive through her heart?'

'Shut up, Jake, I'm being serious.'

Annie's mobile rang and she saw Kav's number flash up on the screen. She put it to her ear. 'Tell me you have some news, please?'

'We have an address and the cell site analysis of Will's phone has come back to within a three-kilometre radius of that address so a couple of plain-clothes task force officers are on their way as we speak to scour the area and do a sweep – and no, I can't tell you where it is because you'll go rushing there and probably end up getting yourself in a whole world of trouble that I won't be able to bail you out of. I just wanted you to know that we're on it and doing our best.'

'What if I promise to sit in the back of the car with you and Jake so I can't get out and get into any trouble? I promise I'll be good – please, Kav, I need to be there when they bring him out. I'll go mad sitting here biting my nails.'

'Arghh, I knew I shouldn't have said anything and just turned up at the house with Will following behind. Wait until they've checked it out and given the go-ahead. If we go storming in, you and I know that it might not end too well for Will. If they think they're going to get caught they might decide to cut their losses and run.'

'Thank you, Kav. I promise I won't do anything stupid. I don't want to jeopardise Will's life. Let me know as soon as you're going. I want to be there.'

'I know you do, kid. Just hang on and let the big boys do their stuff first.'

The line went dead and Annie repeated what Kav had just told her. Jake's radio rang and he excused himself and stepped outside. Annie didn't need to be psychic to know it would be Kav telling Jake to keep a close eye on her but she wouldn't do anything to put Will at risk, at least not until he was safe and then it would be a different matter. If that Amelia thought she was getting away with this she had another think coming.

John took hold of her hand. 'I'm going to go now and prepare somewhere to put Ms Baker's bones. I have a storage box like you described so I'll bless it and fill it with anything and everything I can think of to keep her contained. But I need you to come and collect it tomorrow morning; is that OK with you? I have a busy day tomorrow but we'll get it sorted and have her buried before tomorrow night. Let's just hope that the bishop doesn't get wind of this or I'll be finishing the rest of my life marrying couples in a chapel in Vegas.'

He winked at her and she squeezed his hand back.

'I'm sorry to drag you into this but I don't know anyone else I can trust.'

'Don't be sorry, Annie; I'm a great believer that things happen for a reason. There was a reason you were sent to my door last year and was I glad that you were because I dread to think what would have happened to me or Sophie if you hadn't. I'm the one who is forever in your debt so don't be worrying about any of this. What's the worst that could happen?'

His nervous laugh made her smile. She felt bad for involving him but she knew that he wouldn't have it any other way and that she couldn't do this without his help.

Chapter 21

Megan came rushing into the caravan, making Henry jump up from where he was sprawled on the sofa.

'What's the matter?'

'I've found us a place we can take our victims. It's perfect and nobody uses it. I asked the farmer and he said that the man who owned the field died last year and his son lives abroad. We'll be able to turn it into our little torture chamber.'

'Stop right there; you asked a farmer what, exactly?'

'I was looking at the horses in one of the fields and he was cutting the grass in the field next door. I shut the field gate for him and he stopped to thank me. We just got chatting so I sort of slipped it into the conversation. He was old so he won't remember what we were talking about.'

'And what are we talking about?'

'There's an overgrown field with an old building in the middle of it; there's no one around it. We could take our victims there, tie them up and gag them. If we make it secure so they can't escape it will be perfect.'

'Won't the farmer see us coming and going? It's far too risky. I like your thinking but we need a house somewhere with a cellar that is on its own so if they scream no one will hear them.'

Megan looked as if she was about to burst into tears and Henry felt bad.

'Don't get me wrong; it's a good idea but how on earth would we get a girl, screaming and fighting, across an overgrown field and into a ramshackle barn without anyone seeing us? And what if whoever owns it turns up to see that we've been using his shed for more than keeping chickens?'

'Sorry, Henry, I got so carried away. I'm desperate to do it; I want to kill someone.'

'I know you do but you have to be patient. We can't risk everything that you've spent the last few months planning by taking chances and hoping for the best. That's how people get caught, and I don't want to get caught, Megan. I've never been so happy in my life and it would make me really angry to see it all thrown away because of being impatient.'

Henry knew he was asking a lot. Expecting her to keep her burning desires in check was something he knew was going to be difficult for both of them because the more he thought about murder the harder it became for him as well. All he wanted was to get Miss Graham and have some fun with her and he was finding it all very frustrating. He also wanted to leave this caravan as he was getting stir-crazy, but he knew that it would be a massive risk. He enjoyed his evening stroll around the site and down to the shoreline once it was dusk, but he couldn't be seen going in and out through the day. The scars were too hard to cover; that bloody woman had so much to answer for. She'd stopped him, almost killed him and then burnt his secret room down to the ground; his trophy room was nothing more than a pile of charred wood and ash, thanks to her. It didn't enter Henry's head that if he hadn't splashed petrol all over then the old mansion wouldn't have gone up in flames, because it was easier to blame her, to blame Annie Graham for everything that had gone wrong the last two years.

Megan threw herself onto the bench opposite him. Her legs

looked as if they went on forever in her very short denim cut-offs, and he admired how smooth and tanned they were. The weather had been glorious since they'd arrived and she'd spent all day in and out of the caravan, pottering around in a pair of shorts and a strappy vest top. Being by the sea had agreed with her and she looked a picture of health. She no longer wore lots of make-up and thick black eyeliner or painted her nails in luminous colours; she was very au naturel and it suited her. He'd expected her to sink into a deep depression once she realised that she'd thrown her life away, but he'd been very wrong. She had embraced this life 'on the run' wholeheartedly and was thriving on it. Henry wanted to make her happy; he wanted her to experience everything that he had.

'Henry?'

'Yes, Megan.'

'Are you staring at me again?'

'Yes, Megan.'

'I can tell, you know. I don't mind you having a perv over my body if it makes you feel better, but what would be even better was if you just actually came out and said exactly what it is you want.'

'And what do I want?'

'Me, of course. I don't blame you one bit. I know it's probably been a long time and you know I would like nothing more than for you to ravish my body. I like a good fuck now and again; you could stop being a gentleman for once and drag me into the bedroom.'

Henry grinned. 'That isn't very ladylike, Megan, and of course I would love nothing more than to drag you into the bedroom, but I can't and you know that; I don't want to ruin our friendship with a quick fuck.'

'Suit yourself but the offer still stands. If you're happy enough to perv over me then I'll let you get on with it, but when you decide enough is enough I'll be ready and willing.'

'Thank you, I'll keep that in mind should I no longer be able to contain myself.'

He stood up and went to get a notepad and pen. He wanted to write down some kind of plan. It would be better to put it into words than to just wing it. He could come up with something that would give Megan something to look forward to and keep his mind from wondering about how good it would feel to have her long legs wrapped around his.

* * *

A loud thud and a high-pitched scream jolted Will from his sleep. He had no idea where he was until he tried to move his feet and remembered he was tied to a bed in a cellar. It sounded as if Amelia had finally flipped. There was a lot of muffled shouting and another loud thud; this time a man's voice shouted out in pain. Will found himself rooting for the boyfriend. He wanted him to kick shit out of Amelia and then come and set him free. He had done nothing but sleep yet he was still tired and then he looked over at the bottle of water and cursed himself. They had probably been drugging him – what an idiot.

There was a lot more shouting and cursing and then the door slammed shut and he heard the sound of a car engine revving. It drove off at speed and he hoped that it was her inside it and that a big lorry was coming down the lane to meet her head-on. After five minutes the bolt slid over on the trapdoor and the light was turned on. Will squeezed his eyes shut and waited to see who it was. The figure ran down the stairs and for a second Will wondered if this was it, if he was going to kill him, but then the man lifted his finger to his lips.

'I think she's gone for a drive but she'll be back soon. I've had enough; it's over.'

Will strained to move away from him and the man looked shocked.

'Oh, God, no. Sorry, I don't mean it's over for you. I meant with her; I've had enough. She's a full-on psychopath. I'm going to untie you and lead you to the front door but she's taken the car so you'll have to walk, if that's OK. I'll wait here in case she comes back, then I can stall her to give you a chance to get away. I'm really sorry about all of this and I hope you're OK.'

Will nodded, not sure what to say. His hands and feet were untied and the guy reached out his hand to pull him up. Will wobbled at first but soon found his feet and looked at the man, who seemed genuinely remorseful.

'Thank you, I know it was all Amelia's idea and if it goes to court I'll make sure that they know you didn't have a choice and that she's a control freak who beat you whenever you didn't do as she asked.'

'Thanks, mate; you know I kept your phone. She told me to throw it in the lake but I couldn't. That's what she's just flipped out over. She found it in the boot of the car before, so hopefully your mates will be on the way to come and get you anyway. She said they would have pinged it or something like that. Best thing you can do is to find somewhere to hide not too far away.'

'I will. Are you going to be OK? Why don't you come with me?'

'No, I want you to get away from here and I'd rather take the flak from her so you have a better chance. Good luck.'

He led Will upstairs and to the back door. He opened it up and pushed him out.

'You need to go before she comes back.'

Will didn't need telling twice. He stumbled out into the sunlight and had to lift a hand to cover his eyes. He had been in the dark for a couple of days and it hurt to look at the light. He ran towards the gravel drive in case the man had only been messing around and was actually going to come after him and kill him, but his instinct told him that the poor bloke was in it over his head and needed as much help as him, especially once Amelia came back and saw what he'd done.

Will ran along the road for a while but he knew he had to get off it in case she came driving along. He saw a barn in a field and clambered over the gate. Slipping and falling, he landed on his ankle, which let out a loud crunch and he screamed in pain. Fucking hell, he didn't have time to break his leg. He dragged himself off the ground and, with tears running down his cheeks, he managed to hobble towards the barn. Even if he couldn't get inside it, he could hide around the back and wait for help to come. He fell against the door, the pain making him feel dizzy, and it opened enough that he could squeeze himself through the gap. It was cool and dark in there and he just hoped to God there wasn't a prize-winning bull inside it.

Will dropped to the floor to take the weight off his foot and grimaced as the room swam. He waited for his eyes to adjust to the darkness, thankful that it was empty. He breathed a sigh of relief: no bull – spiders he could cope with. And then he passed out.

1782

Father Sawyer finished his blessings and stepped away from Seth and Joss.

'Now then, let us go and pray for Betsy Baker, God rest her soul.'

He made the sign of the cross whenever he mentioned Betsy's name. Joss stood up and for the first time in weeks he felt better. He had never been a big believer in God but his soul felt lighter, if that was even possible. Seth looked at Joss and smiled, so he must be feeling the same. All three of them left the church and Joss led the way through the village to his cottage on the outskirts. As he walked towards it, he looked up to the bedroom window and gasped. He was sure he'd seen Betsy standing at the window, watching all three of them walking towards her, but she'd disappeared as soon it had registered in his brain that he'd seen her. He nudged Seth.

'Did you see her? She was watching us from the window up there.'

Seth's face paled and he shook his head. 'No, I didn't, thank God. Did she look angry?'

Joss shook his head. 'No, she looked so sad. I can't believe I'm feeling sorry for the ghost of the woman who killed my boys.'

The priest put his hand on Joss's shoulder. 'It's a trick, a devil's trick. She doesn't want us to bless her bones. She wants to be free to run amok and scare everyone to death. Take no notice and, whatever you do, if she appears to you do not look in her eyes.'

'Why?'

'Because her eyes are the portals to hell; she will invite you in and then drown you inside them and you'll be stuck with her for all of eternity.'

Joss considered those words for a moment and then he laughed. 'Come on now, surely you don't believe in any of that?'

'I don't believe in invisible forces bending the solid oak wood of a church door in front of my very eyes either, Joss, but I saw it happen. Never take anything for granted and never mock the forces of the Devil because they say God works in mysterious ways but the Devil works in devious ways and of that I'm positive.'

They stopped at the wooden gate to the cottage and paused for a minute whilst the priest said a prayer, then Joss pushed it open and they stepped in. Minutes ago they had been wiping the sweat from their brows, the sun was beating down so hard upon them, but as soon as all three of them were on the cottage grounds the sun disappeared behind a huge black cloud. Seth followed Joss, who walked across to the small outbuilding where he kept his garden spades. Joss took two of them out and handed one to Seth, who took it. Joss pointed to the uneven mound of soil on the vegetable bed and the priest pointed his finger. Joss nodded at him but, before he could dig the spade in, the priest held up his hand. Joss waited whilst he set about blessing the mound of soil.

The sky darkened and Seth lifted his head as the first heavy drop of rain fell onto his forehead. A huge crack of thunder echoed above them and the priest finished his prayer and, as both Seth and Joss began to dig as fast as they could, the heavens opened and water fell down onto them, making it hard to grip the spades, but they kept on going. Another crack of thunder made Joss look up to see Betsy's skeleton hanging from the porch. She was swaying in the wind and the rain, her bony fingers clawing at the rope around her neck. Joss let out a screech and Seth turned to look in the direction his friend was staring at but he couldn't see anything. Joss dropped his spade, his eyes fixated on the vision before him.

The priest stepped in front of Joss, breaking his gaze, and when he looked back she was gone. Joss couldn't speak but the priest nodded as if to say he knew; he'd seen it as well. The priest bent down and picked up the spade, handing it back to Joss, who took it and began to dig once more. Until the spade hit something hard and he knew it was Betsy.

He dropped to his knees, using his fingers to clear away the soil from her body. He was afraid of touching it but too scared to use the spade in case it did even more damage to her bones. Seth did the same and pretty soon the smell of putrefaction hit their nostrils and they lifted a hand to cover their noses. The priest crossed himself and stepped away from the hole it was so bad. He'd smelt bodies before but never anything like this; it was horrendous. Seth gagged and stopped digging but Joss continued. He wanted this to stop. He couldn't live looking over his shoulder and seeing her corpse wherever he went.

Finally he uncovered what was left of her and was surprised to see how well preserved she was, considering she had no coffin or shroud around her. Her face was pretty just as he remembered, with beautiful black hair and the palest of skin. Her lips were still pink and he wondered if her pale blue eyes were still the same. He looked down at her hands, which were skeletal; most of the flesh had rotted off them.

The priest stepped forward and recited his prayers. He handed

Joss a cross and told him to put it in her hand. Joss cringed at the thought of touching the rotten flesh but took the cross from him and bent down. Trying not to be sick, he pushed it in between her fingers – cold, sharp fingers that reached out and curled themselves around his arm and pulled him forward. They were so strong he could feel the bones digging into his flesh and he let out a scream. Her other hand reached out for him and she pulled him towards her and then her eyes flew open. Joss could hear Seth screaming and trying to pull him away from her but she was so strong and wouldn't let go; he could feel himself being dragged into the hole he'd dug and the smell was so strong he began to heave.

The priest ran towards him, sprinkling holy water all over both him and Betsy. He threw his Bible at her and it landed next to her head. Then he prayed in Latin, loud enough that only Betsy could hear him. Joss could hear nothing but the sound of the driving rain and Seth's screaming. Her grip on him relaxed as she lifted her hands to her ears to block out the priest's prayers and he felt himself being pulled back with such force that he tumbled onto the ground in a heap, landing on top of Seth. Both of them were panting, terrified of what would happen next, and they backed away from her grave.

Joss could hear Seth's sobs and held his hand out towards him. The boy took hold of it and they both prayed together. The rain stopped as suddenly as it had started and the black clouds melted away, leaving the sun to burn brightly and cast its warmth over them once more.

The priest nodded at them both. "Tis done. I've blessed her and sent her on her way as best I could. I think she's gone for good but it's hard to say. She was powerful, though, and didn't want to leave. That was a struggle, one like I've never known, but for now all is peaceful. I suggest that you bury her again and move out of here, Joss, because as long as you live here then she has a reason to come back. I don't think she'll be able to follow you anywhere else but I can't say for definite. She wanted you more than anything in this life, didn't she?'

'Thank you, Father. I don't know what to say. You're right; that was the problem. Betsy wanted me from the day I met her and she didn't want anyone to get in her way. I'm going to board this house up and live in my parents' farmhouse and as long as I live I'll not let anyone move in there.'

They worked quickly, covering Betsy's remains once more, but this time the sun kept on shining and Joss didn't feel the need to look over his shoulder and see her hanging behind him. Once they had done that, Joss asked Seth to come inside the house with him to collect what few belongings he had that were left in there. Seth followed him inside but he refused to go upstairs and waited in the kitchen for Joss to come back down.

Joss had an armful of clothes and two stuffed bears tucked underneath them; around his neck was a silver-coloured chain with a cross on it. Seth recognised it as his dead wife's necklace that she'd always worn and his eyes filled with tears for Joss, who had lost everyone near to him. Joss smiled at him and they left the house and walked up the road towards the farmhouse. Joss didn't turn around to look at his cottage – he had everything he could possibly need. He would send a couple of farmhands to board up the windows and doors tomorrow.

Chapter 22

Jake was on the patio, having an animated conversation with whoever was on the other end of the radio. Annie was half watching him and pouring coffee out for Lily and Tom, who had finally come downstairs. They both looked a lot better for having a good sleep and Annie wished she could do the same.

Jake thundered back in through the patio doors. 'We're on – come on. They're getting ready to storm the house they think Will is in. Kav said you can come, as long as you sit in the back of the car, and if you move so much as an eyelid you're suspended.'

'What are we waiting for? I promise I'll be good.'

Annie hugged both Tom and Lily and ran for the front door, closely followed by Jake. He clicked the patrol car open and she jumped in the passenger seat.

'Do you know where this address is?'

He reeled off a country lane with only a couple of houses dotted along it and Annie nodded.

'Yes, it's not too far away, about three miles. I can't believe it. I hope Will's OK and they haven't hurt him.'

'I'm sure he'll be fine. He has you to put up with.'

Annie was too nervous to actually give him his customary dig in the ribs for being cheeky.

'I need to see him. I've missed him so much.'

Within minutes they were at the entrance to the road and Jake had turned the lights off. There were several cars and vans parked in the car park, which filled the corner of the street opposite. The task force sergeant was being briefed by DS Nick Tyler and Jake told Annie to wait in the car. He got out and jogged over to them and for once Annie did as she was told, not daring to disobey Kav's orders even though it was killing her.

Ten minutes later, Jake came back. 'They're going in and we're to wait here. Apparently, there is no vehicle outside the address so one of them isn't there. Amelia is the only one insured on the car so I'm taking it she isn't home. They want to go in and do a sweep, arrest whoever her accomplice is and get Will out of there, hopefully before she comes back, and then we'll all clear off and wait for her to park up before they arrest her.'

Annie nodded. 'Sounds like a plan to me. God, I hate that woman; I want to kick the shit out of her.'

'I know you do, but we're to stay here and keep observations for her car. You're the only one who really knows what she looks like so if she turns into the road tell me and I'll shout it up. Who knows, we might be the ones to arrest her if she tries to run and then, my little psycho friend, I'll let you have a couple of kicks and punches before we cuff her. Deal?'

'Deal. Have I told you lately that I love you, Jake?'

'No, I don't think you have.'

It was hard watching the armed officers all getting into vehicles, ready to go into the house, which was half a mile down the road along a quiet stretch. Annie wanted more than anything to be with them but here was a good place to be. The cars sped off and Annie crossed the fingers on both hands, praying that Will would be OK. There was a brief silence on Jake's radio and then all hell broke loose.

The three-man door-entry team jumped from the back of the van with the battering ram and with two swings it was put through and they were inside. Luke, who was playing on his Xbox, dropped the controllers and put his hands in the air; two of them ran and handcuffed him. He didn't resist once, relieved it was over. They were shouting to him about Will but there were too many voices and he couldn't understand, so he pointed to the trapdoor. Two more officers opened it and went down in the cellar, to see the bed and the ropes and chains but no Will. DS Tyler came inside the house.

'I'm arresting you on suspicion of false imprisonment and trying to secure money by blackmail. Now, where is Will Ashworth?'

'I let him go about half an hour ago. He's safe and he should be somewhere not too far away. I thought you guys would have found him by now.'

'What do you mean, you let him go?'

'I untied him and told him to run for it before that crazy bitch Amelia comes home. When she sees you lot she's going to lose the plot big time. Can you put me in the back of a car or something because she'll blame me and when she loses her temper it hurts, a lot.'

Two officers escorted him out to the van and put him in the cage, where he slumped back and sighed.

Annie saw the blue car turn into the road and her eyes fixed on the blonde woman who was driving it.

'Shit, she's there. Should we follow her?'

Amelia turned her head and stared straight at Annie. Immediately stopping the car, she began to turn it around in the opposite direction. Jake turned the ignition on and followed her. She floored the pedal and he sped after her. Annie shouted up for assistance on the car radio set as he put the sirens on and went for it. He followed her for half a mile until she reached a turn-off onto one of the quieter roads but she took it too fast and lost control of the car. It spun around and smacked into a stationary car full of passengers. Jake and Annie both jumped out of the patrol car, Jake running to check the car full of people.

He nodded at Annie. 'She's all yours.'

Annie took off, running towards the blue car. The driver's door opened and a dazed Amelia saw Annie rushing towards her and took off running. Annie, who hated running with a passion, had a burst of energy from somewhere inside and caught up with Amelia, throwing herself at her, knocking her to the ground. Annie dropped her full weight on top of her and punched her a couple of times on the side of the head and in her ribs. Jake arrived out of breath and with his handcuffs. He bent down and smacked them across Amelia's hands, locking them on so she couldn't move. He stuck his arm under hers and lifted her to her feet.

'You're under arrest.'

'Did you see that? She hit me. That's police assault.'

'No, I didn't see anything except you running away from the scene of a fail-to-stop accident and assaulting my colleague. So, like I said, you're under arrest for kidnap, blackmail, police assault, failing to stop at a road traffic accident and resisting arrest. Anything else you'd like to add on to that impressive little list of charges?'

Annie had to suppress her giggle as Amelia spat at Jake. Jake wiped his cheek then turned to Annie and grinned. 'Aw, it's just like the old days, and who said you wouldn't miss working with me?'

He winked at her and dragged a screaming Amelia back to his car, taking great pleasure in throwing her inside. He let Annie slam the door shut on her and held his hand up for a high five.

'Come on, let's go and find your man.'

They drove the short distance back to the cottage and the assorted police cars and vans outside. Annie jumped out. There was no sign of Will and she felt her heart freeze. The panic must have shown on her face as DS Nick Tyler came jogging over to her.

'He's not here. We've searched from top to bottom. He was here; there is evidence that someone was kept captive in the cellar, but he's not here now. According to the boyfriend, Luke, he let him go around forty minutes ago because he was sick of Amelia, who has been the one to mastermind it all. I've called for the dog handlers, who will be here any minute, and then we'll do a search of the area. He can't have got far and the trail will be pretty fresh.'

'Where is he then? Why did he not go to someone for help?'

'He might have been disorientated, and there aren't many houses along here.'

'Or he might be injured?'

No one spoke, not wanting to upset Annie. She turned to Jake.

'Come on, I'm not waiting for the dog handler to arrive. I'll go left and you go right; check all the fields and any buildings.'

'Yes, boss.'

Annie walked off, glad to be on her own because her eyes were brimming with tears and she wouldn't cry in front of a bunch of grown men, even though she wanted to. She walked the short distance to the next field and peered over the gate. The grass was quite long but there was no sign of Will lying in the middle of it. She jumped the gate to make sure he wasn't hiding against the hedgerow but it was empty. Climbing back over, she walked along until she came to the next field, which was even more overgrown than the last one but this one had a ramshackle barn in the middle. Her heart raced and she climbed the gate and took off, running towards the barn and calling his name. She reached the door and peered through the gap. 'Will, are you in there?'

A groan made her heart soar with joy and she squeezed through the gap into the darkness. It was gloomy and she blinked a couple of times to adjust her eyes.

'Well, if you aren't the prettiest sight I've ever seen, Officer Graham.'

Annie turned to see Will on the floor. The part of his face she could see through the thick stubble looked ashen.

'Oh, thank God for that.'

She ran across to him, falling to her knees to hug him. He squeezed her back then groaned.

'Did they hurt you? Are you OK?'

He laughed. 'Well, apart from knocking me out and a few sneaky punches from my loving sister, not really. I fell over the gate and think I've broken my bloody ankle; some great escape that was.'

Annie laughed. 'It's good enough for me. I've never been so scared of losing you, Will. I've been a nervous wreck.'

'What, even more scared than fighting off a serial killer and sending scary ghosts back to hell?'

'Yes, far more scary than any of that. It's not the same when it's you who's the one doing the fighting; you don't think about it. I love you so much it makes my eyes water just thinking about it.'

Will sighed. 'Good, because, broken ankle or not, I'm marrying you in seven weeks and you're stuck with me forever.'

Annie kissed him then broke away. She pulled out her phone and rang Jake, giving him directions to where they were and asking for an ambulance.

'No ambulance; I can hobble or you can get the gentle giant to carry me to the car and he can drive me to A & E.'

'You need checking over.'

'Yes, but I'd much rather sit in the back of the car next to you than have to lie in the back of an ambulance. You're not the only one who is hard as nails; I have a reputation to uphold, you know.'

Annie giggled. 'Come on then, tough guy, let's see if we can get you out of this creepy barn and into the daylight.'

She helped him to his feet and he only swore a couple of times. Before they could get out of the door, Jake was outside. There was no need to squeeze through it this time because Jake just pulled the entire door off its hinges and threw it to one side.

'Jesus Jake, don't ruin the door or anything, will you?'

'Am I glad to see you; I mean you look like shit but still, you'd look even worse if you were dead.'

Annie glared at him and he mouthed 'sorry' to her.

'What the fuck is that beard? You look like some hobo. I hope you're going to have a shave before the wedding because, as much as I love you, even I wouldn't marry you with that on your face.'

'Thanks, Jake, believe it or not, they didn't offer me showers and the use of a razor whilst I was tied up for days. Anyway, what took you so long? I thought you were a copper; aren't you supposed to be able to solve crimes? You'll never get into CID at that rate.'

Jake laughed. 'Sorry, Will, I'm glad to see you're OK even if you do look like shit. In fact, can I take a photo to show everyone that you're not always so naturally gorgeous?'

Annie gave Jake his customary poke in the ribs and he swore under his breath.

'Stop messing about and help me carry him to the car. He's got a broken ankle.'

'Sorry, I didn't realise. I thought you were just going for the sympathy card, you know, milking it for every penny.'

Annie looked as if she was about to explode and Jake grinned.

'I best shut up. Come on, William, let's be having you.'

And with that Jake scooped Will into his arms and carried him across the field.

'Don't you be getting jealous now, Annie; do we make a handsome couple?'

Annie laughed and the tears she had battled to keep inside rolled down her cheeks, but this time they were tears of happiness.

Chapter 23

The cottage was almost finished. The builders had been told to work in pairs, which was fine by them, but they wouldn't for all the money in the world work in there alone. They hadn't been near for three days because the last time they were here Eric and Callum had both heard the whispering and the awful sound of long sharp fingernails scraping across the glass. It was Callum who had been running upstairs to finish painting the bedroom window who'd actually seen the woman in the white dress standing at the window he needed to paint. She had her back to him and was looking outside at someone or something. He had jumped but then thought it was Annie for a moment because they both had dark shoulder-length hair. He'd said hello but there was no reply and it was only when she slowly turned and he noticed that her hands were nothing but bone that he'd dropped his paintbrush and screamed.

He'd run out of the house and into the front garden, closely followed by Eric, who had no idea what was happening but he knew enough not to be in the house on his own.

'What's the matter with you?'

Callum pointed to the upstairs window. 'Woman … there's a dead woman in the bedroom.'

They both looked up and saw the pretty face of Betsy Baker grinning down at them and then she was gone.

'She didn't look dead. Have you been sniffing paint fumes?'

'I'm telling you now, women who are not dead have skin on their fingers; hers were just skeletal, with these long pointed nails. I'm not going back in there on my own. What do you think she wants?'

'Shit, I have no idea and I don't want to know either.'

'We need to get it finished. I've done the last of the grouting and you only had that window frame to paint. I'll stay with you while you paint it and then we're out of here. I'm ringing Paul to tell him, to tell Annie. She definitely can't live here with that scary woman hanging around.'

* * *

Will was being kept in hospital, much to his disgust. His ankle was broken and it needed a plate putting in. They had operated on him six hours after he'd been admitted and Annie had stayed the whole time, repaying the favour he'd so often done for her. What a pair they were. Only Will could survive being kidnapped and then break his own ankle trying to escape. She grinned to herself as she fed money into the coffee machine and waited for her latte to be poured. Tom and Lily had both been, and there had been lots of hugs and tears. Tom had looked very sheepish when he'd first walked in, but Will had hugged his dad and told him the past was the past and it didn't change anything.

Before they'd left, Tom had taken Annie to one side. 'Do you think I'll be able to speak to her?'

'Probably, she was remanded into custody, though, so you would have to go to Styal Prison and it depends if she wants to see you. Why don't you write her a letter, then if she wants to talk she can send you a visiting order.'

Tom hugged her. 'Thank you, Annie. I don't know what to

do but I know I can't just ignore her. If it's true and she is my daughter I can't turn my back on her, no matter what she's done. I don't want her in my life but I will pay her solicitor's fees and give her some money for when she is released so she can start a new life. I'm too old to have a guilty conscience.'

'You're a good man, Tom, and I know where Will gets it from. That's very kind of you. Let's hope she appreciates it.'

Lily had wandered out and linked her arm through Tom's. 'Come on, let's get you home. You've had far too much excitement for this month. I want you resting so you're feeling a hundred per cent for the wedding. I can't believe it's so close! Annie, I've booked you and me in for a spa day; after all this stress we need it. Tom, you and Will can babysit each other for the day and have a proper catch-up.'

'That sounds amazing; thank you, Lily.'

Annie hugged them both and walked them out to the car park. She watched them drive away then turned to go back inside the hospital, which was fast becoming her second home. Well, no more; she was keeping out of trouble and so was Will. She'd already put her leave in for the wedding but had decided to take some unpaid time off work to be with Will. Just the two of them could spend some time together and then move into the cottage. Her phone rang and she answered it.

'Annie, it's Paul. Look, the lads are refusing point-blank to go back inside the house now. They saw a woman in there and thought it was you, but …'

He paused and Annie felt a ball of dread forming in her stomach.

'But it wasn't you because she had a face but her fingers were just bone. I know it sounds stupid and they sound as if they've been overdosing on the old cannabis, but I swear to God they're good lads who've been working for me for years. I've never heard them talk like this before or, to be honest, refuse to go in and finish a job because, trust me, we've worked in some right shit-holes.'

'No, it's fine. I believe them. Tell them thank you and not to worry. I know who she is, although I'm not too sure what it is she wants except maybe her house to herself. I'll sort it out. I'll let you know when it's been done so they can finish off. Thank you.'

'As long as you know what you're doing, love. I've never seen grown men with faces so white; I'd have taken the piss out of them if they hadn't been so deadly serious. Be careful, whatever you do.'

He ended the call and she sighed. What had she just said about taking some time out, away from all the drama? If she didn't sort Betsy Baker out once and for all they would never be able to live in their dream home and she wasn't about to let some two-hundred-year-old ghost take that away from her. She sipped on her latte, which was still steaming hot, and then went back outside to phone Father John.

'It's Annie.'

'Evening, my lovely. How is Will? Fabulous news that you got him back almost in one piece. Lily phoned to tell me earlier.'

'He's in theatre, having a plate put in his ankle, but he's fine, apart from a sore head and an aching foot, thankfully. John, we need to sort Betsy Baker out; the builders are refusing to go back inside because they saw her in the bedroom.'

'Right, then. I've dug a hole more than big enough to put her in; as long as she's in a box, contained, I think it will work. I've had to come up with some cock-and-bull story about someone's dearly beloved pet that has died but they didn't ask any further questions so it's all good at this end. I've blessed the box and a cross for you to put in it and there's a bottle of my special holy water. If you and Jake dig her up and bring her to me I'll do the rest. Is that OK?'

'Perfect. As soon as Will is out of surgery I'll drive straight up to yours with Jake and collect the box. What time will it be light until? I'd rather not do this in the dark.'

'Probably about ten-thirty. I'll be ready for you. Give Will my best and I'll see you soon.'

'Thank you, John, I will.'

Before she could phone Jake, as if by magic he appeared, walking across the grass towards where she was standing.

'I need you.'

'Not here, in front of everyone. Have you no self-control, woman?'

'As if, but seriously, we need to do it tonight.'

'Erm … am I being dim or what? What do we need to do tonight?'

'Dig up Betsy Baker and take her to St Mary's, where Father John is going to bless her and give her a proper funeral.'

'Oh, is that all? And here was me thinking you wanted my body, but what you want is for me to help you dig up the skeleton of a two-hundred-year-old serial killer who is scary as fuck then drive her to the church to be buried. Well, you know how to show a guy a good time. I dread to think what you have in store for Will. How is he?'

'He should be coming out of surgery any time soon. Don't say a word to him. He doesn't know anything about it and I don't want him to because he won't let me do it. But if we don't we'll never be rid of her. Please, will you help me?'

She fluttered her eyelids at him and he pushed her arm.

'Oh, go on then. You know I'm a sucker for a pretty lady. Is it going to be dangerous, though? I mean, that Shadow Man was scary as hell; I proper shit myself for months after that.'

'I don't know – possibly. I don't think she'll come quietly but I don't have a choice because if they actually take the time to exhume her properly she's never going to get a proper burial for months, maybe years, and that means she'll be tied to my house forever.'

A nurse called Annie's name and she turned to see her, smiling.

'Will's back on the ward now if you want to come and see him for five minutes.'

Annie and Jake followed her up to the surgical ward, where

she led them to the small private room Will was in. He opened one eye. 'Take me home.'

'No, I will not; you need to rest up tonight. I'll rescue you tomorrow but, unlike someone I know, I'll actually keep my promise.' She winked at him.

'True, but technically that wasn't my fault. Am I forgiven?'

She walked over and kissed him. 'Yes. I love you. Now get some sleep and I'll see you tomorrow.'

Jake patted his arm and Will closed his eyes.

'Don't forget about me.'

'As if. See you in the morning.'

They left him drifting off to sleep and made their way to Jake's car.

'Am I to tell Alex what we're doing – that we're going to dig up Mary Rose, or whatever her name is?'

'No, I don't think so; he panics too much. Tell him you're taking me to pick up some stuff and you'll be home in a couple of hours.'

Jake sent the text then looked at her. 'I hope we're doing the right thing. I haven't got a good feeling about this. I don't know about you, but I'm man enough to admit that I'm scared and I don't want to go to prison when we've just been given the date that we can bring little Alice home.'

'Aw, you've called her Alice; what made you pick that name?'

'Alex chose it. He said he likes old-fashioned names. Do you like it?'

'I love it. I knew an Alice and she was a wonderful, strong, courageous woman.'

'Good. I wanted to call her Annie but then I didn't want to curse her with all your bad luck – one Annie in my life is more than enough.'

'You're right; you couldn't call a kid Annie but it was a lovely sentiment, thank you. You know, if I'm honest, I'm scared too, Jake, but we really don't have any other choice.'

'Trust you to buy a house that was haunted by a psychopathic witch.'

'She wasn't a witch, just a murderer.'

'Oh, well, that makes it all right then. I don't know what I'm so worried about.'

'I'll make it up to you, I promise.'

'I should hope so. You can start by not getting involved in anything remotely violent or scary for at least the next six months. I swear you're turning my hair grey. Alex found a grey hair last night and it's all your fault.'

'I'll try my best. I'm not exactly chuffed about it all. I'd love a quiet life. I can't remember much of what my life was like before I met Mike so it must have been pretty normal.'

Jake shut up; he didn't want her remembering the bad times. They sat in comfortable silence all the way to St Mary's presbytery, where a fully robed Father John was pacing up and down the garden.

'See, he should be ready to retire and you've got him working overtime as well.'

'Shut up, Jake; don't you think I feel bad enough as it is?'

John went inside the house and came back carrying a large plastic box that had a sheet inside and a wooden cross. He opened the boot and put the box in it. Jake wound the window down but it was Annie who spoke.

'Thank you, John. I'm sorry to drag you into this.'

'Annie, you saved my life; it's the least I can do to repay the favour. I'm just a bit jumpy tonight and I'm not sure why.'

Annie knew why but didn't say it out loud; she felt the same. Her stomach was churning so much she wanted to throw up but she hadn't eaten anything for hours so there was nothing inside to bring up. There was one thing: she'd never been so thin so her wedding dress should fit like a dream.

'We'll be back soon.'

John leant into the car and made the sign of the cross on

her forehead, blessing her. Then he did the same to Jake, who nodded his approval. He passed Annie a bottle. She didn't need to ask what it was; she knew it would be holy water John had blessed. Jake wasn't really into religion but he would take all the help he could get.

'Remember to stay close to each other. You are both stronger than you think. Whatever she may say or do, ignore her. It's not going to be easy because she might put up a fight but get her here and I'll do the rest.'

Annie watched the colour drain from Jake's face and knew exactly how he felt. She thanked John and nodded at Jake, who started the engine.

'That's if we make it here; you do know if we were to get stopped with a plastic storage box containing a skeleton we'd be in deep shit, don't you?'

'Look on the bright side; whose beat is it from the cottage to here?'

'I don't know.'

'Mine, you stupid sod, and I'm off sick so no one will be covering it. What could possibly go wrong?'

Jake declined to answer that question and they drove to the cottage in silence. He noticed that Annie kept fiddling with the tiny gold cross on a chain around her neck. If she was scared then it was serious. As they turned into the lane that led to the cottage the sun disappeared behind a huge black cloud, shrouding everything in shadow.

'She knows we're coming for her.'

Jake gulped but carried on driving towards the freshly painted mint-green gate that led to the front garden. He parked the car on the grass verge and got out. Annie followed him. She walked around to the back of the car to get the plastic box out. She lifted the boot and was taking the box out when the lid slammed shut, narrowly missing her arm and hand. She dropped it back inside, snatching her hand away, and turned to the house.

'So this is how you want to play it, Betsy Baker? I'm not afraid of you so you'd best remember this. I told you before: this is no longer your home; it belongs to me now and it isn't big enough for both of us to live in.'

There was a huge rumble of thunder in the distance and Jake looked as if he wanted to get back in the car and drive off but he stood his ground.

'Can you see her, Annie? Where is she?'

'Not yet but she's watching. Please can you hold the boot open while I take out the box?'

Jake lifted the boot and held it with both hands, expecting a sudden weight to force it down, but nothing happened and he breathed out. Annie took the box and they stepped into the front garden as a crack of thunder echoed around the cottage. She put the box down and studied the ground, trying to work out exactly where the vegetable garden had been. She closed her eyes and went back to the vision of the handsome man with a grief-stricken face digging a hole.

Her feet carried her to where she thought the exact spot was and she shouted to Jake, 'There are some spades in the shed; go and get them.'

He ran across to the small outbuilding and opened the door. It was dark inside. He reached in to grab the spades and felt something cold and hard as skeletal fingers wrapped themselves around his wrist. He screamed and snatched his hand back, turning to Annie.

'I can't … there's something in there; it touched me.'

Annie strode over, leant in and grabbed the spades. 'Don't be scared of her, Jake; it's what she wants.'

She took the tools and walked back to where she'd left the box, Jake following. She handed him a spade. They both began to dig at the same time, just as the first heavy drops of rain fell. Within seconds it turned into a heavy downpour, soaking them both through to the skin. Annie kept on digging, even though it was hard to grip the spade and see through the rivulets of water running down her forehead and into her eyes. She lifted her arm to wipe her face and caught a glimpse of Betsy, who was now in the bedroom, her face pressed against the glass of the window with what was left of her hands flat against it. Her mouth was open in a silent scream that only Annie could hear and it ripped through her mind like a hurricane.

Annie lifted her hands to her ears and shouted, 'Stop that now! I'm telling you in the name of the Lord, Betsy, you have to stop this.'

Jake paused. 'Stop digging?'

She shook her head. 'No, keep digging. I meant for Betsy to stop screaming; she's deafening me.'

Annie sang the only hymn she knew. 'All things bright and beautiful, all creatures great and small …' Over and over again in her head so it blocked out the noise, then she picked up the spade and continued to dig. There was an almighty crack above them and a brilliant white flash of lightning illuminated the sky. Jake's spade hit something hard and he shuddered, knowing fine well what it would be. He paused but Annie kept on going until she could see the dirty yellow of Betsy's skeleton.

Jake sensed movement behind him and swung around to see a pretty young woman hanging from the front porch of Annie's cottage. He couldn't move because she was swinging from side to side and grinning at him. She lifted a skeletal hand to the rope around her neck and Jake shuddered. Instinctively, he wanted to run and cut her down like he would for anyone and he found himself walking towards her. Annie looked up to see Jake, his eyes fixed on something only he could see, and she ran to grab him.

'What is it? What can you see?'

'She's there and she's choking, Annie … We have to help her. We can't leave her hanging like that.'

'She's not real, Jake. Well, she's not alive, and we can't help her – she's dead and has been dead for a very long time. It's all a trick; she knows that she can't stay and she's doing everything she can to stop us.'

Annie pulled him back towards the hole and he looked back over his shoulder but she'd gone. He looked down and saw that a ribcage and legs had been uncovered.

'Open the box, Jake.'

Annie knelt down and scraped the last of the soil away with her fingers until she was faced with the whole of Betsy Baker's skeleton. There was a broken cross next to her hand. Apart from that, she was complete; her long black hair was still attached to her skull. Annie couldn't help but notice how long her fingernails were. No wonder she liked scraping them along things; they were lethal weapons. The storm raged above their heads and the rain lashed them both. Annie leant in to try and lift her out and felt the skeletal fingers gripping her arm. Those sharp nails dug into her flesh, dragging her down. Annie lost her balance and tumbled into the shallow grave on top of Betsy's skeleton. Annie opened her mouth to scream and the bony fingers wrapped themselves around her neck, sharp nails digging into the soft flesh and drawing blood.

Jake watched in horror as Annie thrashed around on top of the skeleton. He couldn't see the bony fingers that were wrapped around her neck and didn't know what to do. He knew something was wrong; the only thing he could think of was to take the bottle of holy water out of the box to throw it all over Annie and that scary bag of bones. He emptied the bottle then threw it to one side and leant down, taking hold of Annie by her armpits. With one almighty tug he yanked her with all his force out of the hole, bleeding and covered in mud, and they landed in a heap on the ground.

'Fucking hell, Annie, what was that about?'

Annie couldn't speak she was so shocked, and pointed to the skeleton and the box. Jake grimaced but knew what she meant and leant down into the hole and scooped up the now broken bits of skeleton and put them into the plastic box; he picked up her arms first then her skull. Once they were inside the box Annie leant in and helped him scoop up the rest of it, whilst the rain kept on pouring and the thunder kept rolling. Eventually they had every piece of her and the broken cross. Annie picked up the almost empty bottle and sprinkled the rest of the holy water all over the remains and then Jake slammed the plastic lid down onto them.

They carried it towards the car and put it into the boot, where Jake took the tow rope and wound it around the box as many times as it would go before knotting it and slamming the boot down. Annie got into the car, not realising how much her hands were trembling until she tried to slide the cover back on the sun visor to look in the mirror at her face. Jake clambered in and started the engine.

'Oh, my God … how? I mean, just how? It's not even possible, is it? And you're bleeding; Jesus Christ, that thing has scratched up your neck. You're going to need a tetanus injection. When's the last time you had one? I can't believe it.'

Annie opened the glove compartment and took some tissues out to wipe away some of the blood and soil from her face.

Jake put his foot down; he didn't want that thing in his car for any longer than it had to be. 'What if she haunts my car? Alex will go mental if every time he gets in it there's a dead woman sitting in the back, trying to choke us all to death.'

Finally Annie smiled, snapping herself out of the shock that had been trying to take over. She still couldn't speak but inside her head she kept reciting the Lord's Prayer over and over again. She didn't even complain about the speed Jake was driving through the country lanes to get to Father John. Annie wondered if she'd ever speak again, to be honest. There was a loud thump from the boot of the car and Jake looked into the rear-view mirror.

'Please tell me I just ran a dog over and it's not the dead woman in the box trying to escape.'

He put his foot down and drove, in his own words, like a

maniac to get to the church, glad the roads were quiet, with no slow-moving traffic to hold him up or any buses to run into and kill them all instantly. Finally, the church spire loomed in sight and both of them let out a sigh of relief. There was no more banging from the boot and Jake screeched the car to a halt, almost crashing through the church gates.

Father John came running over, took one look at Annie and crossed himself. 'Come on, no time to lose; let's get her buried.'

Jake got out of the car and put his hand on the boot. It was freezing cold to his touch and he withdrew his fingers, leaving fingerprints on the paintwork.

Annie shook her head. 'No way; we've come this far. We have to finish it.'

She opened the boot and reached in to get hold of the box, which was frozen. Jake took the other side and they followed Father John, carrying Betsy Baker to her final resting place. The box got heavier with every step they took and Jake, who was not the smallest of guys, was sweating with the exertion. Annie wanted to drop the box and forget about the whole thing, forget she'd ever heard of Betsy bloody Baker, but then she thought about Will and how he'd looked to find them the perfect family home and she decided that she wouldn't let some jealous murdering ghost stop them from living there.

She heaved the box up and smiled at Jake. 'Come on; we can do this.'

Father John stopped in front of them at the back of the church next to the deep hole that he'd dug last night. With one last effort they heaved the box over the hole and let it fall into it. It landed on its lid, which was perfect. It would make it even harder for her to escape from her consecrated grave. Father John wasted no time and recited the burial prayers that she should have had when she'd been buried two hundred and thirty-two years ago, then he dropped a rosary onto the box for good measure and nodded at Jake to begin filling in the hole. It was all done in record time and Jake had never worked so hard or so fast in all his life. Annie, who was leaning against the church wall, prayed the whole time for Betsy's soul, relieved it was finally over.

Jake spoke first. 'Is that it? Do you think we're safe now? Because she was one angry woman for a dead bird.'

'I don't know … I hope so. What do you think, John?'

'Let's see, shall we? I believe so, but I'm not the expert here. If things don't improve we might have to call the bishop and request an exorcist from the Vatican, Annie, but I think we may have done the trick.'

The setting sun broke through the clouds and the warmth of it felt good on Jake and Annie's wet faces. Father John wrapped his arms around both of their shoulders and led them away from the grave towards the presbytery.

'Come on, my little ghostbusters, I have a pan of hot chocolate ready to warm up and a huge Victoria sponge cake that needs eating. You both look like you need an energy boost, and we can get you cleaned up, Annie.'

Jake nodded his approval. 'Good, I'm glad you can get her cleaned up because she looks as scary as poor old Betsy Baker.'

Annie leant her arm around John to dig Jake in the ribs.

'Ouch.'

Chapter 24

Henry had a plan. It had taken him all day to figure out where he could find Megan the kind of victim she longed for and it had come to him when he was reading the local paper. He had thought about it long and hard. He came out of his bedroom to see Megan absorbed in reading the paper that had inspired him to commit a murder and that she had become so addicted to.

'I can't believe this; for a small town, there sure is a lot of shit happening here.'

'Why, what's happened now?'

'Some copper was kidnapped and held hostage, taken from the hospital after coming out from visiting his girlfriend who'd been in an accident. Talk about bad luck.'

He sat opposite her and she pushed the newspaper towards him. He picked it up and smiled at the grainy photo in the corner that caught his eye. If it wasn't his fallen angel, Annie Graham, staring back at him with concern etched across her face. There was also a picture of her boyfriend on crutches. This was a turn-up for the books; those two were bad luck magnets, if ever such a thing existed.

'What are you smiling at?'

'Nothing, Megan; it's just an old friend.'

'Who, the copper that was kidnapped? Was he the one that caught you, Henry?'

'Not really, he's more of an acquaintance. No, it's the woman in the corner, his girlfriend. She's also a policewoman; we go back a long way.'

'Really? Henry, you dark horse. You never told me you went out with a copper. I bet she was mortified when you flipped and started killing everyone.'

Henry nodded and pushed the paper away. He didn't want to tell Megan too much. 'I've spent a lot of time thinking today about what you want to do.'

'And?'

'I want you to show me this barn later, just before it gets dark. If it's as secluded as you say we could maybe use it once, just to satisfy your needs. But then we don't do anything else for months; I don't want to get caught.'

Megan stood up and launched herself at him, landing on his lap.

'Thank you, Henry! I'm so excited. I promise I won't mess this up. What are we going to do?'

'Well, that depends on you, Megan. Man or woman? Do you want a quick kill or torture?'

'Can I think about it? I mean, I've thought about it but I want to make sure it's right, that my first is everything that I've been dreaming about.'

'Take as long as you want and when you're ready we'll do it.'

'I think I'd like to get a woman, you know, the ones who always think they're better than everyone else. Wear smart dresses and designer shoes for work but can't actually walk around in them. Someone like that. Oh, and they definitely have to have long hair that they really love and are always flicking it around and running their fingers through it.'

'Why?'

'Because I told you – I hated the girls like that at school; they used to think they were so much better than me and they made my life a misery. I want to gag whoever it is and cut all their hair off whilst they are watching.'

'I'm glad that you didn't need a long time to think about it then; I'd have hated for you to dither around for weeks wondering if you should do it or not.'

Megan ground her hips against Henry's thighs. She bent down and kissed him full on the lips. Henry tried to resist but years of pent-up passion bubbled inside him and he pulled her as close to him as he could. He muttered, 'Just this once.'

'Yes, Henry, just this once.'

Before she silenced him with her mouth once again.

* * *

Annie came down from the bathroom wearing John's faded Rolling Stones T-shirt and a pair of his jogging bottoms. She'd thrown her clothes into the bin. They were tattered and torn and would forever remind her of her fight with Betsy Baker. Her neck was a mess of scratches and bruises, which she had cleaned up, but it was smarting. She sat down and tucked into a slice of cake and sipped her huge mug of hot chocolate, too tired and still in shock to make polite conversation. She listened to John as he chatted about the latest gossip in the parish and was grateful to him for trying to lighten their mood. Grateful for anything that would help to block out the memories of that cold, muddy grave that had now embedded itself into her mind.

When she'd finished, Annie stood up and Jake followed both of them, anxious to get home. 'Thank you John; it's me who is now in your debt. Please let me know if you have any problems with her.'

'Bless you, but I'm pretty sure she'll stay buried this time. What about the cottage? Are you going back to check on it tonight? If not, I would very much like to come and bless the whole house tomorrow, if I may.'

'I don't know about going back right now. I think I've had enough for one night. If we do and she's still hanging there from my front porch I think I'll end up getting sectioned.'

'Fuck that, Annie. Pardon me, Father. I'm not going anywhere near your house unless it's daylight. I've seen enough of ghosts to last me a lifetime. Let's go home. Why don't you sleep at mine tonight then you can go collect Will in the morning? I'm at work but Alex isn't; he'll drop you off and then you can drive Will's car home and you know what your first job is when you get home.'

'What?'

'Sort your car insurance out because being your chauffeur is almost as dangerous as signing up to be a CIA assassin. It's far too stressful for a man my age.'

John laughed. 'You do make me laugh; now, you two take care of each other. You're both very special.'

They left. Annie hugged John before she walked down the steps past the beautiful roses that bordered the path to the gate. He waved and shut the door.

Annie pushed her arm through Jake's. 'You know, one day we'll be able to write a book about our adventures and then we'll both be millionaires.'

'I think you're right. The only problem is: will we live long enough to get it published, with your bad luck?'

'Of course we will; we were destined for great things, you and me, Jake Simpson. We just haven't figured out what they are.'

'I think you've found your calling, Annie, but I'd rather you kept me out of it. At this rate I'll be totally grey by the end of the year or maybe dead. I want to settle down and live a nice quiet life with my little family. I'll tell you what I do need, though – an ice-cold glass of something expensive and strong to help me sleep, otherwise I'll have nightmares.'

They got into Jake's car and he drove away, this time much slower and sticking to the speed limit. He didn't want to push his luck twice in one night; he didn't know how many lives he had left.

Annie laid her head back against the seat, closing her eyes. Her neck was smarting from the scratches and she would ring the doctor tomorrow for a tetanus injection. Then she would be picking Will up and taking him home to bed, where the pair of them could do nothing but order pizza and sleep for a couple of days. It seemed like forever since they'd slept in the same bed. Annie dozed off and was surprised when Jake shook her.

'Come on, sleepyhead, we're at my house.'

She sat up and wiped her mouth.

'Don't worry, you only snored a little and you never drooled once.'

'Cheers, Jake, I feel better now.'

They went into the house, where Alex was waiting with a bottle of wine and three glasses; he handed one to each of them and filled them up.

'So are you going to tell me why you look like shit, Jake, and why Annie looks as if she's had a fight with Freddy Krueger?'

'I don't know if you want to know, Alex, to be honest. It's all her fault; she's a bad influence.'

'Is it going to give me nightmares?'

'Yes, probably, because I think I'll be having them for the rest of my life.'

'Well, in that case I don't want to know; as long as you're both safe and it's over, whatever it is. Is it over? I need to know.'

'Sorry, Alex. I think it's all over but if it isn't I won't drag Jake into it again. I'll sort it out on my own. I promise.'

Jake hugged her. 'You soft cow. Do you think I'd let my best friend fight the likes of Betsy Baker on her own? I'm always here for you, no matter what.'

Annie hugged him back and then followed Alex into the lounge, where she collapsed onto one of the expensive soft leather armchairs and downed her glass of wine.

'Always such a lady, Ms Graham. Refill?'

She grinned and held out her glass. 'It would be rude not to. Thank you, Jake.'

Seven Weeks Later

Annie stared at her reflection in the mirror. Lily had helped her to put on her wedding dress and buttoned her into it. Then she had left her alone so she could get ready herself. The hairdresser had spent ages blow-drying and then putting Annie's thick black curls into a roll and secured them with a beautiful vintage diamanté hair clip, which had been a present from Jake and Alex, leaving fine wisps of curls hanging down to frame her face. The make-up girl had done an amazing job and Annie couldn't remember ever having such flawless skin or such perfect eyes and lips. She hoped Will would think so too. She felt wonderful, even though her stomach was doing somersaults.

She had looked out of the window earlier to see the guests arriving and it had made her feel like throwing up the bowl of cereal she'd eaten earlier. It was an intimate guest list because Annie's only real family was her brother Ben and his family. Her mother, who hadn't been in the least bit interested, had sent her a last-minute Facebook message to cancel, saying she was too ill to travel. Annie knew very well that she wasn't but she wouldn't waste her time worrying about it; there were some things in life that couldn't be fixed and their relationship was one of them. Besides, she had her friends who meant the world to her and that was all she needed. She was looking forward to seeing Kav, Jake and Alex all dressed up in their best suits.

The garden was so pretty. Lily must have bought every string of fairy lights in England because there wasn't a tree or a shrub that wasn't covered in them. She couldn't wait until dusk and they were all turned on. There was a white marquee on the lawn ready to hold the reception, but the wedding was to be held under the gazebo, which was covered in hundreds of white roses, each one with a diamanté in the centre. Annie had told the make-up girl to make sure she used waterproof mascara because she didn't want to risk crying and ruining her flawless face. Not that she was going to cry, but you never knew.

There was a knock on the door and Annie opened it to see Kav standing there in a grey morning suit and pale blue cravat. He gasped when he looked at her.

'Oh, my, are you Annie Graham or have I got the wrong room? You do scrub up well; you look absolutely gorgeous, kid.'

Annie felt her cheeks burning and grinned. 'Finally, you get to see me when I don't look like shit; it's long overdue. I have to say, you don't look so bad yourself, Kav, not bad at all.'

'Will I do? I've been so nervous I almost threw up my bacon bun and pint of lager. I don't want to let you down.'

'You could never let me down. Thank you so much for agreeing to walk me down the aisle. It means an awful lot to me.'

'It's all my pleasure, Annie. I know we're not related but you're the closest thing I've got to a daughter and I even have the stomach ulcer to prove it.'

He stepped forward and hugged her, careful not to crush her hair or smudge her make-up. She squeezed him back and he stepped away.

'This place is amazing but you should see what Lily has done with the garden; it looks like something off a movie.'

'I know, I walked around it before I went to bed last night. I'm very, very lucky. She's such a sweetheart and she's worked so hard.'

'It's nothing more than you deserve, Annie. It will make this old man very happy to see you settled down and being looked after by someone who loves you and would never hurt you – well, not intentionally.'

He winked at her. 'Are you ready then? The man of your dreams is waiting for you and I must admit he looks almost as good as you do, but don't tell him I said that or his head will swell so much he won't fit into the marquee.'

She nodded, and looped her arm through his. He passed her the hand-tied bouquet from the end of the bed; it included old-fashioned roses, sweet peas and every scented cottage garden flower imaginable. The jewelled brooches amongst the flowers sparkled and Annie felt like a fairy-tale princess.

They stepped out of the patio doors and the organist played 'Here Comes the Bride'. Fifty people all turned their heads to watch Annie and Kav make their way to the gazebo, where an extremely handsome Will was waiting with the biggest smile on his face she'd ever seen. Her nerves melted and it didn't matter who was watching because right now all that mattered was her and Will. Father John stood there, beaming and nodding in approval.

Kav passed her over to Will and went to take his seat next to Jake, who was dabbing at his eyes with a tissue. Kav rolled his eyes at Alex, who shrugged his shoulders and laughed. And then everyone focused on the couple in front of them, who looked as if they belonged on the cover of a celebrity magazine. Lily cried throughout the whole service and Tom sat with his arm around her, occasionally passing her tissues so she could dab at her tears. Finally, Annie and Will were pronounced husband and wife and there was a huge cheer when Will was told he could kiss the bride and he didn't waste any time in pulling her towards him and kissing her so passionately that she didn't want him to ever let go.

The day passed by without a single hitch, the sun shone and the champagne flowed freely, the meal and the speeches were perfect, even Jake's best man speech wasn't too insulting and had everyone laughing at his jokes. The sun began to set and everyone sighed in unison as the fairy lights lit up the whole garden and marquee, turning the garden into something so magical it would be the talking point for years to come whenever anyone mentioned the wedding. Annie squealed with delight and hugged Lily then Tom.

'Thank you so much. I don't know what to say except that today has been the best day of my life.'

'No need to thank us; we wanted you and Will to have a day to remember. Nobody deserves it more. We're so proud of you both.'

Will limped over to where Annie stood talking to his parents. 'Are you ready for the first dance, Mrs Ashworth?'

'You can't dance with your ankle, Will.'

'I think you'll find I can. The champagne has helped enormously.'

He took hold of Annie's hand and led her to the dance floor. He couldn't stop grinning and he swung her round and pulled her close, whispering in her ear, 'Mrs Ashworth, do you have any idea how incredibly sexy you look in that dress? I don't know how much longer I can wait before I take you to bed.'

Annie felt her cheeks flush. At this moment she would give anything for it to be just the pair of them and the band but she couldn't let Lily down. She had put so much effort into planning this whole beautiful wedding. She looked at Will. He was so handsome; his top button was undone and he'd taken his jacket and cravat off hours ago but he still had his waistcoat on. He looked like the most gorgeous man on the planet. She had to remind herself that he was hers and always would be. She sighed as he kissed her.

'Is that a sigh because you want me so much?'

She giggled. 'You have no idea how much I want you, but let's give Lily what she wants, a first dance to remember.'

He nodded. 'I suppose I can wait a little bit longer. Tell me, are you wearing stockings and suspenders?'

The band played Annie's favourite song: 'The Way You Look Tonight'. It was Will who had introduced her to the wonders of Frank Sinatra and it was Annie's tribute to his mum, who wasn't around to see her wonderful son finally settle down. It would always remind her of Will and the first time he had danced her round his kitchen singing it to her. Will led her around the dance floor and, even with his broken ankle, they looked like a pair of professional dancers; the classes Lily had insisted they take paying off as the whole room was watching and applauding.

Jake and Alex were standing with their arms around each other and even Stu, who was a bit the worse for wear, was holding Debs, his wife, and smiling at the happy couple. Annie knew in her heart she was finally going to get her happy ever after and she couldn't be happier – dreams did come true.

A cold shiver ran down her spine and she closed her eyes, wondering if someone was trying to contact her, but it went before she could reach out to them. She pushed it to the back of her mind. Whoever it was could wait; this was her night.

* * *

The small silver van parked up outside the town hall. There was a charity gala on tonight and they had been watching the people who had been coming and going out the back for sneaky cigarettes. It was risky – a little bit too risky because the police station was opposite, but there weren't many lights on inside it and Henry had checked out the rear yard when they'd driven past and there were hardly any vehicles parked up. It looked as if everyone was out working hard for a living. The town CCTV cameras were facing the opposite way from where they had parked and Henry was getting twitchy. He'd told Megan if there was a chance of it going wrong they wouldn't do it and she'd agreed.

The woman Megan had pointed out had been outside three times now for a cigarette with a different man each time, clearly a bit the worse for wear and tottering around on heels that were too high for her. This time she'd come out on her own for a crafty cigarette. Her phone rang and she'd walked away from the entrance doors just around the corner, out of sight into the shadows. It was perfect.

Henry nodded at Megan and she got out of the van and walked

over to her. Pulling out a cigarette, she waved it at the woman. 'Have you got a light?'

The woman, who was struggling to keep upright, smiled at her and ended her phone call, then rooted around in her gold clutch bag, finally pulling out a lighter.

'Thank you; it's boring in there, isn't it?'

'God, yes, it is. I hate these functions but, you know how it is – you have to pretend you give a shit when really you don't.'

Megan nodded emphatically, keeping her talking whilst Henry walked up from behind the woman with a plastic bag. He pulled it over her head and then hit her across the back of the head with a hammer. She slumped forward and Megan caught her. He looked around to make sure no one was watching then nodded and they both dragged her over to the small van, bundling her into the back of it. They jumped into the front seats and Henry drove away, taking it easy so as not to arouse suspicion. The whole interaction had taken less than five minutes, around the same length of time as Annie and Will's first dance twenty miles away, and they had their victim.

Megan gave Henry a high five; he drove the van over to the disused barn on Walney that they had turned into a mini torture chamber, ready for Megan's first kill …

The End

Author's note and acknowledgements

This past year has been amazing and I'd like to thank the following people for sharing my journey.

My heartfelt thanks go to my amazing editor Lucy Gilmour and the rest of the fabulous Carina Team. My wonderful readers, who have taken Annie, Will and Jake into their hearts and for following them on their adventures; without your support we wouldn't be on our third adventure. I would like to thank my children Jessica, Joshua, Jerusha, Jaimea and Jeorgia for nearly always understanding that I have to write and putting up with the terrible cooking. A huge thank you to my granddaughter Gracie, who always makes me smile and fills my heart with joy whenever she walks into a room.

A special thank you to my fellow bloggers Jo Bartlett, Julie Heslington, Alex Weston, Helen Rolfe, Deirdre Palmer, Lynn Davidson, Jackie Ladbury and Rachael Thomas, who all form The Write Romantics. You all rock and I don't know what I'd do without you. Finally, my friends at Cumbria Constabulary for keeping it real; it's a tough job but someone has to do it.

Helen xx

Keep Reading …

Ready for the next thrilling instalment in
the Annie Graham series?

THE LAKE HOUSE

Six months on from her last brush with the paranormal, police officer Annie Graham, now Annie Ashworth, dreams of settling down and starting a family. But now that serial killer Henry Smith has escaped, she knows that trouble is coming. She thwarted him once, and he's out for revenge.

When a local man vanishes in mysterious circumstances, Annie realises there may be darker forces at work. And when she takes a glimpse of a monster with a thirst for blood, her worst fears are confirmed.

With a serial killer on the loose and an unknown horror stalking the sewers, Annie is in a race against time to stop them before they kill again. But will she be able to save herself from their clutches?

Out in paperback and audiobook April 2025.

Out now in ebook.

Dear Reader,

We hope you enjoyed reading this book. If you did, we'd be so appreciative if you left a review. It really helps us and the author to bring more books like this to you.

Here at HQ Digital we are dedicated to publishing fiction that will keep you turning the pages into the early hours. Don't want to miss a thing? To find out more about our books, promotions, discover exclusive content and enter competitions you can keep in touch in the following ways:

JOIN OUR COMMUNITY:

Sign up to our new email newsletter:
http://smarturl.it/SignUpHQ

Read our new blog www.hqstories.co.uk

𝕏 https://twitter.com/HQStories

f www.facebook.com/HQStories

BUDDING WRITER?

We're also looking for authors to join the HQ Digital family!
Find out more here:

https://www.hqstories.co.uk/want-to-write-for-us/

Thanks for reading, from the HQ Digital team

H|Q

ONE PLACE. MANY STORIES

Bold, innovative and
empowering publishing.

FOLLOW US ON:

@HQStories